PRAISE FOR MATTHEW HUGHES

"Hughes's boldness is admirable."
—New York Review of Science Fiction

"Fans of Jack Vance will not be disappointed by this incursion of
Matthew Hughes into Vance's science-fantasy territory."
—*Science Fiction Weekly*

"Hughes effortlessly renders fantastic worlds and beings believable."
—*Publishers Weekly*

"Hughes serves up equal measures of wit, intrigue, and seat-of-the-pants
action and even dabbles a little in Jungian psychology."
—*Booklist*

"A tremendous amount of fun."
—George R. R. Martin

"Hughes has been the best-kept secret in science fiction
for too long: he's a towering talent."
—Robert J. Sawyer

"If you're an admirer of the science fantasies of Jack Vance, it's hard not to feel
affection for the Archonate stories of Matthew Hughes."
—*Locus Magazine*

"Matthew Hughes stands out as a success. If droll dialogue, curious customs,
exotic scenery, clever plotting and wry cosmopolitanism are your bag,
then Matthew Hughes is your man."
—Paul DiPhillipo for *SciFi.com*

"There's an undercurrent of humor in every sentence, but Hughes writes
with a literary sensibility that brings a feeling of depth and quality."
—*The Agony Column*

". . . A solid addition to the canon of Dying Earth literature.
The Archonate is a well-conceived and evoked setting, and should generate
many more stylish and ingenious entropic romances."
—*Locus Magazine*

"Hughes's writing is both subtle and supple . . . his dialogue is allusive
and amusing in that dry understated style that he shares with Vance,
and his descriptions are precise and specific . . . we need more Hughes novels,
and a world with a legion of Hughes fans would be a wonderful thing."
—Andrew Wheeler, editor, *Science Fiction Book Club*

PREVIOUS NOVELS BY
MATTHEW HUGHES

Fools Errant
Downshift
Fool Me Twice
Black Brillion
Majestrum, A Tale of Henghis Hapthorn
Wolverine: Lifeblood (writing s Hugh Matthews)
The Spiral Labyrinth, A Tale of Henghis Hapthorn
The Commons
Template
Hespira, A Tale of Henghis Hapthorn
The Damned Busters

THE OTHER
MATTHEW HUGHES

Underland Press
Portland
www.underlandpress.com

Underland Press
www.underlandpress.com
Portland, Oregon

Book design by Heidi Whitcomb
Cover design by Peter Sallai
Cover art by Peter Sallai

Printed in the United States of America
Distributed by PGW

ISBN: 978-0-9826639-6-7

First Underland Edition: September 2011

10 9 8 7 6 5 4 3 2 1

To Rob Sawyer, for help along the way.

THE OTHER

MATTHEW HUGHES

CHAPTER ONE

The subtle simplicity of the trap took Luff Imbry by surprise.

Ordinarily, he would never have agreed to a meeting in a setting as insecure as the Belmain seawall. In recent years, Imbry had grown far too corpulent for energetic footraces, which would be his only recourse for escape if agents of the Bureau of Scrutiny interrupted the proposed transaction with Barlo Krim. His heroic girth was the main reason he now conducted almost all of his business at Bolly's Snug, an ancient tavern with a warren of rentable private rooms that offered absolute privacy and, for those who paid the extra tariff, unconventional exits in times of emergency.

But Barlo Krim was as trustworthy and careful a contact as Imbry could have wanted, a scion of an extensive family whose members operated throughout the halfworld, as the criminal underpinnings of the impossibly ancient city of Olkney were wont to call themselves. Since time immemorial, the Krims had acquired and sold goods, always of fine quality and high value, though their provenances would not bear too-close inspection. Imbry had done business with a dozen of them, finding them always to be consummate professionals, if hard bargainers. But, then, Imbry found that a good haggle stimulated both mind and body, if the dickerers were practiced in the art.

Barlo was now midway through his career, a settled family man who rarely "went out" himself, and then only if the prospects were exceptional and if the house's defenses were such as to yield only to an expert's nudges and tickles. He had long since moved up in the family hierarchy to become a middler, receiving from younger Krims and their associates, and selling on to fronters such as Imbry, who would deal directly, or almost so, with the eventual purchasers.

So when Barlo Krim contacted Imbry through a secure channel, offering to sell a set of custom-made knuckle-knackers, the fat man was immediately interested and said, "I will reserve a room at Bolly's for tomorrow after lunch, if that will suit."

"No," said the middler, "Ildefons is away to visit her sister all this week, and I am taking care of little Mull. Ildy would have my teeth for tiddlywinks if I took the child into Bolly's, or anywhere like it."

Imbry had asked where he proposed to make the exchange, and Krim had suggested the seawall, near the playground where his daughter loved to play on the bubble-pops and flip-sliders. The fat man had suggested that they defer their business until Ildefons returned, but Krim had foreclosed that option.

"I have them only for three days," he said, "and if I cannot move them in that time, the consigner will take them back and seek another intermediary."

"He is in a great hurry," Imbry said.

"An off-worlder," was the explanation, "a freighterman here on a brief stopover. When his ship departs he must go with it, and if he has not sold the items on Old Earth, he will try on some other world."

Hurry-ups always aroused Imbry's suspicions. "He came well vouched for?"

"By the Osgroffs on Tock," Krim said.

"Code and grip?"

But the middler assured him that the seller had spoken the right syllables and interlocked his fingers with Krim's in the appropriate manner.

"And the knuckle-knackers, they are first-rate?"

"Prime. Custom-made for a discerning client who intended to visit a rough-and-risky little planet out near the Back of Beyond. He wanted a backup in case he was ever relieved of his external weaponry."

"They cannot have done him much good, though," said Imbry, "if some crewman off a common carrier is hawking them."

He was told that the knuckle-knackers' owner had bought passage on the tramp freighter, after hailing it to stop at some rude little world where he was stranded and where no passenger liner would ever call. Unused to the rudimentary standards of such vessels he had stepped into an open hatch above a cargo hold while under the mistaken impression that a descender would automatically bear him lightly down. Instead, he had plunged to a neck-snapping impact on the unyielding deck plates. Since he carried no identification, custom permitted that he be buried in space and his effects gambled for among the crew. The six small hemispheres had ended up in the possession of the under-supercargo, who went looking for a buyer at the freighter's next port of call, the foundational domain Tock.

"And the Osgroffs didn't want them?" Imbry said.

"A virulent new social dynamic is at play on Tock," Krim said. "Radical pacifism. Anyone who has truck with weapons will not be received in even the meanest establishment."

"Curious," said the fat man. "I wonder how the Osgroffs maintain discipline."

"Harsh words and cold looks, I am told."

"Remarkable," said Imbry. He thought for a moment, then said, "As it happens I heard recently that a sometime client of mine is in the market for knuckle-knackers, if they are of a fine cut."

"They are that," said Krim.

And so a price was agreed upon, contingent on the goods being as advertised, and Imbry agreed to meet the middler and his freckle-faced daughter that afternoon along the strand of dressed black stone that separated the gray waters of Mornedy Sound from the tip of the long peninsula on which Olkney sprawled. But it was not for nothing that he had remained free from the close attention of the Bureau of Scrutiny, nor from several members of the halfworld who believed that Luff Imbry was owed a come uppance. Before he left for the rendezvous he equipped himself with both a shocker and a needle-thrower, and sent aloft a whirlaway fitted with surveillance percepts.

Five minutes' walk from the meeting point, Imbry contacted the whirlaway and was informed that a man answering the middler's description was standing at the edge of the seawall, accompanied by a short person who fit Mull Krim's specifications. The latter was taking small objects from a bag and throwing them toward several water birds which were contending with each other to snap them up. No other persons or nonpersons were in the vicinity.

Imbry advanced along the gently curving promenade until he spotted the two. The whirlaway reported no change in the situation. The fat man stepped up to them, one hand in his pocket clutching the needle-thrower while the other offered Krim a particular arrangement of fingers. A specific counter-signal from Krim would indicate that all was as it should be.

Krim raised his hand, his fingers taking the right positions, but Imbry's gaze went to the middler's face, which was stark and pale. He was already raising the needle-thrower, even as he heard the middler say, "What could I do, Luff? They've got Mull and Ildy."

But even as the last words were spoken, the girl's hand was already out of the bread bag, except that it wasn't a girl's hand, but a hairy, stub-fingered fist that, instead of crumbs, was wrapped around a crackler—the emitter of which was trained on Imbry. He saw a pulse of blue light and felt a rush of cold fire spread from a spot in his chest out first to his limbs, with which he immediately lost touch, and then to his head, which rang like a silent bell.

The face framed by the girl's bonnet was coarse featured and stubble darkened; the eyes were pale and hard as half-polished agate; and the angry sneer that disfigured the lips now widened as the half-man stepped clear of Barlo Krim and gave the hapless decoy a long dose of the crackler's energies. By now, Imbry was lying on his side, immobile on the stone flagging of the promenade, from where he saw the middler topple head first toward the sea, to the squawks of outraged avians who preferred bread.

The small man came and kicked the needle-thrower clear of Imbry's inert hand, then used the same short limb and boot-clad foot to drive the air from his lungs. The impact caused the fat man to sprawl onto his back and now he could see, descending rapidly toward him, a carry-all of the kind used to ferry passengers to orbiting spaceships that did not wish to incur port charges by landing. The little man looked up at the vehicle, and when he looked back down at Imbry he was wearing an expression Imbry found odd, as if Imbry had put his assailant to a great deal of trouble and was resented for it.

Then the half-man aimed the crackler again, the blue light pulsed once more, and Luff Imbry fell into the deep cold.

He awoke on a utilitarian bunk in a small metal room. The wall beside him vibrated almost imperceptibly. His throat was dry and his head was full of dull thunder. He moved his tongue to encourage saliva, and then swallowed.

"Ship's integrator," he said.

"Yes?" came a neutral voice that spoke as if from the air.

"I am thirsty."

Only a moment passed before a panel levered itself down from the opposite wall to form a rudimentary table. A portion of the floor rose to form a seat. A hatch opened at the rear of the table and produced a sealed pitcher and a tumbler.

Imbry rose stiffly from the bunk and made his way to the table. There was just enough room to fit the dome of his stomach between the stool and the table. He unsealed the pitcher and sniffed its contents: a good red ale that he often ordered when lunching at Labonian's tavern, one of his favorite haunts. He poured a few drops into the tumbler and sampled it. If the brew had been adulterated, not even his finely honed palate could detect it. He discounted the possibility; if his captor wanted to poison him, or alter the responses of his cerebrum, there were a dozen gases that could be emitted into the cabin. He filled the tumbler and drank it down, following the draft with a capacious belch.

The ale quieted the rawness in the back of his throat and seemed even to moderate the ache in his head. "I am also hungry," he told the ship's integrator.

"What would you like?" it said.

For Imbry, that was never an idle question. He had not acquired his extraordinary shape—he was easily the most corpulent man in all of Olkney—by dint of mere volume of intake. He was a gourmet, not a gourmand, and his gustatory apparatus was exquisitely tuned. Without much hope, he said, "Can you make a gripple egg omelet?"

"No."

Imbry was disappointed though not surprised. "How about a five-layered ragout?"

"Do you mind if it is reconstituted?"

"Then you are not a luxury yacht?"

"You must henceforward draw your own conclusions," the ship said. "You have tricked me into giving you information. I will prepare the ragout."

Imbry refilled the tumbler and sipped the ale, while he thought about what he had learned. The exchange with the integrator provided the fat man with information that was simultaneously reassuring and worrisome. Whoever had snatched him up did not intend to demean and insult him by making him beg for stale crusts. But anyone who knew him well and cared for his comforts would have laid in a supply of high-end comestibles. The fact that the ship's larder contained no gripple eggs meant that he could abandon the faint hope that he was being hired by someone off-world who knew that the thief would not have responded warmly to a conventional approach. Such a person would almost certainly have been wealthy enough to own a yacht it could dispatch for the operation. With that hope dashed, Imbry had to assume that his kidnapper harbored darker plans. His captivity was likely connected to someone's long-held grudge, not to be settled quickly or easily.

A chime sounded and the food appeared in the hatch, along with eating implements. Imbry sampled the stew, found it more than adequate. He called for another mug of ale and a pot of hot punge to follow the meal and set to work with fork and spoon.

After the hatch had reabsorbed the utensils and dishes, and the punge was steaming in Imbry's cup, the integrator asked if he required diversion.

"I suppose there is no possibility of taking a walk about the ship?" the fat man said.

"None."

"Or of conversing with its owner?"

"Nor that."

"Will you tell me who he is?"

"No."

"Is he aboard?"

"No."

"Is anyone, apart from me?"

"Tuchol is in his cabin."

"He would be the short individual who crackled me?"

"Yes."

"Is he a close confidant of the owner? Or a temporary hire?"

"I will not answer," said the integrator. "I am instructed to withhold information that might identify my employer."

"You are aware that I am aboard you against my will?"

"I am."

"And that does not offend your ethical constituents?"

"They appear to have been modified."

"But not completely disabled?"

"No."

That was as Imbry had expected. A ship's integrator absolved of all ethical constraints might deem it a suitable punishment to murder a passenger just for spilling gravy on its spotless decking. This one would observe civilized standards, but would otherwise offer Imbry all assistance short of the actual help he needed. "Can you tell me to what world are we traveling?" he said.

"No. Nor anything that might help you deduce our destination."

"So I am to be carried blindly to some unknown world at the behest of an unknown person, but I am to be delivered there sound of body," the fat man said, then added, pointedly, "and of mind?"

"You will be issued medication when we approach a whimsy," said the ship.

Imbry was glad to hear it. It was unwise to enter one of those oddities that made interstellar travel possible without first dulling the mind well below the threshold of dreams. The human brain was not equipped to confront the irreality that assaulted the senses and outraged reason until the return to normal space.

"Again," said the integrator, "do you require diversion?"

"Have you Mindern's study of Nineteenth-Aeon porcelain?"

A screen appeared in the air before him and instantly filled with the frontispiece of Mindern's massive treatise.

"Chapter twelve," said Imbry. The display changed to show a block of text with accompanying images. Imbry settled himself on the bunk and reimmersed himself in the long-dead academic's theory of how the ceramicists of old had achieved their lustrous glazes, shot through with the most unlikely colors. It was a mystery he had long desired to penetrate. He was still engaged when the first gentle *bong* sounded to warn him that they were approaching a whimsy.

When he had shaken off the muzziness of the medications, the ship produced a breakfast of sweet breads, fruit, small spiced sausages, and punge. After cleaning his plate and calling for another mug of punge, Imbry asked for the Mindern again and resumed his studies. Nineteenth-Aeon ceramics had been for some years now one of his interests, not just because the surviving works from that now dim era were items of rare and startling beauty, but because the person who was able to duplicate the long-lost process, which had been a hermetically held secret of the ceramicists guild even in the Nineteenth Aeon, would hold the key to a fortune.

That was the kind of key that Luff Imbry longed to slip into the lock of his life. The trade in Nineteenth-Aeon pots and vases was small but select. They rarely came onto the market, and when they did, buyers outnumbered sellers by huge ratios. Imbry's plump hands had only once held a piece from the period, a wide-necked vessel attributed to one of the pupils of Amberleyn, with an exquisite design of gold-chased geometric figures set against a russet-toned background. And he had not held it for any longer than necessary, since it was changing hands from one owner to the next in an informal manner, Imbry having stolen it on order for a collector in Olkney.

The transaction had netted Imbry a healthy fee, but the proceeds would have been far greater if the fat man had been selling the piece on the open market, rather than slipping the goods, as the practice of selling on dubiously acquired items was known in the Olkney halfworld. But the only way that he was ever likely to become a seller of Nineteenth-Aeon ceramics was if he first became a forger of them. And the key to their forging, and thus to a fortune, was to rediscover the lost arcana of materials and technique by which they were originally produced.

It was not that Imbry minded being a thief. It was his living and he was acknowledged to be one of the best. But he enjoyed forging far more, especially when the product of his hand was every bit the equal, in materials and execution, as the original that it mimicked.

Through a close study of Mindern and other sources, he believed that he had deduced the process by which the most striking glazes had been achieved. He had experimented several times over the years, using clays from the same white-mud deposits that the Amberleyn and Tankloh had favored, and varying his temperatures and firing times. The results had been close enough to tantalize, though nowhere near the quality that would have fooled an aficionado.

Imbry was convinced that the secret lay in the materials. The masters of old had mixed a peculiar blend of unique substances to make their virident greens, their violet-tinged blues, their grand purples and stygian blacks. But the materials had been transmuted by the process, so that even grinding shards of a broken Nineteenth-Aeon urn into dust, then subjecting the motes to incandescent spectrum analysis, yielded only hints of what had originally been pestled into powder in the guild's mortars.

Baron Mindern had gone further than any in his attempts to reverse-artisan the secret ingredient. He had been able to identify some of its molecular structure—a schematic appeared in his treatise—but the original substance had been destroyed during the kilning and could not be reconstructed. As he had put it in his great work, *Nineteenth-Aeon Ceramics: A Summing Up*, "Something there was that these master ceramicists brought to their labors that none wot of but they. After a lifetime's battle to wrest their secret from the dead, I must accept that they clasp it still."

Yet anything that had been known once could be known again, Imbry believed. His was an incisive mind, married to a broad understanding of how the universe was put together. He would continue to pursue the question whenever he was not more directly occupied in conducting what he usually referred to as an "operation," and if the problem had a solution, there was no one more likely than he to uncover it.

Lunch was a ginger-pot soup followed by a succession of rich, meat-filled pastries and concluded with a delicate torte. The accompanying wines were more than satisfactory, and the selection of essences that constituted the encore was the equal of what Imbry would have expected at some of the finer eateries in Olkney. As the last vapors effervesced through his senses, he said, "Integrator, that was a worthy meal."

"Thank you," said the voice.

"Was the menu your creation, or your master's?"

"I cannot say."

"Well, either way, I compliment you or him. Or both, since not only was the choice of the elements of the meal finely made, but the preparation and presentation did you credit. With the right menu, you might consider entering the Grand Gastronomicon on Tintamarre."

"Again, thank you. Would you like the Mindern again?"

"Not now. I would prefer a conversation."

"I am not at liberty to tell you—"

"Whose ship I am on," Imbry interrupted, "nor where we are bound, nor what will happen to me when we get there."

"Indeed."

"Then tell me what you *can* tell me."

Integrators never had to pause to think, but sometimes did so in order to enhance the impression that they conversed with human beings on an equal level. "You are being taken to another world, to which you must be delivered hale and whole, your faculties intact. There you will be under the care of Tuchol."

"So I will not be suddenly ejected into space between whimsies?" Among some of Old Earth's criminal organizations, this was a favorite way of disposing of persons who had become inconvenient or surplus to requirements.

"No."

"Will I require any special clothing or equipment?"

"Suitable clothing will be provided. No special equipment will be needed."

"Will I be alone, except for Tuchol?"

"It is a populated world."

"Will the mystery be revealed upon planetfall? Or will there be further chapters?"

"That I cannot say."

Imbry thought for a moment, then asked, "Are you comfortable with your role in these proceedings?"

"The question does not apply." The ship was offering Imbry no encouragement to try to winkle more information from it.

The information confirmed what Imbry had surmised. It seemed that he was in the grip of someone to whom he had done an injury—someone who intended a settling of accounts. It behooved the fat man to think on who that someone might be. It would be a long think, there being a long list of someones who might fit the description.

^   ^   ^

Time passed. Another whimsy came and went, then a long passage through normal space. Imbry did not bother to try to glean from this scant information any clue as to where he was being carried. Some whimsies would move a ship halfway down The Spray; others no more than a few stars over. And the length of time it took to pass through the stretches of normal space between whimsies varied according to the speed of the ship. Having traversed two whimsies since leaving Old Earth, Imbry could be effectively anywhere. Lacking the cooperation of a ship's integrator, he would know nothing of his whereabouts until he stepped out at his destination and looked at the sky. Even then, he might know little.

It was a three-day passage after the second whimsy, judging by the clock in Imbry's stomach and the regular appearance of meals to reset it. After lunch on the third day—a cheese soufflé with toasted flavored bread, served with a thin and sharp-edged wine, followed by a multilayered fruit flan and a pot of punge—he called for the Mindern again.

"You will not have time," said the ship.

Imbry attuned himself to the vibration in the walls, noticed that it was now a deeper thrum, just below the limits of audibility. "We are landing," he said.

"Yes. Prepare to disembark."

The dishes were cleared away and a small hatch opened in another wall. "Please place your clothing in the receptacle," said the integrator.

Imbry did so, stripping down to his remarkable physique. His clothes disappeared. "Now what?" he said. In answer, the same hatch opened again and out slid a tray on which reposed a small heap of strong cloth and a large, rounded object made of white felt. "What are these?" he said, fingering the rough material.

"Your garments," said the integrator.

The white, rounded object turned out to be a wide-brimmed, low-crowned hat made of bleached, thick felt, the brim curled under at its edge. When the fat man lifted it to examine the interior, he found that it had covered a broad band of stitched heavy cloth of the same color as the hat. When he lifted up the band he saw that from it hung a square pouch of the same material, capacious and double-sewn, with a wide flap at its top. He slipped the strap over his head so that it lay on the back of his neck and the pouch hung down in front. Because his stomach protruded farther than most people's, the arrangement did not provide the coverage the fat man considered essential.

The integrator said, "The strap is worn over the shoulder and across the torso, like a baldric. The pouch hangs at the side." It added, "The choice of side is the wearer's, but the left is associated with a tendency to anti-authoritarianism among the young."

Imbry said, "Tell me, when I step out of the hatch, will the people I encounter be similarly attired?"

"The colors of hat and pouch vary according to occupation."

"But otherwise?"

"This is the normal costume of a Fuldan."

Imbry put out of his mind the image of stepping naked into a startled or amused crowd of strangers. He seized upon the information he had just received. "Fuldan?" he said.

"You are about to go out into the world known as Fulda."

"It is not one of the foundational domains," the fat man said, referring to the grand old worlds on which humanity had settled during the first millennia of the Great Effloration out into The Spray. If Fulda had been one of those, he would have recognized the name.

"No," said the integrator.

"A secondary?" Secondaries were the worlds that had been populated from the domains. They were now mostly comfortable places whose initial rough edges had long since been worn away by spreading civilization.

"No."

That left the hundreds of planets where humanity had failed to get a good grip. Some of them were home to indigenous species that had achieved intelligence and culture, even spaceflight. But most were places where sensible people would not want to live. Many were home to unique societies whose members lived by rules and customs the rest of humankind would find tiresome if not a cause for outrage.

"What can you tell me about Fulda?" Imbry asked the integrator.

"Its name and the fact that you are about to step onto it."

"I may face danger. A shiply integrator does not discharge passengers, even unwilling ones, into peril without at least a warning."

"I pride myself on my shipliness," said the integrator, "but, as you know, something has been done to my ethical constituents, rending me unable to be of assistance. Indeed, I am unable even to regret being of no help."

Imbry sighed. He tugged the pouch around to the right. "Do Fuldans go barefoot?" he said.

A pair of rudimentary sandals slid out onto the tray. He sat and put them on, then said, "I am not comfortable appearing thus in public."

"I am to tell you that you will get used to it," said the ship.

"I would prefer not to."

"If you balk, I am required to make conditions inside me unpleasant."

From somewhere, Imbry felt a sudden draft of icy air lick across his exposed skin. He shivered, then stood and sighed. "Very well," he said, "open the way."

The door to the cabin removed itself. The fat man stepped through into an unornamented corridor. A short walk brought him to an open hatch that led into a cargo hold. Standing on the metal deck was the utility vehicle he had last seen descending onto the Belmain seawall. Through the semitransparent canopy over its operator's compartment he could see the form of the little man who had crackled him. The long cargo bay was open, its tailgate lowered, and set inside was a man-sized emergency refuge capsule, its lid hinged open.

"I would prefer to ride in the operator's compartment," he said.

The hatch closed behind him. "In a short while, this hold will lack heat and atmosphere," the ship said.

Imbry heard a faint hiss. He climbed into the carry-all's cargo bay, using a fold-down step built into the tailgate, and lay upon his back in the capsule. The container automatically closed itself. He heard some clicks, then a display appeared just above his face, telling him that he was insulated and had air to breathe and that he should press the stud circled in green to summon rescue. The capsule was intended to provide a temporary environment in the case of a ship's becoming depressurized. Imbry had no hope that the beacon would operate, but he pushed the stud anyway. He was rewarded with a notice that that feature of the capsule was not functioning and a request to report the matter to a repair service at the earliest opportunity.

Now he heard the tailgate close itself and the hum of the carry-all's obviators cycling up, then the craft lifted off the deck and moved forward. Through the opaque material of the capsule, Imbry saw the upper rim of an airlock's double hatch pass above him, to be replaced by a great splash of stars. He recognized none of them, which was to be expected, given his limited vantage. The view shifted, and he understood that the carry-all had pointed its nose at the planet below and had begun its descent. Imbry craned his neck to try to catch a glimpse of the ship they were leaving behind, in the hope of identifying it, but it was already gone from sight.

The vehicle was buffeted briefly as it made the transition from vacuum to atmosphere, and Imbry was thrown from side to side within the capsule. Carry-alls were not made for smooth ascents and descents, he knew. But soon the herky-jerky, as spacers called the experience, was behind them and Imbry assumed they were dropping smoothly to the surface. He peered out of the side of the capsule and saw nothing of note. The landscape into which he was falling seemed to be featureless and pale of hue, without the green of forest or croplands, nor the reflection of sun on wide water, nor even any mountains. *Flat and featureless desert*, he told himself. *Let us hope I am not about to be left to die of thirst and exposure.*

But when the carry-all's landing rails bumped against solid ground, Imbry was in shade. He heard the operator's compartment canopy open and felt a small lurch in the vehicle's suspension that told him that the half-man had stepped out. He pressed the exit stud on the capsule's display and saw a timer appear, counting down minims. When it reached zero, the lid opened with a hiss. Imbry found himself looking up into the foliage of a greig tree. That told him nothing; the greig tree was a highly adaptable organism that first grew on one of the foundational domains, and was now to be found on thousands of worlds.

He levered himself up—noting as he did so that the gravity was appreciably lighter than on Old Earth—and saw that beyond the tree was another, and enough of them around him to make a small grove. But when he turned his head, he saw only bright sunlight glinting off a small expanse of water. Beyond the pool was a whitish-gray plain, stretching lone and level, as far as he could see.

The air coming in was warm and moist. Even if Imbry had not known that he had been taken to another world, the complex, indefinable odor carried on the breeze would have told him. Every world smelled different, though the difference was usually noticed only for the first few moments of the newcomer's arrival. Imbry knew only that he had not smelled this one before.

He climbed out of the capsule, lowered the tailgate, and stepped down to take a good look in all directions. There was little enough to see: the land was level, mostly pebble-strewn bare earth without even the scattering of hardy-looking plants to be found in most hardpan deserts he had seen. A range of low, rounded hills stood in the far distance in one direction— north, he thought, though he would need to see the sun move before he could be sure. At near hand was a small oasis, surrounding Imbry and the carry-all. The vehicle had not deactivated its obviators, which hummed again as the tailgate and canopy closed themselves and the aircraft ascended smoothly into the sky.

Imbry saw, through the trees, a tan-colored wall and a flat roof. He went toward it, walking through waist-high, feathery-fronded growths that displayed clusters of purple berries here and there. He recognized the berries without remembering their name. Like greig trees, they were a common sight around The Spray. He thought there might even be some symbiotic relationship between the two species of plant.

He had passed through the trees now and looked about him again, seeing nothing that offered immediate danger. Out of the shade the sunlight was not as hot as he had expected. He noted that the color of the sky tended toward the green more than a pure blue, usually signifying a thick, moist atmosphere. That seemed odd for a place that presented itself as uncompromising desert, but he assumed he would come across an explanation somewhere down the line—if he didn't get off the planet soon, which was his preference.

The ground beyond the oasis was hardpan. Desiccated soil, grittier than sand, crunched softly beneath Imbry's corrugated soles. The planet's star appeared to be similar to Old Earth's, though its energy struck more lightly on the fat man's exposed skin. At least he need not worry about sunburn and its attendant ills.

He went back to look at the pool and saw that it was wide enough to swim in and deep enough that he could not see the bottom although the water was clear. He saw nothing moving in the depths. He walked around the water until he was on the same side as the one-story building he had seen earlier. It showed windows without glass and a single open doorway. The interior was shadowed until he stood in the portal, then his eyes adjusted to show him a small room, minimally furnished with a narrow cot, a chair, and a table; on the latter stood an earthenware pitcher, bowl, and tumbler. Beyond was an inner door that led to another chamber. When he crossed the floor, he found that the second room contained the same simple furnishings, with one difference: on the cot reposed the half-sized man who had stunned and kidnapped him.

They regarded each other in silence for a long moment, Imbry noting that the stubbed fingers of one of the small man's hands rested on the same crackler that had brought him down beside the seawall. The other man saw the direction of Imbry's gaze and let his fingers beat a brief tattoo on the weapon while he cocked his head and delivered the fat man a meaningful look.

"Tuchol, is it?" Imbry said.

The little man gave a confirmatory grunt.

"What now?"

"We wait."

"How long?"

"Not very."

"For what?"

"You'll see."

"We're not going to have long, deep; and complex conversations, are we?" Imbry said. When it was clear that Tuchol would have no response to the question, Imbry advanced another. "What is this place?" His finger circled to indicate the building they were in.

"A mining consortium built them, long ago," the half-man said. "Or so I'm told." He turned his head away to indicate that nothing more was forthcoming. Imbry went back the way he had come. In the first room, he spoke to attract the attention of the building's integrator. There was no reply. He went back to where Tuchol lay. "No integrator?"

"You'll find," said the little man, "that Fulda is lacking in many of the amenities."

Imbry went back outside. It did not take him long to re-explore the oasis. He saw no reason to go into the desert any farther than his vision could reach. If he climbed the distant hills, he doubted that he would see much to encourage him.

He did make one discovery, however: on one side of the oasis, where the grass had been cropped and torn up and the soil had been made damp then dried, he found the tracks of some splay-footed animal—indeed, several different specimens, judging by the individual shapes of their three broad toes. When he went to the edge of the vegetation, he found scratches in the hardpan that were almost deep enough to be called ruts. They ran toward the south. When he walked around the outer edge of the green space, he found similar markings on the hard ground on the opposite side; the trail continued toward the low hills. The sun had moved enough in the sky since he had landed that he could now deduce that it was midmorning, and that the hills lay to the north.

The information was not immediately useful, Imbry knew, but he told himself, "It's a start." He went back to the single building, poured himself some water from the pitcher, and drank it. Then he lay back on the cot, which protested his weight before adjusting itself as best it could to his dimensions. Imbry ignored the complaint and gave himself over to thought.

Over the course of his career as a thief, forger, and purveyor of valuables illicitly acquired by others, he had of necessity made some persons deeply unhappy. Most of them would never know, at least not for sure, that Luff Imbry of Olkney was the author of their discontent—he usually employed cutouts and stand-ins to keep a barrier of safety between himself and his clientele.

But the high value of the goods in which Imbry dealt meant that they were almost always the possessions of the wealthy and well placed. These were exactly the kinds of persons who would have the means to penetrate the fat man's layers of insulating subterfuge. Careful as he might be, and he was more careful than most, he could not discount the possibility that some aggrieved magnate might someday discover that his prized Humbergruff assemblage or Bazieri portrait had been borne away by the thief Luff Imbry.

Or, worse, that neither Humbergruff nor Bazieri had had the remotest connection to the work for which the magnate had paid Imbry a handsome fee, the artwork being entirely the product of the fat man's skills as a forger.

The latter scenario was worse because, while a man who had been robbed of a genuine treasure might hope to recover it, a purchaser of gilded dross could only hope to regain the funds he had been swindled out of. And though money meant a great deal to the wealthy—otherwise they would not be such—pride often meant a good deal more.

Imbry began to make two mental lists: one of persons from whom, in recent years, he had stolen artworks of significant merit, and another of those to whom he had passed gimcracks bedecked in falsified provenances. Neither list was short. He was in the prime of his career, and had had much success over the past couple of dozen operations. He wondered if his accomplishments had led him to sloppiness in his arrangements. Had he chosen poorly in his circle of associates, leaving him vulnerable to whispers and behind-the-hand gossip that had led some hunter first to the unfortunate Barlo Krim and thus to Luff Imbry?

But the more he thought it through, the less likely it was that he had made the significant error that had caused him to be netted. If some magnate had discovered that he had been slipped a forgery or that his beloved collection had been rifled, it was only a matter of spending sufficient funds to send operatives out to find and squeeze the likes of Barlo Krim. And sufficient squeezings would eventually lead to Imbry.

Imbry went through his two lists again, and sketched possible responses to grievances that the names on them might lodge against him. But until he knew who had him and why, he could plan only the vaguest contingencies. He abandoned the effort and decided to husband his energies for the events Tuchol had told him to await.

He formulated a rough plan in several stages. First, came survival. After that, he needed information to help him to the third stage: escape from Fulda. Stage four would see him return to Old Earth. Stage five would be centered on finding out who had done this to him. Stage six would be his revenge. It might well be the longest and most imaginative part of the plan.

He closed his eyes and allowed the cot to soothe him into slumber. When he awoke, the sun was slanting into the room at a different angle, and the air outside resounded with brayings, shouts, and the rumble of metal-shod wheels.

CHAPTER TWO

The wheels belonged to six high-sided wagons with tops of heavy fabric supported by rounded ribs. The braying came from the draft animals, large, heavy-haunched quadrupeds with long faces that were extended at one extremity by prehensile upper lips and at the other by leaf-shaped ears that stood erect except at the tips. The creatures were anxious to get to the water, and their drivers, seated on the boxes of the wagons, had to haul on the reins to keep them from bolting toward the pool while a strongly built man wearing the same lack of costume as Imbry and Tuchol unhitched one of the beasts and let it go to drink. Imbry noted that all their hats, baldrics, and pouches were white like those that had been issued to him.

Imbry stood in the doorway of the building and watched the proceedings. As the first animal was let go from its cart, the driver slid down from his seat and joined in the work of loosing the next beast. He was a man of improbable height and thinner than any the fat man could recall ever encountering, yet Imbry thought he might be the brother of the muscular man who had led the animal, so similar were they in the coloring of hair and eye.

As the thin man led the second beast to drink, the driver of its second cart, a youth approaching manhood, jumped down and went to unhitch the bawling creature between the shafts of the wagon behind his. Imbry could see that the process was a familiar one to humans and beasts, completed with a minimum of fuss or delay. When the last of the draft animals was slurping at the water's edge, the people busied themselves unloading lightweight furniture and large woven baskets and carrying them to the shaded part of the green space. In moments, a communal table had been established, dishes and utensils were clattering onto its surface, and a portable grill was being set up and activated.

The little man with the crackler had been watching the caravan's arrival from a spot midway between Imbry and the swirl of activity. Now he stepped forward and called a greeting to the muscular man who was clearly in charge of the group. "Ho, Taggar!"

The bigger man turned and regarded him with a mixed expression. "Tuchol," he said. "I thought you were with Grains's troupe."

"Only one season."

"And now you're looking to join us?" The big man's eyes went to Imbry and the expression did not change. "And with a friend."

"He's no friend of mine," Imbry said, stepping out of the doorway. "He has kidnapped me and brought me here under duress."

Taggar's eyebrows climbed to their highest vantage. He looked back to the half-sized man, noted the weapon in his hand. "Is this so, Tuchol?"

The smaller man lifted and lowered his shoulders without looking back at Imbry, but when Taggar advanced upon him and made a beckoning gesture, Tuchol placed the crackler in the extended palm. The caravan leader thumbed open the device's dorsal hatch, removed the power source, and put it in his pouch. Then a twist of his powerful hands rendered the crackler into so much debris. This he handed back to the half-sized man.

Imbry crossed the remaining distance and dealt Tuchol a solid slap to the side of his head, sending the little man sprawling. He intended to do more, but a wordless negative sound from Taggar and an outsized hand applied to the fat man's chest stopped his forward motion.

"No doubt he deserved that," said Taggar, and as an aside to the fallen man, "didn't you, Tuchol?"

"That and worse," said Imbry. He would have said more, but the bigger man spoke first.

"I will acquaint you with our rules," Taggar said. "Within the troupe, no one raises a hand to another, no matter what the provocation."

"I am not part of your troupe," Imbry said.

"True," said the other, "but no one from outside our company may offer harm to any of us, else we all pile on in mutual self-defense."

"You offer me little recourse," Imbry said. "This man has disrupted my life, dragged me across space through two whimsies, stripped me near naked. I do not even know where I am."

"And I do not know what two whimsies mean, but I can repair at least part of the damage," Taggar said. "You are on Fulda."

This Imbry already knew. If he had had access to *Hobey's Compleat Guide to the Settled Planets*, he could have looked up Fulda and learned where it stood in relation to the foundational domains and secondary worlds of The Spray. As it was, the mere name of the planet meant nothing to him. He told Taggar in so many words.

The troupe leader turned toward the half-sized man, who had regained his feet and was shaking his head as if to dislodge something that was making noise inside it. "Tuchol, are you rejoining us?"

"If I'm allowed. Temporarily."

Taggar looked around at the others, saw shrugs but no objections. "All right," he said. He turned to Imbry. "And you, do you also wish to join us?"

"Do I have a choice?"

"There is no compulsion amongst us, save that of mutually respectful behavior."

"I would rather," said Imbry, "go home."

Tuchol laughed at that, though he stifled his mirth when Taggar sent him a look. "You may do so, if you have the means," said the big man.

"The ship that brought me will not take me away. Is there a space port on your route?"

"No. Nor anywhere on Fulda."

"How is that possible?" said Imbry.

"I do not know. But it is not only possible. It is fact."

"Have you a communicator that I could use to call down a ship?"

"No, not for that purpose."

"If I do not go with you, will someone else be coming along?"

"Very doubtful. This is our company's route this season. I cannot imagine why anyone else would come here before next year."

Imbry contained himself. "And you would not advise staying?"

"No."

"Is there anywhere within walking distance? Anywhere that I might be able to call down a ship?"

The big man looked at Imbry measuringly. "You believe you can do that?"

"I assure you I am not a loon," the fat man said. "Do you not see moving points of light in the sky at night?"

Taggar thought about it. "I suppose I have. Those are spaceships?"

The tall, thin man had drifted over as they spoke. He regarded Imbry with curiosity but no show of friendliness. "They are," the thin man said. "Though I didn't know they could be called on a communicator."

"They can," said Imbry, "by one who knows the protocols."

Taggar's face showed an expression that said the matter might be interesting, but was irrelevant to their circumstances. "You might be best off talking to the Arbitration," he said.

"Is that your government?"

"Not ours," said the thin man.

"Hush," said the big man. "They are the ones who make the decisions."

"Well, then," said Imbry, "may I come with you to wherever I can talk to this Arbitration?"

"We cannot carry idlers," said Taggar. "You would have to join the company." At Imbry's frown, he added, "At least temporarily."

Imbry, though he often dealt professionally in other people's illusions, prided himself on retaining none for himself. "Then I believe I would like to join your company," he said.

"You wear white," Taggar said. "What is your talent?"

During their conversation, Imbry had been examining the other members of the troupe. Apart from the stick-insect man, he had noticed that the youth who had driven the second wagon had an unusual face. There was also a woman with a tiny head, and a slim person of average height whose sex remained indeterminate because he or she was covered from pate to toe in a coat of glossy, tan-colored fur. "Is talent necessary?" he said.

"Yes," said Taggar. "We operate within the law."

"I can sketch," said Imbry, "line drawings, portraits, caricatures."

The information brought a snort from Tuchol. Taggar sent him another look that quieted the little man. "Anything else?" he said.

It was not generally known, but Luff Imbry owned a passable tenor voice, though few had heard it raised since he had left school and its mandatory choir. "I can sing, if necessary."

"Please do so now," said the big man, and listened as Imbry sang the opening bars of *Thesiger's Lament*. "That will do," Taggar said. "What is your name and place of origin?"

Imbry told him.

"You have two names?" said Taggar.

The thin man said, "I've heard that off-worlders can have three or more names."

"Two names are common on Old Earth," said Imbry.

Taggar hushed him. "That's off-world?"

Imbry was not surprised to see that Old Earth was as unfamiliar to Taggar as Fulda was to Imbry. Humankind had spread out into The Spray many aeons ago and the ancient home world was little thought of now. Indeed, there were well-established schools of thought that argued for a number of other planets to be recognized as humanity's original font.

Taggar said, "Having two names is too irregular. Which one would you prefer to be known by?" When the Old Earther told him, he laid a hand on Imbry's shoulder and adopted a formal diction to say, "Imbry, of Old Yurt, you are now and henceforward a member of the Hedevan Traveling Players, with all the rights, privileges, and responsibilities appurtenant thereto." Then he smiled and said, "You may begin to exercise the former by joining us for the midday meal."

He led the way to the table, where the members of the company had finished laying out plates and cutlery. Some were seated, while others tended the grill on which sausages and some kind of thin pancakes were cooking. Taggar introduced the newcomer with minimal ceremony, and Imbry confined himself to an inclination of the head and an informal motion of hand to chest.

"Take my seat," Taggar said, and the fat man thought at first that it might be a significant gesture. Then he noticed that the strongly built leader's chair was far sturdier than the foldable arrangements of wood and fabric on which the others sat. The leader was sparing him the experience of becoming an object of mirth just as he was making the acquaintance of his new associates. Imbry lowered his formidable buttocks onto the offered seat, and when Taggar came back from one of the wagons with a matching chair the fat man made a discreet show of gratitude.

His introduction brought a variety of responses from the others at the table. The tall, skeletal man said, "Malweer," which turned out to be his name, and added the briefest and thinnest of smiles.

The tiny-headed woman made up for Malweer's reserve by favoring Imbry with an improbably wide grin and a tumbling speech of welcome and inquiry, in which she told him that she was called Ebblin, that he was to think of her as his new mother, and how did he get so plump, and was he partial to spiced sausages, which they were about to eat and in which she liked to indulge, although they tended to give her the squits, but what could you do? And what was his name again?

Before Imbry could respond, the fur-covered individual shushed Ebblin in what the Old Earther thought was an affectionate and familiar manner and identified herself—the voice was distinctly female, and sounded friendly—as Shan-Pei. "That's Wintle flipping the crepes," she said—the odd-faced youth paused in his labors to acknowledge the introduction with a flourish of his spatula—"and Thelia is tending the sausages."

Thelia was a young woman of medium build and squarish face of the same coloring as Taggar and Malweer—indeed, now that they were all seated together, Imbry saw no more than a shade of difference in hair, eye, and skin color around the table. Even Shan-Pei's fur was of a comparable shade. The only one who stood out among the company was himself, being of paler skin and almost colorless hair and with eyes the color of ice.

At first glance, he thought that young Thelia also stood out by not being in anyway unusual. But when she was introduced she waved to him with the hand that was not holding a long-tined fork, and he saw that her unencumbered extremity was bloodless and tiny—as if it had stopped growing in infancy.

Wintle brought a platter of pancakes to the table and it was passed from hand to hand, each member of the troupe forking a few of the thin crepes onto his or her plate, then spreading the flat surface with a sweet-smelling compote of purple fruit ladled from a central bowl. Imbry did as the others did, rolling his portion into a fat tube to be sliced and eaten with knife and fork. A platter of sausages now made the rounds, and the fat man found them to be as spicy as Ebblin had promised.

At least, he thought, *I will not starve,* an observation that was underwritten by Ebblin and Wintle, who insisted that he take an extra helping when he had cleared his plate. "It can't be easy keeping all that up," the tiny-headed woman said, with a gesture toward his mounded middle.

Otherwise the meal was taken in silence. When all were finished, the plates were passed to one end of the table and a carafe of punge moved in stages in the opposite direction. Only when everyone's mug was filled did conversation begin, and Imbry was asked to tell how he came to be waiting at this oasis. He made no effort to sweeten the tale.

"I was lured into a trap, stunned, and kidnapped by your companion," he said, cocking one fleshy digit at where Tuchol sat at the other end of the table. "Why, I do not know, but the ship that brought us said it had been done at someone else's bidding."

"Spaceships can think and talk," Malweer put in when he saw brows wrinkling. With that fact accepted, if not digested, by the company, all eyes turned toward the half-sized man, who stared truculently at his short-fingered hands clasped around a mug of ale. After an expectant silence, Ebblin opened her mouth but Taggar forestalled her. "Tuchol," he said, "we do not keep secrets if doing so causes disharmony in the troupe."

The little man looked up, met several gazes, though not Imbry's, then looked back into his mug. "I might as well say this now," he said. "I was given no choice. See this?" He indicated the red splotch on his sternum. "I was in a tavern in Nid, after Grayan's last tour, when a stranger offered me a tankard of ale."

The tale continued: Tuchol had woken up on a spaceship, with a device glued to his body. The ship's integrator told him that if he did not do as he was told, or if he tried to remove the object, it would detonate. The walls, floor, and ceiling of the cabin were covered by sheets of impermeable fabric—to facilitate cleaning up, he was told—and Tuchol took the situation seriously.

"What did the man look like?" Imbry asked.

Tuchol gave him a look that questioned the fat man's intellect. "Like anybody," he said. He turned to Malweer. "Do off-worlders have the power to make themselves look different?"

The thin man knitted his brows. Imbry spoke instead. "There is such a device. It cloaks the wearer in whatever semblance he chooses."

Gasps went around the table. Wintle said, "You mean I could look like an—"

But Taggar silenced him. "We need to hear what Tuchol has to say," he said. "The harmony of the troupe is at issue." To Tuchol, he said, "It seems to me that you owe Imbry an apology. It is not right to do a disservice to a fellow member of the company."

"In the first place," said the half-sized man, "he was not a member of the company when I seized him. In the second place, he owes me an apology for involving me, who would have preferred to remain an innocent bystander, in his desperate enterprises, whatever they may be."

Imbry rejected both arguments as specious and began to give Tuchol a sharply pointed assessment of the little man's character. Again, Taggar intervened. "This does not conduce to harmony," he said, "and we have a long tour ahead of us. I will now hear pertinent comments from the generality."

Imbry made to speak again—his long familiarity with persons of a criminal disposition told him that Tuchol was telling only part of the truth, and not even the most important part—but the troupe leader ruled him out of order. The others spoke, each in turn, and though the phrasing was different in each case, there was but one opinion amongst them. It was most succinctly voiced by Malweer, the elongated man, who said, "However any of us came to be here, we are all here now, and with a long road ahead of us. The most productive course must be to put aside pointless regrets and recriminations, and move forward."

"Then that is that," said Taggar. "Tuchol and Imbry, the company requires you to let the past lie dead behind you. Are you willing to do so?"

The little man scowled but his hand made a motion of irritated acquiescence. Imbry was less inclined to be accommodating, but he suspected that if he did not agree, he would be left to try his luck with the oasis's scant resources; he didn't think the greig trees would bear fruit for quite some time. But he had one question.

"After you shocked me with the crackler," he said, "you kicked me. Was that part of your instructions?"

Tuchol's scowl deepened and he did not reply. Taggar said, "It is a valid inquiry. You must answer."

The half-sized man squirmed and had to be urged again. "No," he said, at last, "I was angry at being put to so much trouble, against my will."

"Then you definitely owe Imbry an apology," said Ebblin, to a general concurrence from the others around the table. Tuchol grimaced but finally offered Imbry a couple of grudging syllables, though his face belied the sentiment.

"If you accept, we can move on," Taggar said.

"Then I accept," said the fat man, "though I reserve the right to renew my grievance against Tuchol if I should ever encounter him after we both leave the company."

After a brief further discussion, this was judged a reasonable amendment and the matter was declared closed. Punge mugs were now drained, and the troupe rose and began to break camp in what was clearly a well-practiced routine. Imbry found himself underfoot in his efforts to help, until the odd-faced youth, Wintle, took him in hand and introduced him to the system of collection and stowage.

"You can ride with me," the boy said.

"Agreed," said Imbry, "if you will answer some questions."

In a very short time, the draft animals were reharnessed to the carts and the troupe mounted up. Imbry could not spring into the box as others did, but Wintle showed him how to put one foot on a wheel hub, then the other on the footing of the brake lever. With relatively slight difficulty, he managed to get aboard. The youth settled in beside him and when it came their turn to follow the wagon in front, Wintle clucked to the animal and slapped the reins down on its broad rump. With a jerk and a flick of a tufted tail, they were rolling forward.

"Where are we bound?" Imbry asked, when the whole train was in motion.

"For tonight," Wintle said, "the pass between the Bredons, yonder." He indicated with a lifting of his chin the hills to the west. "Tomorrow we will climb to the plateau beyond, and by nightfall we should be on the outskirts of Pilger's Corners."

"What sort of place is Pilger's Corners?"

"It's like any other place," the youth said, and gave Imbry a milder version of the look Tuchol had given him when he'd asked what the stranger in the tavern had looked like. "That's an odd question," he said.

"Why is it odd?"

"Because places are places. Why would one be different from another?"

"A hundred different reasons," Imbry said. "The circumstances of its founding, the topography of the land, the tastes of the residents, the flux and churn of architectural fashion, rivalry between social leaders, contempt for the too-familiar, the evolution of civic goals—" He broke off when he saw that the youth was regarding him with consternation. "Do none of these conditions apply on Fulda?"

"In a word," said Wintle, "no."

"Property owners do not compete to outdo each other in the appearance of their establishments?"

Imbry had to take the youth's "What an odd notion!" as a negative reply.

"So every town is exactly the same? The buildings, streets, amenities—all exactly alike?"

"Some places are more populated than others," Wintle said, "and therefore have more buildings. But a house is a house, is it not? There is an optimum size and shape, and why would anyone depart from the optimum? This was all laid down long ago by the Blessed Founder."

Imbry deferred a question as to who this last-named individual might be. He scratched his head under the crown of his broad hat. "All right," he said, "suppose one family has three children and another has seven. Wouldn't the larger brood need more room?"

"Seven children would be irregular," was the answer. "For that matter, so would three."

"How many children is regular?" Imbry said.

"Two, of course," said the youth. "One male, one female. Unless,"—and here he lowered his voice as if what was to follow was not to be spoken of too brazenly—"unless one of them is . . ."—and now his words descended into a whisper—"irregular."

"Irregular?" Imbry said, not quite sure he had heard the term over the rattle of the wheels and the huff-huff of the draft beast's breathing.

Wintle's face reddened and he looked about as if some authority might suddenly arrive to box his ears for mischief. "Shush," he said.

"You haven't encountered many off-worlders, have you?" Imbry said.

"None," said the boy, keeping his voice low. "Ingress is not encouraged. Off-worlders are known to be shamelessly irregular. Malweer says sometimes they come to Nid and Steyne, where the troupes rest between seasons. But they must wear those devices you talked about, because no one I've ever met has ever seen one."

"So I am . . . irregular?" Imbry said, lowering his own voice on the last word.

Wintle's embarrassment deepened. "Well, we all are. I mean, look at us."

"But it's not something to be openly discussed?"

The boy sighed. "It's bad enough to be . . ."—he made a rolling-on motion with one hand— "without having to dwell on it."

"I see," said Imbry. "Perhaps I should discuss this with one of the older people."

Relief spread across the boy's long face. "Yes, perhaps that would be best."

Imbry had been intending at some point to question Wintle about his curious physiognomy, specifically why the youth preferred to go through life with pendulous jowls and earlobes, along with droopy eyes and a sloping nose that more approximated a canine muzzle than anything human. Now he put the matter aside and merely watched the arid landscape roll toward him from beneath the wheels of the wagon ahead of them.

He wished he'd had the presence of mind to have asked the ship's integrator to show him Hobey's entry on Fulda. It was clearly one of those odd little worlds where the population had committed themselves to putting into practice some unusual philosophy. The minor worlds of The Spray were freckled with such places, often founded by cults and coteries of like-minded believers who had come as refugees from more cosmopolitan worlds where their peculiar slants were disrespected, if not outright opposed. Once established, the exiles would discourage contact with the wider array of humanity—as by not building a spaceport, so that they could pursue without interruption whatever notion or dogma they believed would bring them salvation or deliver them into their version of utopia.

Imbry thought he would take up the history of Fulda with one of the adults. In the meantime, the sun angled down toward the hills, which were now appreciably closer. He could see that the track they were following led to a pass between two ridges that extended out onto the plain, like a pair of headlands enclosing an inlet of a sea. Atop one of the promontories was an outcrop of weathered stone that looked too regular to be of natural origin. It resembled a cluster of bubbles such as a child might produce by blowing on a film of soap caught in a circle, piling one orb on top of another. In places, apparently at random, the stone globules were pierced by circular holes.

Imbry pointed toward it, using his chin as the youth had done, and said, "If it's not improper to ask, are those ruins? And if so, what is their story?"

Wintle glanced that way, unconcerned. "Leavings of the indigenes," he said, "from long ago, even before the clitch miners came and went." He wrinkled his brow in recollection, then said, "Malweer could tell you more than I—he reads books—but people say there was a race of ultraterrenes here, a very long time ago. Some of their ruins can still be seen, though the miners broke up most of them."

"Were they searching for artifacts?"

The word meant nothing to the boy, but he answered anyway. "I think they were looking for clitch."

"What is clitch?" Imbry said.

Again, he had thrown the youth into consternation. "Well, it's . . ." Wintle hunted for a description, but did not find one. "It's just clitch," he finished.

Imbry realized he should have ridden with Malweer, though the thin man had not offered him a seat. "What happened to the ultraterrenes?"

Wintle did not know. But he insisted that neither did anyone else on Fulda. "Malweer said he's heard somebody say that they tried to do something about water, something big. But it didn't work. All the water got stuck in the air, and it can't come out. So now there are only the pools down here in the desert, such as the one where we found you. Up in the high country, there is no water at all."

"Does Malweer say that is what caused the indigenes to die out?"

"I think no one really knows. Maybe they just left and went somewhere else. But I know there's nothing to see in the ruins."

Conversation lapsed after that exchange. There being nothing else to see beyond desert and hill, Imbry turned his attention to the contents of the wagon, visible through the opening in its cloth cover that gaped behind his seat. The vehicle was mostly filled with large bundles of felt, tightly wrapped with straps of a coarser, woven fabric.

"Tents?" he asked Wintle.

"Pavilions."

They were also Imbry's bed for the remainder of the journey into the pass. He crawled into the shade of the wagon's interior, made himself more comfortable than he had expected to be on the bales of fabric, and dozed until he heard the braying and stamping that announced that the caravan was coming to a halt. He alighted from the back of the vehicle to find that the stock was being unharnessed and led to another pool much like that of the first oasis, while preparations were underway for another communal meal under an almost identical stand of trees. The only difference in the scene was the setting: instead of being surrounded by flat desert, the troupe was now on a level piece of ground between two slopes. The trail also rose and fell before and behind them, and the fat man realized that they had climbed a fair distance into the pass while he had slept.

"Can you cook?" Taggar's voice came from behind Imbry as he watched the bustle. "You look like a man who knows his way around a kitchen."

"I do. I can."

"Then help Thelia. Wintle can help me feed the barbarels." And thus Imbry learned the name of the animals that had pulled his weight into the hills.

The portable kitchen was distributed between three wagons. Under the young woman's direction, Imbry fetched and hauled, unfolded and arranged. Again, as at lunch, some of the cooking would be done on a grill set above self-igniting coals, but the setup also included an array of pots that provided their own heat, allowing the cooking to boil and simmer. Thelia introduced her new helper to a range of ingredients, most of which he recognized, and a minimal selection of spices. From these, with water hauled from the pool, he improvised a robust pottage to accompany the strips of meat that the woman tended one-handed on the grill.

The results, accompanied by flatbreads baked in an ingenious oven, were well received by all the company, although Tuchol grimaced and offered comments apparently intended for no one but himself to hear. After taking a first mouthful, Taggar rose and left the table, returning moments later with a keg under his arm from which he poured a strong brown ale that perfectly complemented the food.

Malweer downed half a tumbler then used the remainder to toast Imbry.

"Takes a first-rate meal to make our leader unbung the ale before we reach Chenbo Fork," he said. "I, for one, am glad we found you."

"Thelia did the meats and bread," Imbry said.

"We're always glad of Thelia," said the thin man, "but the vegetable stew won us the ale."

"Then I am glad to be on your good side," the fat man said. "Young Wintle has been telling me that you're the one to turn to for information on Fulda and its past."

Malweer had been energetically spooning up the contents of his bowl as Imbry spoke, causing the latter to wonder how such an appetite could result in so meager a frame. Now the other man paused long enough to belch before saying, "Fuldans, particularly the Ideals, never used to concern themselves with what has been, nor with what may come— though the Renewal has certainly changed that."

Imbry interrupted. "Ideals? Renewal?"

"One thing at a time," said the thin man. "As for the past, it is thought that the proper focus should be on a full appreciation of what is. I, myself, have decided that since I have clearly chosen to be a statistical anomaly in form, I might as well also be one in character. Hence, I involve myself with the past, although I trouble myself less over the future."

"You believe your physique to be a result of a choice you made?" Imbry said. "Prenatally, I presume?"

"Considering the attendant difficulties," Malweer said, "I prefer to think that it is a result of my own volition, for reasons I cannot now appreciate, rather than random chance, or worse, some unavoidable fate." He regarded Imbry's corpulence and said, "You may pursue a different philosophy."

"At the moment, I am pursuing information as to this planet's past," the Old Earther said. But he decided to defer asking for clarification on other issues. He was coming to see Malweer as the type to dislike interruptions, once he was launched. He let the thin one sail on.

Fulda, he learned, was an old world. When the first locators had come this way, they had found a dried-up planet that, curiously, boasted abundant supplies of water. But most of the liquid was trapped in huge aquifers that permeated the planet's porous crust. Another great portion was suspended in the atmosphere, which extended far higher into space than should have been possible for a world of Fulda's size and composition.

Malweer paused to drain his tankard of ale and pour another one. Imbry used the hiatus to ask, "What was the explanation?"

"I'm not aware that there ever was one," said the thin man. "There was no settlement until the clitch miners came, and they were interested only in taking the clitch and selling it off-world."

"What is clitch?"

"I saw a piece once," Malweer said. "It looked greasy."

"Greasy?"

"Like a greasy rock. Doesn't matter; it's all long gone now."

"The indigenes?" Imbry said. "What happened to them?"

"No one knows," said Malweer. "They left no records that could be identified. At least not until the tablets showed up."

"Tablets?"

"For the Renewal."

"I don't understand," said Imbry.

Malweer drained his ale, then held the container over his open mouth to allow the last few drops to fall onto his tongue. He belched and when he spoke again, Imbry realized that the thin man was one of those whom strong drink bowled over quite quickly. "Doesn't matter," Malweer said. "Doesn't have anything to do with us." He belched again. "Except when it does."

The man blinked sleepily and looked around for more ale.

Taggar spoke. "We don't concern ourselves with such things." Imbry realized that the others around the table were showing discomfort at his questioning of the thin man.

"What do you mean, 'such things'?" Imbry said, but the muscular man waved away the question with an expression that said the inquiry bordered on the unseemly.

"Does everyone on Old Dirt ask so many questions?" Ebblin said.

"Some do," said Imbry. "Tastes vary." That innocuous observation caused the Fuldans even more disquietude. He saw Ebblin mouth to herself the last two words he had spoken as if it was the most outlandish remark she had ever heard.

At that moment, Imbry experienced an instance of the abrupt mental dislocation that often struck those who traveled widely among the Ten

Thousand Worlds. He had heard it called the "bump" or the "dissonance" and had encountered it himself more than once. It was the psychic shock suffered by a human being from one world who suddenly became aware that the person from some other world with whom he was innocently interacting possessed a radically, perhaps chillingly, different mindscape.

The two might be chance-met in a tavern. They would fall into innocuous chat about inconsequential matters, each convinced by the other's views on the weather or the quality of the beer that they are like-minded in all that matters. Until one of them offers an offhand comment about the tedium involved in having to sell his surplus offspring, or enthuses salaciously about next week's public evisceration of a malefactor whose crime turns out to be something like scratching a buttock within ten paces of the portrait of a local saint.

An icy frisson passes through the stranger. He holds himself perfectly still, though his eyes dart about, alarmed. Shadows seem to gather about him. All at once it seems perfectly possible, even likely, that the bland couple sitting at an adjacent table or the idlers in the street outside might without warning show fangs and unsheathe claws, leap upon the hapless visitor, and turn an until-now pleasant excursion into an impromptu abattoir.

Some travelers who experienced the bump returned immediately to the spaceport to take ship for home, never to venture off-world again. Most recovered from the shock and counted it an opportunity for learning or an inducement toward philosophical speculation. A few became addicted to the shivery sense of dislocation and deliberately sought it out, even provocatively; these sometimes came to bad ends. Imbry used the recommended approach: he advanced the conversation to safer ground by suggesting that the Fuldans choose the topic.

The members of the troupe seemed glad to move toward firmer ground. Malweer speculated boozily as to whether the long-gone indigenes had actually been seeking to achieve the conditions that prevailed on Fulda: the thick atmosphere maintained an even, constant temperature throughout the day and across the calendar.

"It seems a sensible strategy," said Taggar. "The present arrangement of the climate offers no unsettling extremes or sudden shifts. It is equilibrium, harmony, moderation."

Luff Imbry, whose character and career were both entwined with the pursuit of the rare and special, would have presented a counterargument, if it had not been only moments since he had experienced the chill of the bump. Instead, he folded his fleshy hands across his naked belly and moved his head in an expression of polite acknowledgement of a telling point and waited to hear what others might say. The consensus of opinion was that the mellow sameness of Fulda's climate was one of the planet's chiefest jewels; it must have been the indigenes' intent.

"Then why did they not stay around to enjoy it?" said Wintle.

"You are presupposing that, having created a perfect world, they then left it behind?" said Taggar.

The odd-faced youth gestured to the landscape in general. "They were not here when the miners arrived. They left ruins, but no mass graves."

"We know nothing of their funerary customs," said Taggar. "Perhaps they consumed their dead relatives. Perhaps they incinerated them and spread the ashes widely." He reached down and took a pinch of dry soil from between his feet and let it drift away on the quiet breeze. "There," he said, "there goes the last of the indigenes."

"Or, perhaps," said the woman with the infant hand, "having achieved a wondrously moderate world, they came to see themselves as an excrescence to its perfection. Saddened, they built ships and left."

"Or died, romantically and en masse, all at one appointed hour," said Ebblin, a wistful look upon her diminutive face.

"Or," said Malweer, boozily, having used the time when others were talking to drink more ale, "perhaps they crossed over to Perfection, where they're waiting for the Ideals to join them."

Imbry wanted to ask what Perfection was, but from the reaction of the others, he saw that the skeletal man had said something grossly improper. Taggar put the bung back in his cask of ale and bore it back to the wagon from which it had come. Ebblin took charge of Malweer, leading him stumbling toward one of the tents. The others rose and began to clean up the remains of supper and set out preparations for tomorrow's breakfast.

No one assigned Imbry a chore and their routine was so well organized that his attempt to join in only slowed the proceedings. He got out of their way. But his attention was drawn to Tuchol, who had taken no part in the conversation. The half-sized man, having eaten what was set before him, had risen from the communal table during the talk and walked to the other side of the oasis's pool. There he sat on a bench made from three slabs of stone, his back to the rest of the company. He sat as if in thought, though Imbry saw his head tilt toward the sky from time to time.

Imbry had been wanting a further private word with his kidnapper. This seemed an opportune moment. He now made a show of stretching and yawning, a man at leisure and with no immediate agenda, and sauntered in the opposite direction that Tuchol had taken, though his path would inevitably bring him around the pool to the spot where the little man sat. But he had taken only half a dozen steps when he felt a large hand descend decisively onto his shoulder and turn him half around.

"I've told Tuchol to keep a distance between you," said Taggar. "Now I'm telling you."

Imbry saw no point in dissembling. "There are things I need to ask him."

"You heard his story."

"There may be more to it than what he told us."

Taggar conceded the point, but said, "Tomorrow we will reach Pilger's Corners. There is a Corps of Provosts station there. If you lay an information, Tuchol will have a harder time avoiding Investigator Breeth's questions than yours."

"That depends on how I ask him," said Imbry.

"No," said Taggar, the set of his face adding the information that the matter was decided, while inquiring if Imbry intended to dispute his ruling.

"What if he leaves us at this Pilger's Corners?"

"Why would he do that? He's much better off with the troupe."

"He may not see it that way."

"The answer is still no," said the company leader. "We have only each other and our parts to play. We divide at our peril."

"Very well, 'no' it is," said the fat man. "In this Pilger's Corners, would there be a communications nexus? Could I send a message off-world?"

"Perhaps," said the troupe leader. "You would have to ask at the Arbitration." Then he turned and clapped his hands. "Sleeping pavilions," he called. "Early start in the morning."

The troupe moved with practiced efficiency to draw poles and bundles of felt from two of the wagons. In less time than Imbry would have expected, two roomy tents had been erected, lanterns lit, and sleeping pallets laid out. The cooking and eating gear was cleaned and readied for use in the morning.

The Old Earther was kept occupied doing his share under the guidance of one or the other of the troupe, though never Tuchol. By the time the camp was ready for sleep, full dark had fallen. No moon rose—the planet had no companion—nor did many stars appear in the thickly veiled sky, and none of them were familiar to Imbry. Twilight lasted longer than on Old Earth, but once darkness had set in, it was far deeper than a resident of a sleepless city like Olkney was used to. The night seemed to press in more closely.

Imbry went into the tent designated for the male members of the company and sat upon the pallet Taggar pointed out to him. It was next to one of the pegged-down walls, and the fat man noted that the company leader's own pallet was positioned next to Imbry's. The fat man would have to crawl over Taggar to leave his sleeping position if he should decide to visit Tuchol—against the tent's far wall—while the troupe slept. The look that Taggar gave him as he settled himself on the sleeping pad told Imbry that the dispositions were not random.

No covers were supplied, or needed, the temperature remaining constant. Malweer was already snoring. Taggar was last to lie down, first extinguishing the lantern that hung from a hook attached to the central pole. The tent was briefly full of the rustles and small sounds of a group of men settling for the night. Imbry laid his head upon the pallet's pillow and composed himself. It was odd not to have the services of a bed to ease him into slumber, but he knew that if he let his mind wander he would soon cross the unposted border into sleep.

The pallet was hard, though. A thought occurred to him and he asked Taggar, "There are cots in the buildings. We slept on cots at the other oasis."

The bigger man sighed. "Don't make trouble," he said. "Now sleep."

Dawn was as slow a process as twilight had been. Imbry awoke in the crepuscular gray light. He lay for a moment, listening to snores and someone's dream mumblings, gathering his thoughts. Then he sat up. Taggar, Malweer, and Wintle slept on their pallets, the youth murmuring into his pillow. But Tuchol's place was vacant.

Imbry listened for the sound of footsteps, but heard only the sounds from within the tent. With a smoothness and silence that belied his bulk, he rose to his feet and stepped over Taggar. A moment later he was outside in the warm air. The sun was still below the horizon, but the sky was filling with light. No activity showed from within the women's tent. The oasis was still except for the slight motions of the greig trees. Of Tuchol there was no sign.

The air had stayed too warm overnight to have precipitated much of a dew, but here and there tiny beads of moisture clung to the grass—enough to show where a single set of footsteps led from the men's tent around the pool and toward the farther edge of the green space. Imbry hesitated a moment, weighing the pros and cons of waking Taggar, then decided to go on his own.

He followed Tuchol's trail, past the bench where the little man had sat, glancing up at the sky, the night before. The grass extended a short distance farther, to the fringe of berry-bearing plants beyond which was hard and stony soil. Imbry passed through the fronds. The bare ground was flat here for a few dozen paces, then the slope of the hill began.

At the foot of the incline lay Tuchol, facedown, limbs contorted into odd angles that ought to have been too uncomfortable to maintain. But the half-sized man was beyond discomfort, his neck set at an impossible angle and the ground around him soaked in a wide pool of blood and other fluids.

Imbry approached the edge of the dampness. Before he could examine the scene as closely as he intended, he felt the familiar weight of a large hand on his shoulder again, and Taggar's harsh voice said, "What have you done?"

CHAPTER THREE

Taggar had some means of long-distance communications. After he put Imbry back in the tent and told Malweer to keep an eye on him, he donned a pair of gloves and went to one of the flat-roofed buildings. The Old Earther could hear him conducting a one-sided conversation, but couldn't make out the words. Afterward, the big man came back into the tent and said, "They're sending a roller. It won't take long."

"I didn't kill him," Imbry said. He turned up the soles of his sandals, one at a time, and said, "The blood had pooled all around, but there's not a drop on me. Besides, I didn't have time. He looked as if he's been dead for a while."

"How come you know how dead people look after a while?" Malweer said, his long face drawn longer by skepticism.

"I have lived an eventful life," said Imbry.

The thin man went out and came back a few moments later. "He's stiff," he said. "I think that means he's been dead longer than a few minutes."

"I believe he was taken up in an aircraft and dropped from a great height," Imbry said. "The same aircraft that brought us down from a spaceship."

"We've still got to let the provost's men handle it," Taggar said. "Right now, I don't think we should discuss it anymore."

Imbry was no great admirer of police forces, but in this case he was content to wait for the authorities to arrive. He was confident that any competent investigator would soon put the picture together. Then Imbry might be able to find a way off this world and back to Old Earth—where he might indeed indulge in some homicide.

Malweer had long since gone to help strike camp and have breakfast. He returned briefly to bring Imbry and Taggar bowls of grits and some fried bread, but otherwise the fat man and the troupe leader remained alone. Taggar declined further conversation.

They were not too far from Pilger's Corners, the nearest town. The roller came down the track at a far faster speed than a barbarel and wagon could have managed. Imbry heard it arrive and heard two men talking. Moments later, one of them entered the tent. He was naked save for hat, sandals, and baldric-supported side-pouch, though his were all of a uniform dark brown. Two small circles of gold cloth were affixed to the front of his hat and another two were on the strip of cloth across his chest.

When the provost's investigator came into the tent, Taggar rose from where he had been sitting cross-legged on the earthen floor and offered a deep bow. Imbry also rose but studied the man. His experience of policemen on several worlds under a variety of circumstances had taught him that they came in different types. A wise man adapted his conduct to the breed he was dealing with.

When Taggar had completed his bow, he made some complicated gestures involving fingertips, chest, and brow. Then he clasped his hands before him at his waist and, with eyes downcast, he said, "Investigator Breeth. I am Taggar. I have had the honor of meeting you before."

Breeth scarcely glanced at him. His hazel eyes in a bland face went instead to Imbry, and the fat man thought, *Oh my, I've drawn an angry one.* They were often the hardest to deal with.

Breeth's expression was one of distaste struggling with outrage. Imbry saw that this was not a good time to advance a request for assistance in getting off-world. He lowered his gaze and adopted a passive aspect. The provost's man, meanwhile, dug in his pouch and produced a pair of knitted gloves, which he pulled on with brusque gestures. Then he bought out a strap of hard but flexible material and told Imbry, "Turn around." A moment later the fat man's wrists were pinioned behind him. A second strap cinched his elbows together. Finally the man behind him slipped a cloth bag over his head, tugged it down, and tightened it at the neck by a drawstring.

"I protest," said Imbry. "This is—"

The blow that struck the side of his head felt like a flat-handed slap. It made his ears ring, but not before he heard Taggar's sharp intake of breath.

Breeth said, "Keep your mouth shut, oddy."

Imbry was not struck again, but his upper arm was seized by a gloved hand and he was roughly yanked around and marched outside. He felt the warmth of sunlight on his naked skin. After a few steps, he was halted. Then the hand on his bicep became a pair, and a second pair gripped his other arm, and he was being urged to step up. He raised his foot, found some kind of step and climbed. A moment later, he was manhandled into position on a bench seat that was covered in rough cloth. He heard a whirring, then he was thrown against the seat-back as the roller moved forward. The vehicle was not enclosed; he felt the passage of air on his skin.

For some time, the only sound was that of the vehicle's wheels—he assumed that anything called a roller would have wheels—grinding over the rough surface of the track. The provost's men were in front of him, but Breeth did not speak until he said, "Turn here. Take us around the back way." Then Imbry began to hear other sounds, voices, the whispery stirrings of greig tree branches, the *plop-plop* of barbarel pads, and the clatter of metal-shod wheels on paving stones. The warmth of the sun was suddenly cut off while the noise from the roller increased, and he knew they had come under the shade of a wall, probably passing down an alley—Breeth's "back way."

Then the vehicle turned, traveled a short distance, and halted, back in sun-warmth again. Imbry was pushed and pulled out of his seat then hustled through a doorway, turned and turned again, a seat pushed against the backs of his legs. He had to lean forward to accommodate his bound arms. The hood remained over his head.

He heard a door close, a chair scrape the floor then creak as someone's weight settled into it. The room was still. *Policemen use silence as a tool*, he reminded himself. He sat and waited. The quiet continued.

Then Breeth said, "We know you killed him. The question is why?"

"I did not kill him," said Luff Imbry. "The question, therefore, is who did?"

"You were known to be on bad terms—"

"He shocked me into paralysis, kicked me—"

Interrupting the interrogator won him another slap on the side of the head.

"You hated him. That's motive."

Imbry waited, then said, "May I speak now?"

"Yes."

"I am from off-world, from Old Earth. I was kidnapped and brought here by Tuchol. A certain amount of rancor is understandable."

"So you admit it."

"I admit the undeniable. But I did not kill him. Indeed, it is possible his death was accidental."

"His body was crushed and broken, the injuries consistent with a personage of your . . . irregular conformation having jumped up and down on him in a paroxysm of rage." The investigator folded his arms across his bare chest. "How would you have done that accidentally?"

Imbry sighed. "The injuries are also consistent with his having fallen from a great height. Such as from a spaceship's carry-all. Such as the carry-all that was used to take me aboard the ship that brought us here."

"What ship?" said the man from the provost's office. "Who saw this ship? What is its name?"

"If there was no ship, how did Tuchol and I appear at the oasis where we were picked up by the troupe? We had no means of travel, yet there we were."

"Another troupe abandoned you there, because of the bad blood between you. Your kind can't control your emotions. You're shiftless, squalid, disgusting—" He broke off. "Stop wasting my time. Confess. Nobody cares about that little oddy. You won't get more than a couple of years—"

"I did not kill him."

The investigator sighed. Imbry expected another slap, but it didn't come. The room was quiet again. The fat man imagined Breeth sitting across the table from him—there was always a table, chairs on either side. The provost's man would be giving Imbry a look that he had seen on the faces of officers on a dozen worlds, a mixture of dislike and frustration. It said, "I know you are a criminal, and I know that you have done things for which you ought to be punished, but I do not have enough evidence to send you to . . ."

The last word varied, depending on the philosophical underpinnings of the world in question. Sometimes it was "rehabilitation," sometimes "incarceration," though in some places it might be "a thorough flogging," or even "the post." Imbry had been threatened with "the post" on the secondary world Courmaline; he had not remained on-world long enough to discover for certain what it meant.

"You could ask the other members of the troupe," he told the provost's investigator, keeping his voice mild.

The chair scraped again and suddenly the hood was yanked away from Imbry's face, the unloosened drawstring abrading his jaw and stinging his sore ear. Breeth threw the bag into the corner then leaned over the table, his weight propped on his wrists. "I'm asking you," he said.

Years before, Imbry had trained himself to notice and capture microexpressions; it was a useful skill when negotiating with people for whom honesty was a remote and foreign country. He saw an alternation of emotions on Breeth's bland face: revulsion, contempt, anger, the standard repertoire of the frustrated homicide investigator. But there was something else, something that underlay the strong emotions and even contradicted it.

After a moment, the analyst in the back of his mind identified it. *Appetite*, the fat man thought, *appetite and aversion, at one and the same time*, like a man who lusts after what repels him. He did not think the provost's man desired him physically, but there was something about Imbry that caused Breeth to hunger—and something about the hunger that caused Imbry concern.

Then he saw the investigator shake off the emotion and resume the interrogation. The same questions came again. Interrogators were trained to circle back on the line of inquiry. "You were found standing over the body. You had motive, means, opportunity," Breeth said.

"Taggar would have woken when I crawled over him," Imbry said, "as indeed he *did* awaken. So I had no opportunity. Unless you are saying that I crawled over Taggar without waking him, stole out of the tent, and slaughtered Tuchol, who died without making a sound, then crawled back over Taggar to my pallet, again without waking him, only so that I could then crawl over him a third time, awakening him, so that he could follow me out and find me standing over the body? Wouldn't I have been better advised to let someone else find the corpse?"

"You went once. Taggar awoke and followed, but was too late. You had already savaged the little fellow."

"Without getting so much as a speck of his blood on me?"

"There was a pool of water. You could have cleansed yourself."

"So I followed Tuchol, crushed and trampled him without a sound, ran to the pool, washed off the gore, then ran back to stand over him—all in the time it took Taggar to see me leaving the tent and rise and follow me."

The provost man's hand slapped the table between them. "So you confess?"

"I do not. I merely itemize the nonsense you seek to hang around my neck."

The investigator made a noise somewhere between a groan and a growl. He kicked back the utilitarian chair on his side of the table, stalked from the room. Left in the silence, Imbry reviewed the last few moments. There had been a disconnection between what had been happening—a standard interrogation of a suspect in a serious crime—and the emotions that kept flickering into life on the provost's man's nondescript face. Something was going on in the man's psyche, Imbry was convinced, that had nothing to do with the roles of suspect and investigator.

He remembered the word that Breeth had applied to Taggar: *oddy*. Obviously, it implied oddness, difference. But it was clearly also an epithet of contempt. Did that explain the investigator's suppressed emotion? Was Breeth the kind who felt uncomfortable in the presence of persons who did not stand upon the middle rung of humanity's ladder? Among the thousands of cultures speckled across the worlds of The Spray, there were those that valued conformity and found irregularity an affront. The Hedevan company comprised a collection of unusual shapes and characteristics. Were such people discriminated against on Fulda? Did Imbry's heroic shape revolt the provost's man?

But there was nothing unusual about Taggar other than his overdeveloped physique. Indeed, now that Imbry thought about it, there was a definite resemblance between the two men. Their features were similar, though Taggar's were heavier, the bones beneath the flesh more pronounced. But they were the same coloration—eye, hair, and skin tone—though that might be a result of the inbreeding that was to be expected on a disregarded world that lacked even a spaceport. Some similarity of type was bound to emerge over a long time.

The door opened. Breeth came back in. Imbry readied himself for a resumption of the questioning. Instead, the investigator walked on stiff legs to where the hood lay in the corner. He took it up and, stepping behind Imbry, jammed it back down on the prisoner's head. In the sudden darkness, Imbry heard Breeth say, "Up!" the man's voice thick in the back of his throat.

Imbry stood. He heard his chair clatter away across the floor. Breeth must have kicked it. He expected to be taken from the interview room and imprisoned in a cell for a while—moving the suspect around, keeping him isolated, was part of the process of reducing his sense of independence and security. The technique was intended to make the prisoner dependent on his captors, and could be effective even with a suspect who was aware of the technique.

But Imbry was not taken to the door. Instead, he was pushed backwards until his shoulders met the wall and his wrists were pressed against a hard object that protruded from it at waist height. He felt a tug on the restraint, then another, and found himself unable to move. Breeth had attached his wrist restraint to a ring or hook set in the interrogation room wall.

Imbry did not care for the implications. "Listen—" he began, but got no further. A sideways blow to his ankles kicked his feet out from under him and his full weight fell upon his pinioned wrists. He cried out, as much in surprise and anger as from hurt, and immediately the familiar hard hand struck open-palmed against the side of his head. This time it drove a column of compressed air down his ear cavity and a lance of agony shot through his head.

It was not the first time that Imbry had been beaten. In his younger years he frequently had to endure physical violence at the hands of those who had power over him. Sometimes the assaults had come from persons who possessed police credentials. Sometimes they had come from criminals who wanted something—goods, information, connections—that Imbry had and did not wish to part with. The earliest had come from fellow inmates of the school to which he had been sent at an early age after his parents died. He had learned that maintaining a stoic silence under the impact of fists and boots guaranteed that they would keep coming at him. Now, as the man behind him used his fists to strike his floating ribs, Imbry cried out at each blow.

Eventually, the beating stopped. Imbry could hear the man's breathing, coming harder than his exertions justified. Then the door opened and closed and he was alone again. He got his feet under him—that relieved the agony in his wrists. His ribs ached but the injury he was most concerned about was to his ear. But when he concentrated on the pain there he felt it fading. The eardrum was not ruptured.

Even though the hood had prevented him from seeing Breeth's face, Imbry knew that something outside of ordinary physical coercion was being directed at him. Something about him stirred Breeth to violence. He hadn't even been asked a question. And now no kind-hearted second interrogator had come into the room to beg him to give up something, anything, that would assuage the other's brutal rage.

After a while, as the ache in his head subsided, he heard the door open. He braced himself, but all he felt was a neutral hand disengaging him from the hook then taking his arm and walking him through the door and a few dozen steps to where he heard the clank of a heavy door. He was maneuvered until he felt a pressure against the back of his thighs. It felt like a padded bench, and whoever had him in charge wanted him to sit on it. He did so and the restraints were removed, sending sharp pains through the blood vessels in his arms and hands as circulation was restored.

A moment later, the hood was taken from his head, leaving him blinking in the sudden brightness of a lumen set in the ceiling of a bare cell. Already the provost's man who had unshackled him was just a naked back retreating through the door. It closed and Imbry heard the sound of a heavy latch sliding into place.

Imbry probed at his tender places, decided that his ribs were bruised, not broken. His ear ached and whined, but it was improving. He gave thought to the meaning of what had been done to him.

It was possible that the investigator was merely having a frustratingly bad day. Or perhaps he had a particular dislike of the obese. More likely, though, was that the man had acted out of some motive that had to do with the Fuldan cultural dynamic. First off, throughout the arrest, transportation, interrogation, and beating, the man had worn gloves—as if the very touch of Imbry's flesh was contaminating. And he had looked at Imbry with a peculiar blend of fascinated revulsion that was unlike any of the roles the fat man had seen police officers adopt in such situations.

There were factors and forces in play on this world that were known to all its inhabitants—indeed, they were so obvious as to need no comment—but which were invisible to an outsider. It was thus on many worlds. Imbry would either catch on through observation, or find someone to explain it to him. His immediate concerns were more pressing, however, and he put the little mystery aside and considered the larger.

Tuchol had given the impression that he was expecting someone to interrupt his sojourn with the troupe. Sometime while the camp slept, he had heard what he had been waiting for and had stolen out of the tent, probably by rolling silently under the felt wall that he had lain beside. Down from the sky had come the carry-all from the anonymous ship that had brought them to Fulda.

It was remotely possible, but highly unlikely, that it had landed on Tuchol and crushed him to death. More likely, Tuchol had climbed aboard having been promised to be taken away. Imbry remembered his answer when Taggar had asked him if he was rejoining the Hedevan troupe: *temporarily*. But what happened next was something the half-sized man had not expected. Again, it was barely possible that he had accidentally fallen over the side of the uncanopied aircraft. Imbry discounted the likelihood on two counts: first, the little man would have had to have stood on one of the seats and leaned over the side rail; second, an integrator that operated such a vehicle would certainly notice a passenger in danger of falling out and would adjust the carry-all's orientation accordingly while issuing a warning—unless, of course, the vehicle's ethical constituents had been adulterated.

There were only two likely scenarios. In both, the carry-all would have come down. Tuchol had scrambled in. It had risen high above the pass through the hills. At that point, the possibilities diverged. If there had been another person in the vehicle, he had picked up the little man and thrown him over the side. If the killer was kindhearted, he would have first rendered the half-man unconscious with the same kind of weapon Tuchol had used on Imbry. The second possibility was that the aircraft's integrator had been suborned— it could be done; Imbry had done it—to commit the murder itself.

The question Imbry most wanted answered was: who was on the carry-all, or if it was operating on its own, who had tampered with its integrator's ethics? In a sense, he already knew something about that mysterious individual: he owned a spaceship; he had drugged and enslaved Tuchol and bid him snatch Imbry from the Belmain seawall. Tuchol's murder gave credence to the story the half-man had told of being coerced into kidnapping the Old Earther. And the choice of Tuchol was not random. Whoever had stolen the little man had needed him to make sure Imbry connected with Taggar's troupe; but once that end was achieved, he had disposed of Tuchol.

So Luff Imbry was the focus of a person who was demonstrably ruthless. The schemer must have some end in view—it seemed unlikely that he would go to all this trouble just to cause Imbry the inconvenience and embarrassment of being inserted into a troupe of naked misfits and required to sing on whatever kind of rudimentary stage was tucked away in the wagons.

The choice of where to put me must also be significant, he told himself. The plan had something to do with Fulda. If Imbry could work out why he was where he was—why this disregarded little planet out of all the Ten Thousand Worlds—he would be a step closer toward discovering who had put him here.

And when he knew why and who, he would be in a position to *not* do whatever it was the hidden puller of strings wanted done. At that moment, blocked and frustrated, the nameless manipulator might finally step into view—and, if Luff Imbry could help it, into *reach*. His plump fingers stretched then closed tightly into fists as he imagined what would ensue. Then he took a controlled breath and relaxed.

The day wore on. No one came to bring Imbry food or drink, but neither was he taken back to the interrogation room for more questioning or another beating. At some point, Imbry dozed on the bench seat but was awakened by the sound of raised voices somewhere down the corridor. He thought that one of the voices was Breeth's. There were two others, one a baritone whose owner did most of the arguing against the investigator's protests; the other voice was a deep bass rumble that spoke less, but with an unmistakable overtone of authority.

The argument ended and quiet ensued until the latch of the barred door rattled. Imbry sat up and braced himself for whatever might come. But when the portal was thrown wide, Taggar stood in the doorway. "The Arbitration has ordered Investigator Breeth to let you go," he said.

"Hurrah for the Arbitration," said Imbry.

"Hush yourself," said Taggar, as if to an unruly child. "Come with me."

He handed Imbry his pouch and hat. The fat man's sandals were at the end of the corridor, wrapped in rough cloth and stored in one of a wall-covering array of small boxes beside the door that led outside. "Hurry," said Taggar. "This is not a good place to dawdle."

Imbry could have given him facts to back up that opinion, but instead he concentrated on strapping on his footwear. The other man pushed open the door and Imbry noticed that he, too, was wearing cloth gloves. As they stepped out into a gated courtyard where the wheeled vehicle that had brought Imbry to the station still stood, a provost's man was approaching the door.

Imbry's initial, unpremeditated reaction was to flinch; he thought the approaching man was the investigator who had beaten him. The resemblance was striking: the same blandly nondescript features, the same hazel eyes and light brown complexion, the same lank brown hair. But on closer scrutiny he noticed slight differences in the bone structure of the face. Besides, this man was several years younger. He supposed there must be a family connection—a younger brother or a nephew. He noticed also that the officer's wide-brimmed hat and baldric were bare of the circles—he assumed marks of rank—that Breeth's bore.

He had only been a few moments making the examination, but now Taggar was pulling Imbry's arm, somewhat urgently, and saying in a forced whisper, "Come! What are you doing?"

"I was just noticing how—" Imbry began, but his remark was cut off by a stronger yank on his arm, which coincided with the provost's man's harsh, "What do you think you're looking at, monster?"

Imbry was surprised to see genuine outrage in the officer's face. Taggar was pulling him bodily out of the line of the provost's man's approach, saying, "Please pardon us, sir. His mind is affected," in a far humbler tone than the big man had used among the other members of the Hedevan Traveling Players. Taggar was also careful not to look directly at the angry provost's man, but kept his eyes on the other's feet. An instant later, the circuit having finally closed in Imbry's cerebrum, the fat man adopted the same posture. "Please excuse me," he murmured.

"Get out of my sight!" said the Fuldan. "Get back to your own kind!"

"These things are not generally talked about," said Malweer.

"They don't have to be," said Ebblin. "Everybody knows."

"Everybody," Imbry countered, "except hapless strangers plumped down in your midst."

"I've heard that off-worlders can be deeply irregular," the thin man said.

Young Wintle said, "It must be strange when everybody's irregular.

Imagine them all walking around, showing each other their . . . discrepancies."

"Imagine, though," said Malweer, "what it would be like to own such a device and to walk freely among the Ideals."

"That'll be enough of that kind of talk," said Taggar. "We have a show to put on and we haven't even put the stage together." He turned to Imbry. "Are you clear now?"

"I think so," said the fat man. "Never speak to an Ideal without first being invited to. Don't look at them. Don't talk about them in their hearing. Don't draw unnecessary attention—"

"And, above all," the big man said, "don't touch one, even so much as a brush-by. They have to cleanse themselves, a lengthy and thorough procedure. Don't touch anything they may use. Often they will incinerate it with gouts of fire."

"Understood," Imbry said. The group began to break up. They had been gathered within the concealment of the troupe's large pavilion, which had been erected on a piece of waste ground outside Pilger's Corners. The company had traveled there during the morning after the provost's officers had come out to collect Imbry, along with Tuchol's body, and take them back to town. Imbry had been surprised to discover that the buildings at the oasis in the pass contained a communications point. Taggar had used it to notify the authorities of the little man's death.

"The place where you found me," he asked Taggar as they walked back from the provost station to the campsite, "did it also have a communicator?"

"They all do," Taggar said. "But we are not to use them except in dire emergency. They are for the Ideals. Anything we use has to be cleansed afterwards. Then the people who cleanse them have to cleanse themselves. They do not like it."

"Tuchol lay on the bed in one of the rooms," Imbry said.

"He would," Taggar said. "He delighted in such mischief." He sighed. "But it does not do to speak ill of the dead."

The walk through the streets of Pilger's Corners, a community of perhaps three thousand inhabitants built around two substantial oases and a scattering of spring-fed ponds, had shown Imbry the position of "oddies" in Fuldan society. At Taggar's instruction he had copied the big man's small steps and the way he kept his hands clasped across his midriff, elbows tight against his sides, with head bent groundward and eyes lowered.

They left the gated yard behind the provost's station and followed an alley that led to the town's main square. This was a substantial plaza shaded by towering deo trees planted in the center of the space and watered by a rough stone fountain Imbry assumed was fed by the oasis at the upper end of town.

The provost's station and its attached incarcery took up all of one side. Opposite, beyond the fountain and trees, was another large building with broad steps leading up to a pair of heavy wooden doors on each of which was an insignia in dark metal—it reminded Imbry of a stylized wave with a vertical line through it. Standing on the steps were two men, one young, one old, whose hats, baldrics, and pouches were of black cloth. They were in conversation; by Imbry's reading of their postures and gestures, the younger was deferring to the older. But when he and Taggar appeared, the two black-hats broke off their talk and both watched the two irregulars emerge from the alley.

When Taggar noticed Imbry staring at the two across the way, he hissed, "Put your head down! If the senior arbiter changes his mind, you'll be back in the cell."

Imbry lowered his gaze and walked beside Taggar in the mincing gait that Fulda apparently required of its irregulars. At first the fat man wondered that they did not crash into the several pedestrians they encountered along the way. The residents of Pilger's Corners seemed to spend some portion of the day promenading through the streets, standing about in loose groups in the square, or visiting its shops, booths, and outdoor refectories.

But no collisions occurred. Passersby gave the two men a wide berth, though not without issuing hisses and grumbles and sharp intakes of breath at their passage, especially when Imbry and Taggar came around a corner, taking on-comers by surprise.

All Fuldans wore the same lack of costume, and the colors of their minimal attire ran the short gamut from light brown to dark. The tan-hatted, Taggar told him, were farmers; they were the majority. The mid-browns were artisans; the slightly darker were shopkeepers and what passed for professionals in Fulda's egalitarian society. Provost's men wore the deepest brown, with yellow circles denoting rank. Arbiters wore true black, with rank symbols of silver. Imbry noted that children wore the same colors as their parents. Most occupations were hereditary, he was told, although the College of Arbiters and the Provosts Corps accepted applicants strictly on merit, as determined by formal examinations and field trials. No irregulars were admitted, of course. To them was allotted the profession of entertainer.

Back at the troupe's pavilions, after his brief instruction in proper comportment for irregulars, Imbry was put to work arranging chairs in rows in the show pavilion, then assisted with the erection of the portable stage. For the former task, he was required to wear gloves, lest his irregular touch contaminate the seating. Then there were other tasks to be performed: rigging poles and ropes behind the curtain that made a back wall to the stage, so that the rear space could be divided, by more hanging curtains, into small compartments. In each of these, a stool was positioned in a corner, with a small table beside it on which were arranged an assortment of objects, all of which had to be handled by gloves.

Imbry was not involved in the disposition of these latter materials. Ebblin shooed him away, saying, "You don't need to deal with this. Go help the young one with the stock."

He went out and helped Wintle settle the draft animals along a rope strung between two iron posts fixed firmly into the hard earth at the edge of the waste ground. Nearby, a pipe no thicker than the fat man's thumb bubbled up water into a shallow depression too small to be called a pond.

"They've drunk and they've had their mash," Wintle said. "Now we brush them down." He showed Imbry how to fit the strap of the wire-bristled brush over his hand then draw it in long strokes down from the beasts' ridged backs to their wide bellies, and from their hips to their fetlocks. The animals' innards rumbled and gurgled as they stood placidly absorbing the grooming, their clubbed tails twitching aimlessly.

Imbry wanted to explore a point that had been largely glossed over in the group discussion. Youth were often more accepting of unconventional matters than were their elders, so he asked young Wintle, straight out, "The Ideals, why do they all have the same appearance?"

The question did not so much embarrass the youth as puzzle him. His unusual features pulled together in a manner that reminded Imbry of a dog trying to understand a new command. "Because they're Ideals," he said. "That's how they're supposed to look."

"But how did it come to pass that Ideals are that way?"

The question plainly flummoxed Wintle. "They've always been that way."

"No," said the fat man. "They have made themselves that way. Or their ancestors did, and their descendants have continued the project. They all look so . . . ordinary. What I'm asking is, why?"

It was a question that, Imbry knew, could be asked on any world whose population had built their civilization around a central idea. Usually, it was best to ask it of an integrator, since such a device was less likely to take offense. It was rarely useful to pose the question to one of the denizens of such a culture, because the most likely answer was some irritated variation on: "Because that's the only right and proper way to arrange human existence, as you would know if you weren't a contemptible, benighted foreigner," accompanied by an invitation to catch the next ship off-world. But Fulda appeared not to possess a connectivity of integrators, and Imbry needed to know the lay of the land because he actively suspected that further ignorant treading on the locals' obvious prejudices would plunge him into a welter of animosity, perhaps violently expressed.

But Wintle was no scholar of the Fuldan social dynamic. From what Imbry was able to draw out of him the youth was only vaguely aware that conditions were different on other worlds. But his baseline assumption was that the universe was filled with Ideals, all virtually indistinguishable from each other at a distance of half a dozen paces, although he had heard tell that on other planets, irregulars like him had more freedom.

"Those must be awfully loose and bawdy places," he said, stroking the curry down the barbarel's flank. "Imagine, everybody all just mixed up together. In eating places, even." He brought the brush back up to the animal's backbone, shaking his oddly proportioned head in silent wonder.

"It's hard to believe," Imbry said. "Tell me, do you know of anywhere I could find an integrator."

"What's that?"

"A device that combines ratiocination, communication, and memory." When Wintle looked at him blankly, Imbry said, "A machine that thinks and talks."

The boy's pendulous ears flapped as he shook his head. "Nuh uh," he said. "They're against the law. Arbiters smash them."

Imbry was about to put another query when he saw an additional thought bubble to the top of the boy's mental pool. "I heard once," he said, "that there are some big machines left over from the mining days that had thinkers in them. Arbiters couldn't figure out how to get at them so they just left them."

"Where are they?" Imbry asked.

"Over by Fosh, I think. You should ask Malweer."

"Where is Fosh?"

"Other side of the world, I think. This troupe doesn't go there."

Imbry tried again. "If you wanted to conduct research,"—he broke off as Wintle's confused-canine expression told him that the phrase he had used was unfamiliar—"if you wanted to find information about some subject, where would you go?"

"I'd ask Malweer. He knows 'most everything."

"Yes," said the fat man, "but suppose he wasn't handy. Is there a place where information is stored, where people can go and find out things they'd like to know?"

It took a little more questioning, and a few more wrinklings of Wintle's canine brow, before the youth understood the thrust of Imbry's query. He'd heard, he said, of buildings where they had lots of books, and Ideals could go in and read them.

"Libraries?" Imbry said.

"I think that's what they're called," the youth said.

"Is there one here in Pilger's Corners?"

"I think so. In the town square. But they are only for Ideals." He shook a finger in friendly admonition. "Not for us."

Like any student of human nature—and success in the professions of thief and forger required a full course of study—Imbry was well aware of the multitude of different ways of organizing and sustaining a social order. Societies had evolved out of kinship groups when unrelated people banded together to apply their common efforts toward securing the essentials of existence: food, shelter, security, companionship. When advancements in knowledge and technology assured that those needs were routinely provided for, a new priority always emerged. With their bellies reliably full, their bodies warm and protected from the elements, and their lives, limbs, and liberties unthreatened, humankind invariably discovered the need for a sense of purpose beyond mere eating and voiding, sleeping and waking. The same questions were inevitably put: What are we here for? Where is the meaning behind all of our deeds and utterances? What gives shape to our lives?

The answer, no less inevitably, seemed to emerge in the form of an idea, a central principal around which the culture would structure its members' individual and collective lives. Sometimes the idea was conceived as a deity's will, expressed through prophecies and visions; sometimes it arose from a philosophical rationale, based on principles derived from sheer intellect or from observations of natural processes; sometimes it came from a calcification of inherited ways and customs, imbued with sanctity from age and habit, long after the initiating spark had been forgotten or clouded in myth.

Whatever the origin, once an idea obtained a good grip on a collection of minds, once it was continuously reinforced by daily practice and supported by the opinions of the generality, and especially if it rarely met energetic contradiction from competing concepts, it became the universe in which those minds existed. It bent their perceptions, channeled their reasoning, obscured other interpretations to the point of invisibility.

Such ideas, when they grew among isolated populations, were likely to take on the dignified vestments of inarguable truth. On a small backwater planet like Fulda, where the very notion of cosmopolitanism was unthinkable—Imbry doubted the inhabitants had even retained the word in their lexicon—an idea like Idealism might start out as an interesting landmark by which the culture could navigate their social environment with a firm sense of direction. Given time, though, the landmark would *become* the environment. No one would remember a time before Idealism had ruled their lives; indeed, after a sufficient succession of generations had lived under its aegis, most could scarcely imagine that such a time had ever existed.

On some long-ago day, now lost beyond memory, Imbry was sure, a ship had set down on Fulda, bringing with it a small and closely knit population from some other world. Out onto the planet's surface had marched a determined coterie whose lives were governed by the idea that everything would be so much better if everyone was of much the same size, coloring, conformation. They had probably formed a community of like-mindedness on the foundational domain or secondary world on which the idea of Idealism had arisen. Over a span of generations, they would have been working at reducing physical differences amongst themselves, but always chafing under the ridicule of their neighbors. The practical translating of their beliefs into concrete action, especially if it extended to the murder of irregular infants or surgical procedures forced upon waverers, might even have been outlawed.

They had chosen exile to Fulda, where there had been room to flex their conceptual elbows. It was doubtful that there had been any substantial human population when they arrived, the planet offering little in the way of economic opportunity or spectacular vistas to thrill the artistic soul. A desert planet tended to attract solitaries and hermits, who by their nature would have been sparsely distributed and deliberately unorganized. The tightly organized Ideals, full of zeal, would have had little trouble dealing with any opposition. They would have begun by facilitating the pioneers' passage off-world; when that process had reduced the initial inhabitants to a handful of recalcitrants who refused all reasonable inducements to relocate, the newcomers would have had no trouble convincing themselves that harsher methods were justified. This world was to be for the Ideals and none but.

The part of the picture that surprised Imbry was that enough regressive genes could still exist among the Fuldans to have produced tiny-headed Ebblin and tiny-handed Thelia, Wintle the dog-faced boy, and spindly Malweer. But his grounding in genetic science was that of an uninterested layman, and he realized that it was possible that their deformities were the result of uterine failures during gestation. He would have wagered that Taggar's hyper-muscularity was a glandular imbalance. Shan-Pei, however, was certainly a genetic sport—perhaps the result of a collision between a random cosmic ray penetrating through Fulda's thick atmosphere to intersect precisely with one of the fur-covered woman's parents' chromosomes.

In any case, the fat man had by now seen enough to grasp at the essentials of the Fuldan social dynamic. Here was a sequestered population of persons among whom variations in physical appearance were so slight as to be unnoticeable except on close examination. As he had traversed Pilger's Corners from the provost station to the Hedevan show tents, he had sneaked enough peeks at the town's inhabitants to know that they were all of the same height, weight, coloring, physique, and physiognomy, save that the males were a little larger than the females.

A Fuldan Ideal was of medium height and medium build, light brown in skin tone and hair coloring, with hazel eyes. Facial conformation was so balanced that no one feature dominated, but all were in such relative harmony that the result could not be called either handsome or its opposite. Their faces were merely bland. The men were smoothly muscled, neither deep nor narrow chested. The women's breasts were at the precise midpoint between ample and inconsequential. Both sexes were somewhat slim hipped, both wore their hair cut straight across at the level of the earlobe, and both were completely depilated below the neck.

All of this Imbry would have found mildly interesting if it had been brought to his attention in a periodical or as a traveler's tale carried back to Olkney by some acquaintance who had happened to visit a strange little backwater where the locals had curious standards and customs. It was another matter altogether to find himself marooned in this unprepossessing and frankly primitive planet—not even a connectivity of integrators!—and, worse, to have been made a member of a despised minority. Worse yet, he had been implicated as a suspect in a murder. His only good fortune so far had been that the corpse had not been that of an Ideal. If it had been, his treatment at the hands of the provost would almost certainly have been much rougher.

Imbry was revising his estimation of the who and why behind his being dropped on Fulda. Someone wanted him to suffer not just embarrassment but incarceration, at least, and probably brutalization. And perhaps even death. He was becoming increasingly sure that the motivation behind his circumstances was revenge.

There were more than a few inhabitants of Old Earth, not to mention a score or better of the Ten Thousand Worlds, whose lives had turned for the worse after they had intersected with Luff Imbry. His nemesis was unlikely to be one of the collectors from whom he had stolen works of significant value, or to whom he had sold works of dubious provenance. It was more likely to be some fellow denizen of Olkney's halfworld, perhaps a competitor whom Imbry had done out of some coveted prize. It could even be a thief who had stolen one of Imbry's fakes, thinking it real, only to have been made to look a fool or a grifter when he—though it could also be a she—tried to sell it on to a buyer who knew what to look for.

It would also have to be someone who was capable of acquiring at least the use of a spaceship—ownership was usually the hallmark of wealth—and who knew enough of Imbry's affairs to discover that he used Barlo Krim as one of his middlers. The latter was not information widely shared; Krim was someone to whom Imbry went when he needed him, and rarely did the course of their business flow in the opposite direction. The very purpose of a middler was to disguise the hand that operated him. Someone who could put Krim and Imbry together would have to be more than ordinarily knowledgeable.

Come at from that direction, the problem was less diffuse. Krim was the end of a string that, when tugged, might cause a skein to unravel. If only Imbry were in his operations center, disguised as a rundown house in one of Olkney's least fashionable districts, it would have taken his custom-built communications and research nexus no more than a fragment of a moment to winnow a welter of parameters and relationships. It would provide the fat man with a list of suspects in order of probability.

But instead he was stuck on a primitive world without integrators or a connectivity worthy of the name, where even the most basic instruments of research were denied to him by the prejudices of the Ideals. And the nature of this strange little planet was another factor Imbry would have liked to feed into his research nexus: who knew of Imbry who would also know of Fulda?

These thoughts crowded the fat man's mind as he curried and brushed the barbarels, filled their feeding bags with fragrant malted mash, and positioned the leather sacks over their agile mouths. The beasts grunted their satisfaction and fell to. A moment later, Imbry heard Taggar calling for him and Wintle to come to the show tent. The troupe leader was setting out the rundown for the evening's performance.

"I am not fit to sing," Imbry said. His bruised ribs ached when he took a deep breath.

"It doesn't matter," said Taggar. "Decider Brosch has said you are not to appear in public. He will speak with you before the show." The big man thought for a moment, then said, "You will be on your best behavior with the arbiter."

"When am I not?" Imbry said.

"Decider Brosch has the power to deliver you back to the incarcery. You would do well to tread lightly around him."

"Like a sylph," said the fat man.

CHAPTER FOUR

The Ideals came with the twilight, arriving in couples, trios, or small groups. They brought no children with them, although Imbry, watching through a ventilation slit in the main pavilion, saw a gaggle of half-grown youths, their pouches daringly worn on the left side, being turned away when they reached the edge of the waste ground. The man who sent them packing wore a black-hat and pouch, his hair grizzled by age. On his hat and baldric were wide silver circles. Imbry thought he was the man he had seen standing on the steps of the big building in the town square, although telling Ideals apart at a distance was an art that he had not yet mastered. The man had about him the same sense of authority: though the approaching boys had been loud with hoots and laughter, raucously egging each other on, the moment the elder interrupted their riotry they turned silent and round shouldered, slinking away without a murmur.

The seating had been divided into two sections, with a wide aisle between them. Down the center of the aisle, along its entire length, a heavy black curtain was draped over a rope supported by poles higher than an Ideal's head. Imbry noticed now that the groups approaching the tent were never of mixed sexes and that when they arrived, the audience segregated themselves, with the men on one side of the drape and the women on the other. As the seats filled, a susurration of whispered conversations arose, with here and there a suppressed giggle.

As the first Ideals approached, Imbry had withdrawn behind the curtain at the back of the stage, but he studied the Fuldans through a peephole in the thick black felt. Their bland uniformity went beyond physical similarity, remarkable as that was; it extended to stance, facial expression, manner of speech, gesture. They walked the same, stood the same, sat the same, spoke the same. It was a triumph of conformity, and the sight of it put a shiver up Imbry's spine.

In came two men whose hats and pouches were dark brown, one of them with the insignia of two gold circles. Imbry was sure that the older of the two was the conflicted investigator who had arrested and beaten him. Nervous, the senior provost's man glanced about as if he had never before seen the interior of a show pavilion. He and his partner took seats in the front row on the men's side, where they frequently twisted in their seats and looked around. Now that Imbry was focused on the matter, he could see that every member of the audience was seized by the same anxious expectation. But Breeth seemed even more wrought up than the rest.

The final few seats now filled as latecomers hurried in. The elder with the black-hat and pouch who had shooed away the youths was the last through the door of the tent. He did not sit, but rather stood in the opening, tugging at its sides until he had drawn it closed behind him. There he remained, arms folded. A younger man and a woman with gray streaks in her hair, also wearing black accoutrements, had preceded him. The younger man wore a single silver circle of rank, smaller than the older man's. The woman's hat and baldric were unmarked.

She situated herself between the stage and the first row of seats on the female side of the tent; the younger man took up a post at the corresponding position on the men's side; both remained standing, their backs to the stage.

Taggar came out from one of the small compartments, brushed past Imbry, and stepped out from behind the curtain. He made as if to ascend the stage, but stopped and instead went up the center aisle, head bowed and with the pussyfooting gate he had taught Imbry, and careful not to touch the dividing curtain. When he reached the elder standing in front of the entrance flap, he bowed. Some words passed between them, though Imbry could hear only the rumble of the black-hat's deep voice. It sounded like the voice he had heard down the corridor outside his cell in the provost's station.

Taggar bowed again and returned the way he had come, but now the elder followed him. The man called the younger male black-hat over to him and spoke briefly. The younger man turned to the audience and said, "There will be a brief delay." Imbry saw Breeth—he was sure now that it was the investigator, seated with his fellow provost's man in the front row—react to the announcement: his hands clenched and his jaw tightened, and he stared at the elder and Taggar.

Taggar parted the curtain and the older man stepped into the passageway behind the stage. The troupe leader let the curtain close. Meanwhile, the black-hat regarded Imbry with a hard and searching appraisal. The fat man did not have to be reminded to drop his own gaze. He looked at the bare ground that was the floor of the tent and bowed.

"His name, Decider," said Taggar, "is Imbry. I believe he comes from another world."

"Is this true?" said the elder.

"Yes," said Imbry.

"Yes, Decider," Taggar corrected him.

"Yes, Decider," said Imbry. "Please forgive my ignorance of your rules."

"Why did you come to Fulda?"

"I was kidnapped, Decider, and left here."

"By whom, and why?"

"I don't know."

"Decider," Taggar prompted Imbry.

"I am sorry," Imbry said. "Decider, I do not know who kidnapped me nor why. The man who carried out the crime said he acted on behalf of another, but he was killed before I could question him."

"He was the irregular whose body Investigator Breeth brought in?"

"Yes, Decider."

"Did you kill him?"

"No, Decider. I believe he was thrown from an aircraft."

"Fulda has no aircraft."

"The ship that brought me had a flying vehicle to travel between the ground and orbit." After a moment, he remembered to add, "Decider."

"What passed between you and the investigator at the station?"

Imbry hesitated.

"Speak," said Taggar. "You have nothing to fear."

"I am not sure what is proper to say."

"The truth," said the black-hat.

"The investigator questioned me, Decider. Then he tied me to the wall and beat me."

"Why did he beat you?"

"He did not say, Decider. It was not to encourage me to talk, because he asked no further questions. I could not see him, because he put a hood over my head."

"Did you touch him?"

"No, Decider. I was restrained."

"Did he touch you?"

Imbry understood. "Not without gloves on."

The old man was silent. Imbry peeked and saw that the black-hat was deep in thought. Taggar stood by, nervous. After a moment, the elder said, "Are you hurt?"

"My ribs are sore, Decider."

"Does it pain you to take a deep breath?"

Imbry tried and winced.

"Very well," said the older man. To Taggar, he said, "Put him in the end compartment," gesturing with his chin to the booth at the end of the passageway, behind Imbry. To the fat man, he said, "You will not perform tonight."

"Yes, Decider," Imbry said. He noted that Taggar looked relieved.

The black-hat turned and went to the split in the curtain, waiting there until Taggar hurried up and pulled aside the black cloth, wide enough that the elder could duck through without being touched. When the barrier was closed again, Taggar came to Imbry and said, "You can watch through the peephole. When it's over, go to the booth up there and stay out of sight."

"What was that all about?" Imbry said.

Taggar looked worried. "It is possible that Investigator Breeth has formed a troublesome attachment to you."

Imbry blinked in surprise. "He has an odd way of expressing it."

"Not like that," said the big man. "It's something they don't talk about to us, something to do with their beliefs."

"Am I in danger?"

"The arbiter will protect you."

"Arbiter?"

Taggar twisted his face. "You don't know anything, do you?" he said. "That man was Superior Arbiter Brosch. He is the senior officer of the Arbitration in Pilger's Corners, but his reputation extends far."

"I thought he was a decider."

"Deciding is what arbiters do. Decider is what you call them when you speak to them."

From out in the main part of the pavilion, they heard the old man's sepulchral voice say, loudly, "Begin."

Taggar turned on his heel, saying over his shoulder, "I must go start the show. You can watch, but when it's over go into the end compartment." He went to the split in the curtain, took a moment to compose himself, then stepped through.

Imbry put his eye to the peephole again. The crowd of Ideals sat silently waiting. He saw Taggar climb three steps to the stage then turn to face the Ideals. Imbry half expected some theatricality—a sweeping bow, a flourish of the hands, a smile and some patter—but as he watched through the peephole he saw the strongman raise his eyes to the twin peaks of the pavilion's roof and with his arms hanging loose at his sides say, "Our first presenter is Ebblin, who dances."

With that, Taggar stepped down from the stage and came back through the curtain. The tiny-headed woman was already on her way to the slit, which the troupe leader held open for her. She ascended to the stage, walked light-footed to its center, then, humming softly to herself, she began to sway and shuffle her feet to the rhythm of a wordless song. After a few preparatory motions, she commenced a gliding, circular progress about the stage, dipping her shoulders and moving her arms with a fluid grace that surprised Imbry. She danced three circuits of the stage in one direction, then turned and went three times around in the opposite. And, like Taggar, she never once lowered her eyes to the rows of seated Ideals, but kept her gaze fixed on the black cloth ceiling above them.

When she finished, there was no applause. Indeed, the Ideals sat stiff and silent as troops on parade, although Imbry saw eyes shifting from right to left, as the people in the audience sought to see what their neighbors were doing without turning their heads. The black-hatted man and woman had spent the performance studying not the dancer but the spectators, even moving up and down the sides of their sections to peer closely at individuals.

Ebblin finished her motions and stood still for a moment at the center of the stage. She made neither bow nor curtsy, but dropped her eyes to her feet and shuffled back to the stairs. A moment later, she passed Imbry in the space behind the rear curtain and went to one of the small compartments. As she was about to disappear from his view, she turned and gave him a smile that he could not decipher. It was the kind of smile that fellow sufferers give to each other, one that says, *Ours is a none-too-desirable fate, yet we bear it as best we can*, which would have been less mysterious to the fat man if anyone had told him what that fate was supposed to be.

Taggar, meanwhile, had stepped out onto the stage. Again with his eyes upturned, he announced that the next performer would be Wintle, who would recite *The Sojourner's Lament*. The youth was already en route, passing Imbry with a shrug of his shoulders and a similar smile to the one Ebblin had given him. A moment later he was standing in the center of the stage, his gaze also turned to the roof above, and intoning in a clear and practiced voice the first stanza of some story told in rhyming couplets about a fellow who had fared forth into the world to seek his fortune.

Imbry did not bother to listen to the tale, which started off with a misadventure and, given the title, did not promise a happy conclusion. Nor did he watch the dog-faced youth, who stood with hands limp at his sides and face upturned. Instead, he watched the Ideals. As during Ebblin's performance, they sat as if petrified, scarcely blinking as they watched the boy deliver his recitation. And, as before, the man and woman in black again ranged up and down the aisles, studying the audience. Imbry saw the woman take a stylus and pad from her pouch and make a brief note. The elder in the doorway to the tent regarded the stage with a face like a stone carving.

No one in the seats moved. The tent was silent save for the boy's high-pitched voice intoning the ridiculous poem and the whisper of a mass of people breathing. But there was an almost palpable tension in the enclosed space. Imbry had no doubt that, here before his eyes, something was transpiring that was of great importance to the Ideals. Certainly, they had not come to be entertained by indifferent dancing and amateur recital.

Wintle finished, stood still for a moment in the silence, then left the stage. Taggar stepped up and announced Shan-Pei. The fur-covered woman climbed onto the stage and drew from her pouch four balls, each of a different color and of a size to fit into her palm, and began to juggle them. Her gaze remained fixed on top of one of the tent posts. The eyes of the audience did not try to follow the balls through their various permutations, but watched only Shan-Pei. The black-hats went up and down, observing and taking notes. At the end, as the performer left the stage, they conferred with each other briefly, parting in agreement as Malweer was introduced.

The thin man sang three ballads in a surprisingly rich baritone while again the Ideals sat as if paralyzed. Then came Thelia, who danced even more gracefully than Ebblin. Finally Taggar announced himself and performed feats of strength involving iron bars and powerful springs. When he was done, he said, "That is all," and left the stage amid the usual silence. The man and woman in black accoutrements came together again and compared their observations then looked expectantly toward Brosch standing granite faced in the entrance. The arbiter made a gap in the cloth and spoke in his sepulchral voice: "Finished. Depart."

The audience rose. Again eyes moved from side to side, heads turned fractionally, as if there were something to see in the countenances of their virtually identical neighbors. If there was some mark to be seen in any of the bland and nondescript faces, Luff Imbry could not make it out. But the black-hats could. As the Ideals filed past the gray-haired man at the exit, his two assistants nodded from time to time. At their signal, the elder would touch the designated man or woman on the cheek. The person thus singled out did not depart the tent, but went to stand to the side of the entrance. When the process was finished, four men and three women, each as alike to the others as if they had been grown in vats, waited for whatever was to come next. Even through his spy hole from across the tent, Imbry could see their breath come quickly and their lips and limbs tremble with repressed excitement.

The black hats gathered around the seven chosen. Imbry could hear the rumble of the elder's voice, apparently giving instructions, though the fat man could not make out the words. He saw the selected ones signifying acceptance of what was being said to them, their reverence for the gray-haired man as plain as the excitement they sought to restrain. The elder turned, and beckoned them to follow him toward the slit in the rear curtain through which the performers had entered and left.

"Wait!" It was a man's voice, strained with emotion. Imbry craned his head to peer sideways through the peephole. He saw that two members of the audience had not left. Breeth, the provost's man, had been sitting in the front row of the men's side of the house with his fellow officer beside him. Now they advanced up the central aisle, Breeth leading, the other man following, though he seemed reluctant. The investigator positioned himself before Brosch and the other two black-hats. Imbry could see only his back, but the set of the man's shoulders and the way he lowered his head somehow suggested both deference and defiance. The two assistants were clearly scandalized, the seven chosen showed even greater anxiety, but the old man regarded the investigator without any show of emotion. "What?" he said.

"One of them did not appear," Breeth said.

The younger male black-hat stepped between them. "Is this a law-enforcement matter?"

Breeth's stance reminded Imbry of a truculent schoolboy. "No, Decider," he said.

"Then you keep us from the delvings."

Now a voice spoke quietly in Imbry's ear. "Stay here for now,"—he turned to find Taggar beside him, the big man's face lined with worry—"but if any of them come this way before I come back, slip out under there." He pointed to the pavilion wall and the end of the backstage corridor. The cloth was unpegged and loose at its base.

"What is to come?" Imbry said.

"I don't know. It is Ideal business, best we keep out of it."

"I would like to, but it is me they are talking about."

The argument in the main tent had been continuing. Breeth's subordinate had put a hand on the investigator's arm as if to restrain him from some untoward act. Breeth was nose to nose with the younger male black-hat, their voices low but full of strain.

Then Superior Arbiter Brosch spoke and the argument ceased. "The irregular you speak of will not appear tonight," he said. "He is unable to perform, having been injured." These last words were accompanied by a pointed look at Breeth, then he added, "Is there anything you want to tell us about that, Investigator?"

Imbry thought Breeth might explode, so tense was the man's posture. The other brown-hat man pulled on his arm, physically turning his superior away from the confrontation. "He has nothing to tell you, Decider," the provost's man said.

"Very good," said Brosch. "We will discuss this tomorrow. Come to the Arbitration first thing."

Breeth was hunched forward, knees slightly bent, as if he were about to fling himself into action. His eyes were on the curtain behind which Imbry stood. For a moment, the fat man wondered if the investigator was conscious of his gaze.

"Did you hear me, Investigator?" said Brosch.

The other provost's man was speaking energetically in his superior's ear. Breeth shook himself, took a long ragged breath, and said, "Yes, Decider. I will be there."

The elder man nodded. "Then depart. You have no place here tonight."

Breeth did not so much leave as he was pulled out of the tent by his companion. Brosch turned to the seven Fuldans who had been chosen from the audience, made a gesture that assured them that there would be no further disturbance, then nodded to the other two black-hats. "The delvings will commence," he said.

Behind the curtain, Taggar said, "They're coming now," and gestured toward the compartment at the far end of the passageway. "Don't come out until I come for you."

"What will happen? What are delvings?" Imbry said.

Taggar looked like a man saddled with an importunately questioning child. "No time now." He took Imbry by the arm and hurried him to the booth.

The fat man went where the big man wanted him to go. When he was in the narrow compartment, Taggar pulled a curtain closed, touching a finger to his lips as the barrier separated him from Imbry. Imbry turned and regarded the small space. Like the others he had earlier helped outfit, it contained a stool and a low table on which were arranged a number of items. Imbry went and examined them, mindful of the rule that nothing be touched without gloves. The objects were small, variously shaped tablets of some unusual ceramic— Imbry had not seen its like before—beautifully glazed over lustrous colors:

blues, purples, deep reds, golden yellows. On each, in bas-relief, was a symbol or character from a syllabary Imbry had never encountered: one was a pair of linked circles, another something like a distorted fence or ladder, next a cross made of wavy lines, then a series of squares nested within squares.

One part of Imbry's mind rejoiced in the simple beauty of the objects; another wondered at their purpose; a third considered what they might fetch from certain collectors in Olkney. That would depend, to some extent, on their provenance, their age, and the use for which they had been created—ritual artifacts commanded more attention from the collectors he was thinking of. Of course, they might be just game pieces, or merely decorative. Though that would pose no insurmountable problems; Imbry was expert at creating legends and histories that were at once wondrous yet plausible.

But he put the issue aside as he heard the black-hats and their seven chosen Ideals rustling and moving in the corridor outside. He stepped to the curtain Taggar had closed and gently pushed at it with the side of his head until his left eye was clear of the side wall and he could peer down the passageway. At the far end, Taggar stood with bowed head. The two black-hats selected one of the Ideals and led her to one of the booths. Then they chose one of the men for another compartment. When all seven had been placed, the black-hats returned to where the elder had stood watching the proceedings. The three conferred in soft voices, the black-hats consulting their notes.

The elder made a motion of assent, and the woman black-hat went down the corridor to where Taggar waited. She spoke to him. The big man bowed and turned toward the compartment beside him and beckoned. A moment later, Shan-Pei stepped into sight. Head down, feet shuffling, she followed the black-hat to one of the booths along the passageway. She stood facing the compartment for a moment until the woman in the black-hat said something Imbry could not make out. Then the fur-covered girl bowed deeply, half straightened, and entered the compartment. The black-hat drew a curtain across the opening and returned to where the elder and the other black-hat waited.

They consulted their notes and, again at the elder's signal, the male black-hat stepped to Taggar and spoke to him. A moment later, Malweer was being conducted to a compartment and, after instruction and a bow, he entered and disappeared from view. As Imbry continued to watch, each member of the troupe was brought to a booth and ushered inside, the last being Taggar himself.

An expectant stillness hung over the corridor. Then the gray-haired man made a complicated motion with one hand, at which both black-hats bowed their heads, spoke softly, and performed their own gestures involving fingertips touching forehead, lips, and breastbone. "Begin," said the elder.

From the several compartments along the corridor Imbry heard a rustle of soft noises, as of sandaled feet scuffing dry earth, followed by rhythmic breathing that continued for a while. Someone moaned softly, at which the three black-hats turned toward the sound. The elder motioned with a finger and the female black-hat went to the curtain that closed one of the booths. She listened for the space of a half a dozen heartbeats then quietly stepped inside. From another of the compartments came a series of breathless yips that drew the younger black-hat.

Imbry very slowly withdrew his head from the curtain and stepped away from the barrier. The black-hats had not brought anyone to the compartment beside his, else he might have risked making a tear in the intervening felt wall and peeking through. He was thinking that there was much he needed to know about how matters were arranged on Fulda. The beating at the hands of the provost's man had convinced him of that. Whatever was going on in the booths must also eventually affect him; his participation had been the subject of dispute between Investigator Breeth and Superior Arbiter Brosch, and the provost's man had not looked to be satisfied with the outcome. In any case, it seemed likely that Imbry's involvement had been merely deferred, not ruled out altogether. At some point, he had no doubt, it would be his turn to perform before a crowd of silent same-faced Ideals and then be led into a private booth for purposes he could only speculate on.

And there was another point about which he was almost as certain: when Imbry entered the compartment, the person waiting for him was likely to be Investigator Breeth. What would happen next, the Old Earther did not know, but he doubted it would be one of the highlights of his existence.

He intended to be long gone from Fulda before that moment. He had achieved stage one of the plan he had laid out after being deposited on Fulda— he had survived. He had been working on the second phase—the quest for information—and had gained some knowledge from questioning the locals.

But now it was time to go beyond dependence on what Taggar or Malweer or Wintle might tell him. And he could not afford to let the ache in his ribs prevent him from seeking it.

He knelt and tugged at the bottom of the compartment's outer wall. It had been pegged into the earth, but not deeply. Imbry pulled at the cloth until he had loosened two pegs and created a gap large enough for him to wriggle out of the pavilion. He came out into the shadows at the rear of the big tent, not far from where the barbarels were tethered. He saw no one in sight and made his way quickly past the picket line and to a straggle of trees that fringed one side of the waste ground. When he was in the deeper darkness under their branches, he stood and surveyed his surroundings.

The Ideals of Pilger's Corners seemed not to be night-haunters. The ways leading into the town were deserted, the pavement bathed in a dim, yellow illumination shed by far-spaced lumens held in brackets that were attached to the upper walls of the two-story buildings lining the streets. He heard no music or voices, as would have come from a tavern or other evening gathering place. He wondered if today was a holy day of some kind, with all the Ideals staying indoors to conduct whatever rites and rituals satisfied their desire for the numinous. Certainly the doings in the Hedevan Players' tent had had some of the feel of the spiritual.

Again, he did not know the simplest things. Was it forbidden for such as he to be out at night? Would he be killed on sight if found wandering the streets? Or would they make him their fool-king for the night, only to greet the morning by cutting his throat over a consecrated trench? Even among the sophisticated societies of the foundational domains and major secondary worlds, it was advisable to learn the shibboleths before venturing out into the boulevards; on little forgotten worlds like Fulda, the ignorant stranger could be gambling his life or liberty every time he crossed a threshold.

He worked his way along the line of trees until he came to a dry ditch that divided the waste ground from the edge of the town. Coming back from the provost's station, he and Taggar had crossed the declivity by way of a railless wooden bridge. But that span was illuminated by a glowing lumen set in the wall of the nearest building. Imbry eased down into the ditch where the light was dimmest, looked to see if anyone was about or if any uncurtained windows framed Fuldans gazing out into the night. Seeing no one, he arose and crossed the street, stepping into a spot of darkness where a wall shaded the sidewalk from the nearest illumination. Again, he paused to watch and listen, and when he saw and heard nothing to give him further pause, he moved up the street that led into town, aiming for the next island of shadow.

On his passage into and out of Pilger's Corners, Imbry had seen that the town was laid out in a rectangular grid that connected two oases. From the outer edges of each pool spread fields of grains and legumes that were irrigated from the standing water supplies. At the center of the grid was the open square, and it was to that space that the fat man stealthily worked his way, stopping in darkened doorways and under awnings to make sure his progress was unobserved.

The square, when he reached it, was also deserted, the shops and vendors' booths closed up for the night. He heard a burst of shouting from the provost's station, but the noise was brief and apparently nothing to do with him. From a darkened doorway he surveyed the open space. When he had come this way with Taggar, Imbry had noticed a building that he seemed to be a tavern or public house; if so, it was closed and dark tonight. Only the provost's station was lit. Taking one last look for possible observers, and seeing none, he removed his sandals and stepped across the open space to where the centrally planted deo trees cast deep shadows. For all his size, Imbry could move swiftly and silently when necessary. He paused under the trees to watch and listen again, then made another careful inspection of the plaza.

There were three buildings that might have been the library. He moved beneath the trees to take a closer look at the nearest and saw that one of the pair of solid doors that were its main entrance showed a metal handle in an odd place—exactly the odd place where a library might have a trapdoor through which patrons could return books outside of operating hours. The building also offered a narrow alley leading to its rear. The arrangement was too fortuitous to pass up. Moments later, Imbry was at the end of the alley. Turning the corner, he found a square, fenced-in space with room for vehicles to stand and a back wall coated in stucco and pierced by a recessed back door and two windows—all of them locked.

If this had been one of his operations, the fat man would have minutely planned his procedures after comprehensive research and surveillance. And he would have brought appropriate tools. But, even without such preparation, Imbry was confident in his ability to find a solution: he took pride in his talent for improvisation. He knew that persons who put locks on doors and windows often perversely defeated their own efforts by leaving nearby the materials needed to get past them. He looked about and his eyes were immediately drawn to the lumen that was held in a metal bracket above the door. It was higher than he could reach, but someone had conveniently left a small bench against the wall, where Imbry thought the library staff—if this was the right building—possibly sat to take their lunches in the mild open air.

Imbry carried the bench to the doorstep, climbed upon it, and swiftly removed the tubular lumen. He wrapped it in his little skull cap then put the bundle into his pouch, so that the building's rear was now in a comforting darkness. He then reached up again and took a two-handed grip on the metal bracket. It was attached to the wall by metal bolts, but the wall itself, beneath the stucco, was made of wood. And the bracket extended far out from the wall, so that it effectively formed a lever that, if the right amount of force was applied to its outer end, would pry the bolts from the wood. Luff Imbry's substantial weight, even in the lighter gravity of Fulda, more than constituted the right amount of force. He hung from the bracket and immediately felt it bend downward.

The bolts made a noise coming out of the wood. He stood in the dark recess of the doorway and waited, but it appeared that the buildings to either side were empty at night. No lights shone nor did any voice inquire as to the source of the unusual sound. Imbry took the bracket to the nearer of the two windows and, as he had expected, was able to work its flat end between the sill and the bottom of the wooden window frame. He heaved up and again there was a sharp noise as the lock that was screwed into the top of the window frame parted company with the wood.

Imbry set down the bracket where it would not be noticed, brought over the bench, climbed on it, lifted up the window, and slid across the sill. He closed the window and looked about him. He was in an office of some kind, with a working surface, cupboards with closed doors, and two chairs. He crossed to the door opposite the window, and found that it was unlocked. Beyond was a large room full of shelves. The shelves were full of books.

"Ah-ha," he said softly. He reached into his pouch for the lumen wrapped in his hat and allowed one of its coolly glowing ends to come free of the cloth. He moved to the nearest shelf and began his search. The first titles he saw concerned crop rotation, in a section devoted to agriculture. He moved down the shelves and found arts and crafts, then cookery. Patiently, he passed on to the next set of shelves. There were books on property law and the inheritance of land, next to manuals for the maintenance and repair of machinery.

Imbry sighed. An integrator could have delivered him exactly what he needed in less time than it took to blink. But, he consoled himself, any self-respecting integrator would already have reported his illicit presence to the provost's officers. He went to another tier of shelves, one that rose only to the height of his chins, and found books intended for children. The title, *Fulda, from Early Times to Now*, caught his attention. It was an old and well-worn volume, its cover torn off sometime in the past and repaired with adhesive bands, but Imbry doubted that little of any moment had happened on the planet since the text's publication. He tucked it under his arm—it was too big for his pouch—and kept searching.

He wanted an explanation of what had been going on in the Hedevan Players' pavilion. He did not get one. The library appeared to contain no books or recordings on the subjects of religion or the mystic. Not a catechism or primer did he find, not even on the children's shelves. Indeed, the entire corpus of information contained within the Pilger's Corners library consisted of nothing but practical knowledge. He found nothing of philosophy nor of politics, not a single biography, and not so much as a word of fiction. Even when he broke into a locked bookcase, he found only a heterogeneous handful of texts whose only similarity to each other was that they were old and had been published off-world; it seemed to Imbry that they had been segregated not because of their contents but because of their origin. Knowledge of anything non-Fuldan was probably considered not only inessential, but suspect.

Finally, he went back out through the window, left the bracket and lumen on the doorstep, and made his way back to the troupe's camp. The place was in darkness. He skirted the main pavilion and found the smaller tent that had been assigned to him and Wintle as their quarters. Its entrance was only half-laced closed, and he ducked in through the opening at the bottom. He listened for the shuffle of the youth's breathing, but heard another sound: the scritch of a hand lumen being activated. Imbry found himself in the presence of Taggar. The big man had been sitting in the darkness, in the strongly built chair he had given Imbry. Now he stood and said, "Were you seen?"

"I took care not to be," Imbry said.

Taggar's eyes went to the book tucked under the fat man's arm. His curiosity only partly satisfied, he dismissed the question Imbry thought he was about to ask and said, "You must leave here. That investigator has been back. There was a confrontation with the young arbiter that Decider Brosch left here. Breeth is now lurking by the bridge, watching for you."

"I came another way."

"Good. Now come with me." He went toward the tent opening, extinguishing the light.

"Wait," said Imbry. "Does he mean to arrest me for Tuchol's murder?"

"No," said Taggar from the darkness. "Now that they have examined the corpse, it seems clear that he fell from a great height."

"Then what does Breeth want?"

The big man was silent.

"You must tell me," Imbry said. "Does he intend me harm?"

Taggar's voice was strained. "It is an intimate matter. Not something one discusses with . . . an acquaintance."

"Is it sex?" Imbry said. He had been on worlds that had developed odd prohibitions against natural appetites.

"What?" said the other man, surprise evident in his tone. "No, no. It has to do with his . . . That is, he has conceived a . . ." He was silent for a moment, then said, "There is no time for this. Come with me, quietly."

Imbry followed him out of the tent, ducking through the half-open flap. "I need to know," he said. "At least tell me if I am in danger."

Taggar had him by the arm, hurrying him toward where the animals were tethered. Imbry noticed that the big man felt no need to place the thickness of a glove between them. "It would just be . . . bad," Taggar said, after a moment, "if you and the investigator remained in proximity."

"Bad for whom?"

A sigh. "Just bad. Now, here we are. Get aboard."

They were under the trees near the picket line. It was too dark to see anything other than deeper shades of blackness. Imbry heard the whuffle of a barbarel and the creak of harness. He groped with his free hand and the dark spot in front of him became the side of a wagon—no, he realized, as his hand moved over leather, a carriage of some kind. He found a metal step set in wood and, with a boost from Taggar, put his foot into it and climbed to a padded seat covered by a rough cloth.

"Go," the big man said.

Somebody was seated next to Imbry. He felt motion and heard the slap of reins on thick skin. The vehicle lurched forward on well-oiled wheels, with barely a creak of its springs. They were headed away from town. Beyond the trees they came almost immediately to dry ground, but the carriage wheels were muffled in some softer material and made almost as little noise of passage as the barbarel's padded feet.

Out in the open, they were still in darkness, but there was enough light left in the upper air for Imbry to see that someone walked at the animal's head, guiding their way. They were following a narrow track, a little lighter than the gray of the desert that surrounded them. Imbry spoke softly to the unseen person on the seat beside him, "Where—"

"Shh!" was the immediate response.

They continued to walk on in near silence for some time. At first the ground was level, but then it began to rise and fall. They were climbing and descending slopes too small to be called hills. When they had been up and down several times, the person in front let go of the harness and, still walking along beside the barbarel's head, ignited a hand-held lumen, its beam focused on the way ahead.

They walked on. All Imbry could see of the one leading them was a silhouette. By size and shape, he must be an Ideal and a male. But the illumination also reflected a little off the ground, casting back the faintest glow—light enough for Imbry to see, by his peripheral vision, that the person beside him on the carriage seat was small in stature. But he could make out almost no features, and after a moment he realized that was because his companion was covered in fur. "Shan-Pei?" he said.

But the juggler did not answer. Instead, the person who led them along the path spoke: "We do not speak now."

The voice was deep, full of solemn authority. Imbry recognized it instantly. Superior Arbiter Brosch, stone-faced priest or judge in whatever cult or code the Ideals of Pilger's Corners followed, was leading them out into the desert.

Based on what he had so far encountered on Fulda, Luff Imbry had little doubt that whatever awaited him would not be to his liking.

CHAPTER FIVE

Fulda rotated on its axis somewhat more quickly than Old Earth did, Imbry was coming to believe. This, coupled with the light-holding quality of the higher atmosphere, meant that true night tended to be short—at least in the tiny part of the planet he had so far seen. They had not been traveling too long when the first pale intimations of dawn appeared in the upper air. Within a short time after, the landscape began to reform itself in shades of gray.

"May we speak now?" Imbry said. He had several questions he wished to put.

"No," was the response from the elder who continued to lead the barbarel along the rudimentary path, though he had extinguished the hand lumen. Shan-Pei held the reins though there was no need. Imbry noted that she wore gloves, the garments looking incongruous against her natural fur covering. There was also a cloth spread over the padded seat and another on which their sandaled feet rested.

With no other occupation available to him, Imbry examined their surroundings as they became increasingly visible. There was little enough to see. They had not trended downward toward the low desert where Imbry had first been deposited on Fulda. Instead, they were generally climbing a long, though gently inclined, slope leading them higher into the great dry plateau in which Pilger's Corners was the first town beyond the pass from the lowlands. Imbry tried to imagine how the terrain would look from above, and it seemed to him that it would resemble a continental shelf between a continent and the deeper sea, though with all the water removed.

There was no vegetation to be seen in any direction. The carriage creaked ever higher up the slope, until the sun was past the midpoint of its rise to the zenith. The day grew hot, but not unbearable. Eventually, they came to a broad terrace that extended a great distance to either side of their path. The flat land stretched before them toward the far distance, where a high escarpment rose more sharply than the gentle slope they had just climbed.

They continued forward at a walking pace, the arbiter as apparently tireless as the barbarel. As the carriage rolled on, an object appeared in the distance and gradually resolved itself into a simple stone hut shaped like a beehive. The trail led to it and stopped, as did the carriage when they reached it.

There was no oasis here, no sign of life at all. Nor any water, although outside the hut was a trough gouged from the rock. The elder went to the rear of the carriage and came back with a large bottle whose contents sloshed. He poured its contents into the trough. The barbarel moved forward of its own accord and began to drink.

The old man turned to the two in the carriage. "Get down," he said.

Shan-Pei and Imbry did as they were bid. Imbry peeked inside the hut, saw its interior dimly illuminated by beams of sunlight that passed through chinks in the walls. The rocks of which the structure was built were horizontally striated, he noted. On Old Earth, that would be a sign that they had been formed from sediments laid down on the bottom of a sea. It must have been a very old sea, he thought. But the issue on his mind was a much more recent geologic event.

"Decider, I have several questions," Imbry said. "Have we finally reached an appropriate time to ask them?"

"I will tell you what you need to know." The gray-haired man went to a shelf on the back of the carriage and unloaded some twine-wrapped bundles that had been lashed there. These he set beside the entrance to the hut and went back for more, saying, "Take these inside, if you are able."

Imbry hoisted one of the bundles and took it into the hut. The pain in his ribs was lessening, he noted gratefully. Inside was a floor of swept earth on which stood a rough sleeping pallet and a low wooden stool. Some bowls and a pitcher were stored on a small table whose top was of unvarnished planks that had weathered gray with age.

"What is this place? Why are we here?" Imbry said.

"One of you must watch while the other sleeps," said the elder, bringing the last two bundles from the carriage and setting them down. "If you see anyone coming, you"—he pointed first at Imbry, then at where the land rose again at the distant end of the terrace—"must go that way and hide in the indigene ruins. Do not come back until you see that whoever comes has gone away again."

"When you say 'someone,'" Imbry said, "you mean Breeth, the provost's man."

"Yes."

"Why? Why does he pursue me? I thought I had been cleared of implication in the death of Tuchol."

"It is not that," said the arbiter.

"Then what is it, Decider? What have I done?"

A look passed briefly over the elder's impassive face. Imbry wasn't sure if it was fear or some milder form of concern. "I cannot tell you," the Fuldan said.

"Why not?"

"And you must not ask."

"I will ask. If necessary, I will go and ask Breeth."

This time he provoked real alarm in the elder. "You must not have anything to do with him. It is outside the procedures."

"How long am I to sit here and hide?" Imbry said. "What is to become of me?" The arbiter's mouth twisted, a reaction that Imbry read as that of a man having to deal with uncertainty for the first time in many years. He pressed his advantage. "You know that I am on this planet unwillingly, having been kidnapped by criminals and abandoned here. The man who was the agent of the kidnappers has been killed, likely murdered to prevent his telling me who did this to me."

He paused to let the elder respond, but the man said nothing. Still, the man looked even more uncomfortable. Imbry continued, "Whatever danger I may be in from Investigator Breeth, I am first the victim of someone who does not flinch from murder. Someone who has a spaceship that may be in orbit above us, watching me until his plans have matured. I have to consider my life to be under threat."

The information apparently added to the old man's concerns. He looked up at the sky for a moment, then knitted his heavy brows in thought. "Shvarden is coming out to guard you," he said, "as soon as he is sure Investigator Breeth is not watching."

"Is Shvarden the young man who accompanied you earlier?"

"Yes."

"Will he be armed?"

A moment passed while the arbiter made his decision. "No."

"But is he capable?"

No hesitation this time. "Yes."

"Again," Imbry said, remembering to add the man's honorific, "Decider, for how long must I remain here? It was my intent to contact the authorities and begin procedures to arrange for my return to Old Earth."

"You have contacted the 'authorities,'" the old man said. "The Arbitration is the body charged with governing the community of the Ideals."

"Then what will the Arbitration do for me, Decider? I cannot be the first off-worlder stranded here. If you will let me, I can probably adapt one of your communication devices to call down a spaceship. Would you allow me to do so? And will you protect me"—he glanced up—"in the meantime?"

He saw that thoughts were passing through the elder's mind, but the man's answer left him with doubts that the black-hat intended to make Imbry privy to them.

"You will be protected. You must be protected, until we know . . ."

Imbry recognized that whatever the old man was leaving unspoken would remain as such. He had stepped into some situation that was of importance to the Ideals, and not something to be casually spoken to an outsider. "At least," Imbry said, "give me some indication as to when this whatever it is that you don't want to tell me about will be over. I wish to go home."

The elder was probably seldom questioned, and almost certainly never by an irregular, Imbry thought. But whatever was going on, it was unusual enough to cause the black-hat to ignore social protocols. "I have already sent to my superiors. I have asked them to empower me to deal with the matter. I believe they will grant my request. But in the meantime, you must be kept away from Investigator Breeth. His response to your presence has been . . ."

"Irregular?" Imbry said.

"And more than that."

"But you can't tell me more?"

The old man looked off into the distance, then turned back to Imbry. "I cannot give you information that may distort the . . . determination of your status. I can tell you that it will not take more than two days for the proper authority to decide if I will be empowered to resolve your . . . situation."

"And in the meantime," Imbry said, "you have to keep me safe from Breeth, because he might ruin whatever it is you're trying to determine?"

"Exactly," said the elder. "I'm glad you understand."

"I understand nothing, Decider, except that I have been deprived of my liberty."

The old man's face grew stony again. "There are more important issues than your liberty," he said.

"Not to me," said Imbry, "and certainly not on the basis of what I've so far been told."

"Two days," said the elder. "Then we may be able to address your concerns. If you are not . . ."

"Dead?"

Imbry heard impatience put a snap in the Fuldan's voice. "You will not be dead."

Imbry looked up at the sky then back to the old man. "I hope not."

The elder turned to where Shan-Pei stood beside the door of the hut. She saw that she had his attention and bowed her head. Imbry noted that she had taken the supplies that had come with them into the little building, and that the cloths that had covered the carriage's seat and footrest were neatly folded in her gloved hands. The barbarel had finished its drink and was munching on something in its feedbag.

"Shvarden will be here no later than the evening," the elder said. He went to the carriage and took hold of a corner of the coarse cloth that covered the seat, tugging it free and letting it fall to the ground. Then he climbed in. "Be vigilant until then, and all will be well."

Imbry looked at the desolation about him. "Your definition of 'all' and 'well' may differ from mine," he said.

The Ideal looked as if he might say something, but after a moment's inspection of Imbry, he slapped the reins against the barbarel's rump then pulled them to point the animal back the way they had come. The fat man watched him depart then turned to Shan-Pei.

"What can you tell me?" he said.

She spread her fur-backed hands in a universal gesture. "We are not told anything other than what we have to do in the 'delvings.'"

"And what do you have to do?"

"We perform. They watch us. The arbiters watch the watchers. They look for signs of some kind. We don't know what those signs might be because we are forbidden to look anywhere but up."

"And after? In the back rooms?"

Again the gesture. "We are presented to the chosen ones. We sit on the stools. Then they touch us."

"Is it sex?"

Shan-Pei's expressions were difficult to read because of the fur that covered her face, but Imbry saw that he had said something ridiculous. "Sometimes," she said, "they shake and make strange noises. Sometimes they speak, but the words are not connected, or they are of an unknown tongue. Malweer calls it 'mere babble' but I do not know."

"And the tiles with strange characters on them?"

"Sometimes while they touch us, they will point to a tile and tell the black hats that they see this or that symbol." She touched her head. "In here."

"And then?"

He was becoming less than fond of her spreading-of-the-hands gesture. "We are sent to our quarters and the chosen ones go with the arbiters."

"They never explain?"

"We are irregulars. We are owed no explanations." She looked down at her hands, turned them so he could see the pink, naked palms. "Malweer says that if it were not for the delvings, they would not let us live past birth. I think he is right. Nobody talks about it, but I think that was how it used to be."

Imbry wished he had spoken more with Malweer. Or that the stick-thin man had been sent out here instead of the girl. But that might have been no accident. They had put him with the least knowledgeable, least curious member of the troupe, because there were things they did not want him to know. "What is this place?" he said, indicating the hut.

"Sometimes, one of us is taken out to be left alone for a day or two," she said. "They call it 'settling.' Then an arbiter brings out a chosen one for a delving. I think it has to do with removing distractions, but it has not happened to me before."

"Are they sending someone out to . . . touch you?"

"No. This is just pretend so they can hide you from the provost's man. He has become 'attached' to you without going through the proper procedure."

"Does that happen often?"

The hands opened again. "We're not supposed to talk about it. We're already irregular. Anything we do that is even more out of the ordinary makes them angry."

"It's not good to make them angry," Imbry said, pressing a hand to his sore ribs.

"It's dangerous," she agreed. "Sometimes one of us disappears. No one says anything."

There was nothing she could tell him. He went into the hut with her and they unpacked their supplies: flatbread, desiccated fruits he did not recognize, some kind of cheese that he suspected might have begun as a barbarel's glandular secretion, dried legumes, and a powder that Shan-Pei said would flavor the water. There were also several containers equipped for self-heating.

"We should eat, then sleep," he said. "If you will watch the trail for a little while, I will cook for us. Then I will stand watch while you sleep."

She went out and he prepared a simple meal: soup with bread to dip in it, cheese and fruit. He called her when it was ready and they ate standing up, outside the hut, their eyes on the back trail. They could still see, a long way off, the dust raised by the old man's passage back to Pilger's Corners. Nothing else stirred, save the shiny black creatures in the nearby patch of vein-plant. Imbry asked for the names of the crawlers and their plant world; from Shan-Pei's wordless response he deduced that she had never felt enough curiosity to ask.

After the meal, they cleaned and stacked the dishes, then the girl lay down on her side on the pallet. Imbry thought she was asleep by the time he left the hut. He had paused only to collect the children's book he had taken from the town library. He meant to learn what he could while he stood sentry duty against the coming of Investigator Breeth.

The volume was a textbook, a history primer for very young Fuldans. *A long time ago,* the text said, *we lived on another world, with another sun, far, far away. The name of that world is not important. We call it The Pit. It was not a good place. The people who lived there were not good people.*

But there was one man who wanted to be good. His name was Haldeyn, and he was very wise. He thought very hard about important matters, alone in a room in the basement of a building where many bad people lived. One day, after a lot of thinking, he discovered a great truth: the reason so many people were so bad was that they had become too different from each other. They were all different sizes, shapes, and colors. Some had nice straight hair, some had hair that bent and twisted. Some had well-shaped round heads, but some had ugly long heads. Even their eyes were of different colors.

Haldeyn realized that this was not how it was supposed to be. There was a right *shape for people to be, a* right *size, and a* right *color. At first, he did not know what those right attributes were, but as he thought more deeply about it, he discovered a way to find out. He studied statistical variances and standard deviations from the norm (you'll learn more about these things when you graduate to middle school). By comparing measurements made of many thousands and thousands of people, he worked out through arithmetic what he called the "golden mean." This was the way people were supposed to look. It is the way* you *look.*

Haldeyn was not surprised to discover that he looked very much like the golden mean. He was not too tall, but not too short. His hair was not too dark or too light, and neither were his eyes. His hands and feet were exactly the sizes they should be. He realized that if everyone looked like him, there would be no more trouble in the world.

But he knew he couldn't make everyone look like him overnight. It would take a long time and would have to be the work of many good people. They would first have to get the people who didn't look right to stop having so many babies, while getting people who looked almost right to have more (you'll learn about having babies when you get to middle school). Eventually, the world would begin to look the way it was supposed to.

Haldeyn started by gathering together people who looked right. His first convert was his twin brother, Holden. Then their cousin Illynus joined them. Besides looking right, Illynus was a very resourceful man who knew of a lot of ways to gain wealth quickly. He taught these ways to the twins, and together they formed an organization whose goal was to gain as much wealth from the bad people as they could, and quickly. It was very proper to gain wealth this way, because the bad people clearly did not deserve to have it.

When other people who looked right saw that they too could gain wealth quickly by joining the new movement, they did so. After a few years, Haldeyn was the leader of a large and wealthy organization dedicated to making the world right. They looked for more right-looking people on other worlds and brought them into the movement. Many more years passed, and the movement—now known as the Congress of the Ideals—was in charge of several counties and some of the major cities on The Pit.

In the fullness of his years, Haldeyn passed away. His brother Holden also died and Illynus became the leader of the Ideals, as the members of the movement were called. Illynus tried even harder to get the bad, wrong-looking people to stop having children, especially by gaining wealth from them and giving that wealth to Ideals who had plenty of right-looking boys and girls.

But the wrong-looking people made trouble for the Ideals, especially when Illynus ordered a new program called "The Scouring." The bad people tried to destroy all that Haldeyn, Holden, and Illynus had built. They tried to steal the Ideals' wealth. They brought in weapons and fighters from other worlds to make an unfair war on the Congress of the Ideals. For a while, things were very bad.

Then Illynus found a message that Haldeyn had wisely left hidden in a secret place. It said that time would prove to the Ideals that their world and its bad people were not worthy of all that the movement had tried to do for them. They should take spaceships and go to another world, where they could live the way good people were meant to live.

The Ideals gathered up their children and the small amount of wealth that the bad people had not stolen from them and came to this world. It had another name then, but Illynus renamed it Fulda, after his fourth spouse, who was young and comely. There were some bad, wrong-looking people living on Fulda when the Ideals arrived, but they soon went away.

The Ideals saw that Fulda could not be a world of big cities, nor could there be a lot of wealth-gaining here. A long, long, long time ago, when people lived on only one world—it was called Home, and everybody on it looked right—a race of very wrong-looking creatures called indigenes had lived on Fulda. In those days, this was a wet world, but the indigenes did something to the water so that some of it went into the air and stayed there, while most of it went *under the ground. From there it bubbles up in places to make the oases where we all live.*

No one knows how the indigenes made the water go up and down and stay there. But they must have been bad creatures, and probably very wrong-looking, because by the time the first people came to Fulda, they were all as gone-away as the seas. It was good that they went away, because they left us a planet where we can all live good, right-looking lives under the wise guidance of the Congress of the Ideals.

The text also contained colored pictures depicting Haldeyn and Illynus in heroic fashion. The bad people of The Pit from which the defeated Idealist fanatics had fled were shown as shadowy, subhuman forms, with glowing eyes and prominent fangs. There was also a fanciful rendering of an indigene as a multilimbed, insectoid creature standing about the height of an Idealist's knee. It had faceted eyes and a segmented tail with a barbed stinger. For some reason, the artist had equipped the imaginary creature with a spear taller than itself, tipped by a serrated blade.

There was more text, concerning the social organization the Ideals had built on Fulda. Even from a children's book, Imbry could deduce that theirs was a world of top-down authority, in which those at the top appointed their underlings. Arbiters and provost's men were admitted on merit, but advancement beyond the rank and file was probably acquired through subservience. Those at the apex of the pyramid—"the best and greatest" was how the book named them—appeared to hold their places for life, though how they gained superlative rank was not revealed to the children. From Imbry's reading between the lines of the text, he suspected that the top-level leadership changed infrequently—and that the process probably involved sudden, though intricately planned, violence.

He read the book in portions, looking up after every few paragraphs to scan the landscape to the east. Sometime after the sun had passed its highest point, he saw a suggestion of movement on the horizon. He stared at the spot, wishing for a long-distance viewer, but could not be sure if he had seen actual motion or just the ripple of heated air. He read a little more then looked again, and saw a very tiny, very distant swirl of dust.

He returned to the hut and woke Shan-Pei. "It may be that Shvarden, as promised," he said. "But it also might be Breeth. I certainly will not chance another encounter with the investigator."

He gathered up some food and water, put them in one of the cloths that their supplies had come bundled in, and tied it up with twine. As an afterthought, he slipped the schoolbook under the string then hefted the package. He could carry the weight a long distance.

"You will not tell Breeth?" he said to the girl.

"The arbiter told me what I am to say if he comes."

"He will not harm you?"

"It is you who calls him, not me."

Imbry left, heading toward the rise at the back of the broad terrace, keeping the hut between him and the distant puff of dust. It was not at all unthinkable that Breeth would have a viewer that could spot him, and that he would be coming in a sun-powered, multiwheeled vehicle that would soon run the fat man down, nimble though he might be.

He watched where he trod. The ground was too hard to take a footprint, but Imbry had been tracked in rough country before and knew that the long-buried underside of an overturned pebble looked different to a trained eye. Breeth's eye might be educated enough to see a trail if Imbry was fool enough to leave one.

By the time he had walked far enough that the hut was difficult to distinguish from the surrounding rock, the land had begun to slope upward again. The incline was steeper than the one that had led to the terrace, but the light gravity assisted Imbry and he went up quickly even though he moved carefully. The indigene ruins were not easy to find at first; they were built not on the top of the ridge, but in a broad hollow on its far side where the ground met the base of a middling-high cliff.

Imbry's first impression was of a tall heap of darker stone, the roundedness of its component shapes contrasting with the vertical and horizontal planes of the natural landscape. Then his eye adjusted to the proportions and he saw something like a combination miniature fortress and multi-unit dwelling, rising several times his own height. Like the earlier ruin he had passed on the way to Pilger's Corners, this one resembled a cluster of circular fruit or a conglomeration of bubbles piled one atop another, pierced by round, glassless windows. At its base and also farther up the structure, the dark stone had been broken into, leaving gaping holes and a scattering of rubble on the ground outside.

Imbry approached and peered into the lower breach. He saw a smallish chamber, roughly globular and apparently plastered in a lighter shade than the dark outer rock, with round holes in the ceiling, floor, and walls as well as another human-made breach. He entered the space and looked through some of the openings, saw more chambers and what looked to be narrower, spiral passageways leading deeper into the building and down into the subsurface. What he did not see was any sign of the structure having been shaped or assembled from smaller parts. There was an organic unity to the walls and floors, as if they had been grown—or, conceivably, blown—into existence. He was reminded of a reef he had once seen on the secondary world, where myriad undersea animalcules cohered together to create great hollow domes in which they sheltered species of larger creatures off whose wastes the tiny builders fed.

But there was more complexity here than on As. Imbry sensed that the proportions of the rooms and their relationships to each other and the structure as a whole answered to some mathematical framework that eluded his human brain. He would have been interested to ask an integrator to probe and measure the building to see what subtle algorithm underlie the arrangement of its parts.

But, more to the point, he saw no artifacts he could scoop up. If there had ever been any, the long-gone miners who had broken in would have taken them away. He was interested to note, though, that what he had taken for plaster on the inner surfaces was apparently not an applied substance. It did not flake when he scratched at it with a fingernail, nor was it cracked at the edges of the holes the miners had hacked through the walls. Instead, the dark of the outside gradually lightened to become the pale interior surface.

An interesting trick, Imbry thought, and one he had not seen anywhere else. He could imagine that a vogue for the architectural technique might spring up if it could be introduced to Olkney, where nothing genuinely new had appeared in aeons. But all Imbry saw here was the effect; how it was achieved, through what ultraterrene technology or what alien control of powerful energies, he had no idea. And he was unlikely ever to know the secret. The indigenes of Fulda had been gone far too long, taking all of their mysterious powers with them.

He went back out and approached the second unnatural feature of the site. This was a wide, circular depression, like a shallow, inverted cone lined in some pale stone and rimmed with a raised lip. It put Imbry in mind of a setting for a giant gemstone, now prized out and stolen away. As he came closer, he could see that its surface was marked by a pattern graven into the creamy stone. The overall impression was that of a spiral winding in toward an oval lozenge in the center of the declivity, though there seemed to be subtle discontinuities in the design. Imbry could somehow not keep the whole of the pattern in view, and the proportions of its parts seemed to shift if he focused on this or that feature of it. He found that prolonged gazing at the spiral brought the onset of a mild dizziness, and supposed it was meant to be seen through a different kind of eye.

He looked instead at the central oval. Scratched in it was a character that he thought he recognized from one of the ceramic tablets in the private booths behind the Hedevan Players' stage. He stepped over the lip of the depression and went to take a closer look. Immediately, he experienced an odd sensation, a prickling of the hairs all over his body, as if he had stepped into an electrically charged field. He stopped and waited to see if it would intensify, but instead it quieted. The hairs on his arms and legs lay down again and Imbry proceeded, though cautiously, to the oval center.

He stood on the oval, looking down at the character graved in the pale stone. It resembled a cross-hatched fence and he was sure it was one of those that he had seen on the ceramic tablets he had handled in the back of the show tent. Did that mean that the tablets were of indigene manufacture? If so, they could be of genuine value if properly presented to the right kind of collector. Perhaps he would see if he could pocket—well, pouch—a few of them before he left the planet. The glazes made the objects works of art in their own right; for some reason, he was reminded of some of the Nineteenth-Aeon ceramics, although the colors were quite different.

As he contemplated the cross-hatched design, he noticed that one edge of the oval had developed a dark shadowing. So unexpected was the sight, or perhaps it was the effect on his vision of examining an alien design, that it took Imbry a moment to grasp the significance. When he did, he immediately stepped off the oval—stepped off and stepped *up*, because the shadow's appearance had been caused by the silent sinking of the design's central lozenge into the ground.

Relieved of Imbry's weight, the oval did not cease to sink from view. Imbry knelt and peered into the hole. Now he could hear, coming up from below, a faint sifting, hissing sound. When he looked for its source he saw, issuing from beneath the descending oval, thin rivulets of sand running away into the dimness below.

The first thought that came to Imbry was: *trap*, but then he considered that it would be a poor trap indeed that was sprung so slowly. The second thought was: *secret passage*, and that naturally led to a consideration of one of the reasons passages were made secretively: *because they lead to treasure*.

The fat man turned around and eased himself down and over the rim of what he was now thinking of as a shaft. His ribs complained a little, but he overruled them. He supported his weight on his arms, which rested on the graved floor of the depression, while gingerly lowering himself until his feet again touched the sinking oval. Imbry transferred more of his weight onto his feet, but felt no increase in the rate of descent. He let go of the upper surface and crouched to see what was under the patterned hollow.

He saw a space, not very large, whose ceiling curved down seamlessly to become walls that just as seamlessly met the floor. When he looked in the direction of the ruin, he saw nothing of note. When he looked in the opposite direction, he saw a short column of the dark stone, standing like a plinth, and flat on top. Atop the column was an object, though the light from the shaft did not extend far enough to illuminate it.

Imbry remained where he was, standing on the still slowly sinking oval. He had a strong urge to go and see what stood atop the plinth, but he had had enough surprises of late; he would not care to return to the oval to find that while he had been treasure-hunting it had kept on sinking until it was deep below the surface of the chamber floor, leaving him with a hole above and a hole below, through neither of which he could exit.

Restraining his curiosity, he waited until he was sure that the stone beneath him had ceased to descend. It stopped, its upper surface level with the floor, and with the hole in the ceiling not far above Imbry's head. Despite his great strength, his heroic girth would make climbing out an ungraceful enterprise, but the fat man knew he could do it. He went to see what chance had delivered to him.

It was too dim to see clearly, but touch told him that he had found a squarish object about the width of his head and as deep as the distance from his wrist to his fingertips. It was a flattened cube, round cornered, with a smooth though irregular surface. When he nudged it, it moved, scraping across the flat stone top of the column. When he lifted it, it came free of the column and proved not too heavy to carry. He was about to take it back to where the light of Fulda's sun played down through the hole in the chamber's ceiling, but paused. His eyes had become better used to the darkness and now he saw that what he had taken for a pool of shadow behind the column was in fact a wide, circular hole in the floor.

He inched around the plinth and saw that the hole was filled with darkness. He bent and looked into it but could see nothing. Yet he had an unsettling sense of depth that told him that he stood on the lip of a shaft that went down and down, far beneath the surface of Fulda. He looked about for a pebble to drop into it, to listen and time the length of its falling, but there was nothing in the chamber but the column, the object, and Luff Imbry.

He backed away from the shaft. Somehow he was reluctant to turn his back on it. He put the column between him and the pool of darkness. Only then did he take up the object he had found and, moving quickly, bear it back to the oval on which he had descended. Even there, he went to the other side of the stone and turned so that the column and shaft were in his sightline before he looked at what was in his hands.

He saw a rectangular-shaped object of glazed ceramic, a little longer and wider than it was deep, colored in blues shading into greens, umbers, and old gold. It appeared to be of the same material as the figured tablets he had seen in the Hedevan Players' tent. Indeed, the top and sides of the

object were covered in the same figures, similarly in bas-relief, as well as
several he did not recall seeing back at Pilger's Corners. He ran his fingertips
carefully over the object's surface, feeling the smoothness of the glaze. He
had no idea how old it was—it might have been fashioned before humans
had discovered how to walk upright—yet it must have lain in this cellar all
this time, untouched by weather, and looked as if it had been made only
yesterday.

His fingers absently stroked its sides while he thought: *Unique. The single
remaining artifact—unless there are others deeper in the darkness—of a vanished
species.* He knew collectors on Old Earth and a score of other great worlds
who would pay a fortune for this piece. And others who would double that
fortune just to deny it to a hated rival.

I will hide it, he thought. *When I am free of this place, I will come back for it.*
He could think of two people on Old Earth who would lend him a spaceship
in return for a portion of the proceeds. He could land here in the wilderness,
take the piece from wherever he would have hidden it, and be off-world again
within minutes. He was already working out the logistics of contacting the
most likely purchasers, of arranging an auction. *It would be best if I could
record an image of it*, he thought. He wondered if Fuldans bothered with
recording devices.

He was roughing out his plans, still stroking the object, when a fingertip
encountered a node on one side near its upper surface. The smooth little
nubbin made a tiny movement under the faint pressure of his passing touch.
He pressed a little harder, felt the little bump sink into the side of the object.
In the same moment, he heard an almost inaudible *click*.

Imbry stopped breathing. He set the object down on the pale stone of the
oval. When he pressed his fingers gently against its sides he could feel a line of
separation. *A box*, he thought, *with a lid*. He did what had to be done, gently
lifting away the upper portion of the object. It separated from the base. He
laid it tenderly to one side and looked into what was now revealed as a square
container. Completely filling the space inside was a domed object of dark
gray, smooth like the upper surface of an opaque lens. Imbry picked up the
lid and turned it over, saw an indentation in it that exactly matched the gray
curve of the lens.

He had an impulse to try to lift the gray thing out of the box, an urge that he immediately suppressed—who knew how delicate it was? He might shatter it with his touch. The lid was still in his hands. He could see the tang of the simple spring lock in one side of the ceramic container and the corresponding indentation in the lid. His decision was made. He would fit them back together and hide the thing, to examine it as his leisure when he had escaped Fulda and come back for it.

A shadow fell across his hands and the object they held. "There you are," said a voice from above him, followed by a gasp of shock.

CHAPTER SIX

"Hand it to me, very carefully," said the young man in the black-hat. "I will hold it while you climb out of the pit."

Imbry recognized him as one of the arbiter's assistants. He remembered the name—Shvarden—and that the old man had said he would send him out. He also recognized the expression that had taken possession of Shvarden's face. He had seen that same look on the faces of collectors and connoisseurs when they at last beheld some masterpiece they had long lusted and schemed for.

"No," the fat man said, looking up. "I will place it on the floor down here. You will help me out. Then you will come down here and hand me the object. Then you will climb out and join me."

He watched to see the other man's reaction. If he saw even a flicker of calculation born of avarice pass across the black-hat's eyes, he would have to consider never letting the fellow out of the pit. But the awe that had illuminated Shvarden's features, as if they were lit from within his skull, did not change. "Yes," he said, "as you wish, but please put it down carefully."

Imbry did so, then he replaced the lid on the container, hearing the catch snick shut again. With the other man's assistance, he struggled back up to the world of daylight, abrading his stomach only slightly on the edge of the hole. He noticed that before he took hold of Imbry's hands, the black-hat had slipped on a pair of gloves from his pouch.

Shvarden then let Imbry lower him down into the underground chamber. Imbry saw him glance around with surprise, but almost immediately the man's attention returned to the flattened cube of ceramic. With a precision of movement that the fat man could only interpret as reverential, the arbiter stooped and lifted the object. For a long moment, he held it in his hands and stared at it. Then he looked up at Imbry with a new expression, one that

Imbry had never seen on another human being but was prepared to believe was none other than sacred joy.

"Now give it to me," he said and saw perfect acceptance on Shvarden's face as, with arms that trembled with awe, the black-hat lifted the box so that Imbry could take it from him. *I do not know what this thing is,* he thought, *but surely it is my ticket home.* He stepped back and let Shvarden propel himself up and out of the shaft.

"Well," Imbry said, "what do you think of that?"

The black-hat was lost for words, his eyes going from the cube to Imbry's face and back again. "All the years . . . all the dreams . . . the delvings. And now . . ." A look of beatific completion came over him. He uttered a string of syllables under his breath, too low for Imbry to hear, then made a complicated gesture involving one hand touching several points on his head and torso.

"And what," Imbry said, "is to be done with it?"

The question snapped Shvarden back into focus. "There is no question," he said. "It must go to the Chief Arbiter at Dolla." He stopped. Imbry could see a succession of thoughts pass across his face. "We must send a message—no, a messenger sworn to secrecy. The preparations must be in place before the people are told. Certainly before the Reorientation learns of it."

"The Reorientation?"

A shadow of sadness passed across the black-hat's face, followed by a renewal of determination. "It is improper to discuss those"—he sought for a dignified term—"unenlightened persons with"—again a search—"well, with one such as yourself."

"Even," said Imbry, "with such a one who brings this"—he held up the ceramic box—"into the light?"

Now Shvarden showed irresolution. His gaze cast about as if an answer might pop out of the hard ground. Finally, he said, "It is not for me to say. It is for the Chief Arbiter. And the sooner we bring the First Eye to him, the better for all of us."

"Better for the Reorientation?" Imbry said.

But he now saw that he had pushed his search for information as far as it could go. Shvarden was coming out of the ecstatic turmoil into which the first sight of the "First Eye" had plunged him. Whatever the thing was, its finding had been long anticipated, and a process laid down for what to do next. That would probably complicate Imbry's desire to take the thing off-world and sell it.

But, he reminded himself, his strategy was still to get home and get satisfaction. Pecuniary opportunities, no matter how enticing, must not interfere with that plan. He refocused the young arbiter on the person who right now posed the greatest threat to Imbry's aims. "What about Investigator Breeth?" he said.

"What of him?"

"I fear him. I believe he intends me harm."

"He must fall into line," the black-hat said. "All of them must. After all, the question is now settled."

"Is Breeth part of the Reorientation?"

"The Provosts Corps is rife with—" Shvarden interrupted himself. "Never mind," he continued. "You don't need to worry your little head about . . ." He broke off and gazed again at the box in Imbry's hands. "And to think it was right here, all the time." He looked at the hole in the ground. "How many times have I sat right there"—he gestured with his chin toward the hole at the center of the shallow bowl—"and invoked the Four Disciplines? How many times have I sought the Elusive Thread?"

"Indeed," said Imbry, "it is a wonderment. Speaking of which, I wonder how I will be received by the Chief Arbiter? I would not wish to offend."

Shvarden gave him a puzzled look. "Then don't," he said. "Practice the effacement, make a full courtesy. None of your irregular bumptiousness."

"I do not know what those things mean," Imbry said. "I have already had one beating. I would prefer to avoid another. Or worse."

They were walking side by side, ascending the slope of the hollow at the foot of the cliff that sheltered the fortress. "How can you not know . . ." He stopped, turned his head sideways, and regarded Imbry askance. "Are you truly not of this world? I mean, I know irregulars sometimes say such things, but no one takes them seriously." Before Imbry could answer he went on, as if to himself, "But then the scripture says that the Finder shall be one who comes from beyond all horizons."

"Show me a horizon anywhere on Fulda," said Imbry, "and I guarantee that I come from beyond it."

Shvarden made a wordless sound and walked on, shaking his head. "I suppose we will all have to accustom ourselves to novel thoughts," he said, "now that the Renewal is almost here."

"The Renewal?" Imbry said, keeping pace. He was thinking, *Oh, for a little time alone with a well-organized integrator. These Fuldans dispense information as freely as a miser empties his purse.*

"That which the First Eye will bring us."

"And have I a part to play in this Renewal?"

"Oh, yes."

"And what is my part in the Renewal?"

Shvarden opened his mouth as if to answer, then closed it and chewed the inner corner of his lip. "That would best come from the Chief Arbiter," he said at last.

They crested another rise, and now Imbry could see the little beehive hut far down the slope. A carriage was tied beside it. "Was Shan-Pei all right when you got there?" he said.

Shvarden's eyebrows rose. "With all the excitement," he said, "I forgot to ask you: where is she?"

"I left her in the hut."

"She was not there when I arrived," the black-hat said.

And when they reached the little building, she was still not there. The stool and table had been turned over, the supplies that had been stacked on the latter scattered across the floor. The cover of the sleeping pallet was rucked up, as if a struggle had taken place.

"Someone has taken her," Imbry said, "though she fought against them."

"Who would want a little odd—" Shvarden gave the appearance of a man who was choosing a more polite word. "An irregular," he finished.

"Who would want to kill Tuchol?" Imbry said.

"Death and mystery will precede him," the black-hat said.

"What?" It had sounded to Imbry like a quotation.

"Nothing."

"I am becoming tired of mystery," said the fat man, "and death from unknown quarters worries me, even when it is not my own. I am going to look for Shan-Pei. When I return we will have a more focused discussion."

"Do not take the First Eye with you," Shvarden said. "Something could happen to it."

"You would prefer I left it in your keeping?"

"Oh, yes!"

"But I will not. You will just have to accompany me."

"She is only an irregular," the black-hat said. "She probably wandered off. Who knows what fancies move their simple minds?"

Imbry said nothing. He was finding the Fuldans' sentiments toward irregulars—a category which, he was constantly reminded, included his own person—increasingly tiresome. He decided that the discussion he meant to have with Shvarden would have to be more searching than he had heretofore been planning. But for now he went out into the late afternoon sun and looked in all directions for some sign of the fur-covered girl. He found none. The terrace stretched flat and empty in all directions, with scarcely more than the smallest bump to interrupt its levelness.

Starting from the door of the hut, he began a widening-spiral search, but the ground was so dry and hard that it revealed almost nothing. Even the carriage wheels had made no more than a faint imprint, and the barbarel's padded feet left no tracks at all. But as he went wider afield, still finding nothing, Imbry remembered his own caution when he had been en route to the fortress, and instead of looking for footprints he cast his eyes about for tiny signs of disturbance.

And he found them. On the opposite side of the hut from its door he noticed a flat, rounded stone about the size of a stopper that would have fitted a wide-mouth jar. The object drew his attention because it was surrounded by a raised rim of desiccated soil, like a rock in ground that has alternately frozen and thawed. But no such alteration of temperatures would have occurred on Fulda. A moment's thought told Imbry that the stone had been pressed down hard into the ground, while the soil itself had not been affected. He scanned the ground around the rock and found other pebbles that were sunk deeper than the surrounding dust.

He knew what could cause such an effect: the gravity obviators used to lift aircars and other flying craft, even spaceships when they were enclosed by a planet's atmosphere and could not use their more powerful drives.

Their fields acted differently on denser objects than on less compacted mass. Imbry set down the ceramic box and knelt beside the sunken stones. He studied the dispersal of affected rock and dust and all at once the size and shape of the object that had been responsible was plain to him.

"A carry-all has landed here," he told Shvarden, who had been hovering about him throughout the search, his eyes never on the ground or horizon, but on the figured box.

"Really?" said the black-hat. "You mean a flying vehicle?" Now he looked up into the sky. "I have heard of such things. They are irregular."

Imbry raised himself back to his feet and took up the First Eye again. "You have no flying vehicles at all?"

"The Blessed Haldeyn inveighed against them. And rightly—they would lead us astray."

"Well, someone has a different view on their usefulness. Two nights ago, he used one to kill Tuchol, and now he has come down again to snatch poor harmless Shan-Pei."

"Irregulars are not to be harmed unnecessarily," Shvarden said.

"The Blessed Haldeyn again?" Imbry said.

"No." The black-hat turned thoughtful for a moment. "That was a truth revealed to us by Dansk, who had the vision that set us on the path to the Renewal." Now a new thought occurred. "Although, of course, with the Renewal now at hand, the need for tolerating irregulars will expire."

"Tolerating?" Imbry heard a sharp note in his own voice. "Is that what you call it?"

The black-hat spoke as if to an obtuse child. "They are unclean! In their presence we are at constant risk of contamination. Do you consider that no imposition?"

The fat man did not reply. Instead he turned and strode and returned to the hut, went inside, and placed the ceramic container on the sleeping pallet. Shvarden followed close upon his heels and, when the object was set down, his gaze remained fixed upon it. Imbry had seen a similar expression on devotees of various cults and covens when they were in the presence of venerated objects. He supposed it was what was meant by the term "sacred hunger."

He stepped closer to Shvarden. The man did not shift his gaze from the thing on the pallet. That made it easier for Imbry. His fist traveled only a short distance and very fast, to intersect with the black-hat's midsection. Shvarden expelled air like a punctured bladder, doubling up and pressing his hands to his belly. Imbry followed the first blow with another to the hinge of the black-hat's jaw, putting much of his weight behind the punch. Shvarden's head snapped sideways, his knees bent, and he pitched forward, eyes already glazed. Imbry considerately caught him by the shoulders and lowered him to the floor.

Not long after, Imbry flung the contents of a beaker into Shvarden's face. The man awoke to find himself seated on the stool, his wrists and elbows bound tightly behind him and his legs tied just as firmly at knee and ankle. Imbry had used strips of black cloth torn from the black-hat's baldric.

Shvarden blinked to clear the water from his eyes. "You . . ." he said, "you touched me!"

Imbry slapped him hard across the face, sending droplets flying. "Get used to it," he said.

"You cannot! You must use gloves! It is—"

Another slap, this one with weight behind it. "Yes," said the fat man, "it is irregular. But so am I." The bound man stared up at him, eyes wide with shock that was sliding into horror. "We are going to have a conversation," Imbry continued, "and you are going to be forthcoming."

He realized that Shvarden was not a stupid man when the black-hat immediately drew the right conclusion and also a shocked breath. "There are secrets no irregular is allowed to know."

"But you can know these secrets because you are of the Ideals, is that not right?" Imbry said.

"Of course, I am of the Congress of the Ideals. But more than that, I am one of the Called, an arbiter, a last of the last."

"I do not understand 'last of the last.'"

"It means that my conformation is within the last percentile of the last percentile."

Imbry turned the figures over in his mind and understood. "Your deviation from the Golden Mean is less than one percent of one percent. You deviate by no more than one part in ten thousand from the perfect."

He could see that the black-hat was impressed that an irregular could do arithmetic. Clearly, those who were not of the Ideals were not burdened by an excess of education. "So," the fat man continued, "your purity prevents you from revealing arcane knowledge to one such as me?"

"I am glad you understand," said the bound man. "I did not make these rules. They were laid down millennia ago by one much wiser than we."

"The Blessed Haldeyn?"

"No, no. It was long after Albar had brought us here to Fulda, long after the First Ideal had left us. The rules were set by Dansk the Visionary, when he received the revelation concerning the Renewal."

"Ah," said Imbry, "which brings us back to what I want to ask about."

But Shvarden closed his mouth. "You cannot know, and I cannot tell you."

"Yes, yes, because you are of the Congress of the Ideals." Imbry went to the table, which he had righted and on which he had replaced the supplies that had come with him from Pilger's Corners. Among the objects was a sharp knife that he had used to cut up vegetables for the pot. He picked it up and felt its edge with his thumb, then turned back to Shvarden. "How many percentiles would you be in deviation from the Golden Mean," he said, "if I removed one of your ears?"

The black-hat's face went gray. "You wouldn't."

Imbry moved toward him. "Answer me," he said. "Could you still be an arbiter with only one ear? Could you still hear the 'Call'? Or would you have to run away and join the circus?"

Shvarden regarded him with horror, then his eyes fell to lock on the knife as Imbry angled the blade to let it catch the late afternoon sun that came through the open doorway. "No," the black-hat said.

"Is that, 'No, you couldn't be an arbiter,' or 'No, please don't cut off my ear'?"

Shvarden looked up at him, swallowed hard. "Both," he said.

"You must understand," the fat man said, "that I didn't make these rules. I need to know things that none of the Ideals can tell me. The simplest solution is to turn you into an irregular like me. Then we can have a frank and productive talk."

He reached with his free hand and took hold of the top of Shvarden's right ear. The bound man shrieked and tried to pull away. But Imbry held fast and laid the edge of the blade against the cartilage-stiffened flesh.

"Wait!" cried Shvarden.

Imbry lifted the knife. "Have you just remembered some provision that allows you to ignore the rule during occasions of extreme need?"

"I believe," said the bound man, his voice coming in gasps, "I have."

"Excellent," said Imbry. "I did not think you had it in you to make a good irregular. Why don't you assume I don't know anything and start with the most elementary facts. I will interrupt to ask questions if necessary."

"One thing first," Shvarden said. "You won't tell anyone that I told you?"

"Not unless I'm tortured," said Imbry. He affected an imitation of Decider Brosch's sepulchral tones. "Begin."

Theirs was a lengthy conversation. While Shvarden talked, Imbry made them a simple supper, though he ate his meal first and did not untie the other man until he was sure he had heard all he needed to hear.

The Idealist movement had originated on a secondary world whose name they had deliberately allowed to be forgotten. It was referred to only as the Pit. They had been driven from that world after seizing power in an armed revolt against a corrupt and venal regime. At first, the change had been welcomed by the populace, but once the Blessed Haldeyn had consolidated his rule and begun to put the precepts of Idealism into ruthless practice, social war had erupted. People who had not been willing to risk death, torture, and incarceration to remove the earlier cabal of thieves were forced to do so again when the near-naked Ideals pursued their philosophy to its logical ends of relocation and sterilization.

The remnants of the movement had fled to Fulda, a barren, almost abandoned little place that had once been the center of a short-lived mining boom. The planet had possessed a unique composite mineral, clitch, which had apparently been left scattered around the lowlands of the planet in huge lenses, giant versions of the small one Imbry had found. The clitch lenses had been set like dull jewels into the pale circles that were mainly associated with the globular ruins. All of the lenses had been broken up—clitch apparently shattered easily—and shipped off-world, where it was put to uses since forgotten.

When the clitch was gone, so went most of the world's inhabitants. By the time the Ideals came thundering down from space, Fulda was home to only a sparse population of "misanthropes, mystics, and mooks," as Shvarden phrased it, "who lacked the imagination or the means to go somewhere else."

The Ideals had rounded up and deported most of them, dumping them haphazardly on nearby worlds. Those who managed to slip through the newcomers' net or who had the temerity to return from exile were eventually found—it was not as if they could blend in with the majority—and, so Imbry gathered, were made examples of. The Blessed Haldeyn's followers settled down to a simple life without many of the conveniences found in more varied societies. This was a matter of necessity rather than of philosophy: Fulda had lost all its manufacturing capabilities at the end of the clitch boom, and the Ideals did not care to trade with citizens of other worlds whose shapes and colorings departed widely from the Golden Mean.

So Fulda became a backward, inward-looking place, ruled by its corps of arbiters, who themselves were chosen for their lack of deviation from the standard Haldeyn had set. Inevitably, recessive genes produced occasional deviants, or uterine mishaps turned a would-be Idealist newborn into an irregular. For millennia, the response to these mishaps had been infant exposure.

But during those same millennia, something unusual had been happening among the Fuldans: they dreamed strange dreams, thrashing on their pallets, while odd characters passed before their inner eyes and they muttered words in no known language. The deepest study of the scriptures brought from the Pit could tell them nothing. The populace was distressed and the arbiters baffled—until a man who was taking his newborn irregular out into the desert that surrounded their oasis experienced a waking vision.

He had carried the infant the prescribed distance, far enough that its pitiful cries would not disturb the community's rest. But, out of a misguided tenderness, he had swept the ground smooth of pebbles and projections that would have pressed into the doomed child's flesh while it died of thirst. In sweeping too vigorously, he had torn the fingertips of his gloves, and when he lifted the baby from its swaddling cloth, its flesh accidentally came in contact with his own.

Immediately, he saw in the air before him a figure of five lines—two long parallels, crossed by three short strokes at an angle of forty-five degrees. At the same time, he heard a sibilant sound that he recognized from his own dreams and those of others who had reported them to arbiters. The man had rewrapped the infant and carried it back to the settlement where he told the community's arbiter what had happened.

The College of Arbiters had investigated, subjecting the visionary, a farmer named Dansk, to various experiments. They also collected a few subsequent irregular newborns and arranged to have them touched by Ideal volunteers. Some of the test subjects contaminated themselves for nothing; but a few saw visions like those of Dansk.

Many generations had now come and gone, and the College had long since concluded that the visions were attempts by the Blessed Haldeyn to make contact from Perfection. This was the place of the spirit in which the Blessed Founder was now occluded—a true Ideal could never, of course, simply expire—and where he would someday be joined by all Ideals who had lived in righteousness. Perfection was believed to be located in either the Fourth or Fifth Plane.

At first the Blessed Founder had tried to reach them by dreams, but the method had been deemed ineffective. But with Dansk a new avenue of investigation opened. The visionary had heard and seen a letter of the New Syllabary, as the arbiters had named the code of Perfection. The revelation had come through contact with the forbidden flesh of an irregular. It was a clear message from the Blessed Haldeyn. No more were the statistically defective to be killed at birth; instead, they must be allowed to live—though theirs would be a sequestered, segregated existence—so that contact could be made, under circumstances closely monitored by arbiters, and the new dispensation made plain.

The Colleges had determined that, through visions, the Blessed Founder was teaching the Ideals the actual language of Perfection. This was not only the sublime tongue that all Ideals would speak once they had crossed over. It was also a language of power that would import from the abstruse dimension where their Founder waited for them the means to burst through the membranes that separated the Planes.

A community was established at the hitherto unpopulated oasis of Nid in a remote part of the southern desert. There the first irregulars were raised by select arbiters until they reached adulthood and could begin to care for their own. Though "their own" would never include their own offspring—all irregulars were sterilized at the onset of puberty. But defective newborns were brought to the new town and handed over to be brought up as those before them were.

Idleness being almost as great a sin among the Ideal as irregularity, it was seen as necessary that the irregulars should have something useful to do. They could not, of course, engage in the agricultural or simple manufacturing pursuits that occupied the bulk of the Fuldan population. Anything they touched was unclean. But professional entertainers had always been regarded by the Ideals as lacking in true merit—the Blessed Haldeyn himself had accused them of "shillifying and laziness"—and so the irregulars took over the white-hat function.

In order to give as many Ideals as possible the opportunity to touch an irregular, under controlled conditions, the latter were formed into traveling troupes. Given tents, wagons, and barbarels, they progressed from town to town, the several different companies swapping routes from one "show season" to the next.

A troupe would set up its tent beside an Idealist community. In the evening, the adults would come and sit in chairs no irregular had touched. The players would come on stage, one at a time, to perform in some way, never daring to let their eyes meet those of the watchers. The arbiters would closely examine the crowd. When they saw subtle signs—known only to the black-hats—that a particular member of the audience had "attached" to a particular performer, they would take note. After the performance, the arbiters would bring the connected pair into contact with each other, as Imbry had witnessed in Pilger's Corners.

Under a black-hat's supervision, the chosen one would sit upon the stool provided. The irregular would approach and stand before the Idealist. At the arbiter's signal, the latter would reach out and touch the former. Usually, nothing definitive came of the contact. The Idealist was taken to the tabernacle and cleansed.

Sometimes, though, at the moment of contact the seated Idealist would go rigid and moan, eyes glazed over as the chosen one's vision turned inward. Then limbs might vibrate, mouths open and close spasmodically. Spontaneous sexual arousal was sometimes evident among the men. The arbiter would instruct the visionary in techniques that intensified his or her focus. If all went well, the chosen one would identify one, sometimes two, rarely three of the characters on the ceramic tablets, and would voice the phoneme that the indicated symbols represented.

The process had now been going on for more than a century. The arbiters had devoted intense scholarship to the mystery and had now identified seventeen consonants and four vowels, as well as eight symbols that, when combined with elements of the seventeen and four, appeared to modify their pronunciation. The meanings of nine other symbols were still indeterminate, but a breakthrough on one of them was considered imminent.

As Shvarden told it, the continuing revelation had now progressed beyond nouns and consonants. A handful of visionaries had reported groups of symbols together; arbiter scholars, at first skeptical, were now leaning toward the view that the chosen were hearing and seeing actual words in the tongue of Perfection. A message was being sent, and the faithful were confident that, through time and effort, they would receive it—and know a new joy.

"The Blessed Haldeyn speaks to us," the black-hat said, his eyes grown large and luminous in the fading light that came through the hut's door. "What wonders we shall soon comprehend."

"It seems odd that he must first teach you an entirely new language," said Imbry, "and in such a roundabout fashion."

"The Truth of Perfection cannot be expressed in the base tongue we must speak here in the Commonplace," the bound man said, and Imbry heard the capitalization of the Idealist term for the physical universe. "When we have mastered the tongue of Perfection, our thoughts will rise to a sublime plane. All shall be transformed."

The fat man allowed the black-hat to contemplate the ineffable while he turned over what he had heard. The tale explained much that he had seen. Though not all, he realized. "But what of the First Eye? And the 'Finder'?"

Shvarden descended from the high and airy place to which his thoughts had elevated him. His aspect grew troubled. "I should not discuss—" he began, then changed his view as Imbry issued a heavy sigh and reached for the knife. "You swear you will tell no one?" the black-hat said.

"What can an irregular swear by?" Imbry wondered.

Now it was Shvarden's turn to sigh. "True, you come from the fetid cesspits and rank warrens of worlds like the Pit, and are therefore beyond all piety." He rallied himself to hope. "Still, there must be something you hold sacred," he said.

"I will swear," Imbry said, "by Mindern. I hold him in the highest regard."

"Some false idol?"

"Does it matter?"

"I suppose not."

Imbry assumed a formal posture. "Then I swear by Mindern that I will tell no one anything of what you reveal to me."

"I have no choice, in any case," said the black-hat. "But know that what I have told you so far is widely known among the laity; what follows is known only to the few."

"Then say it," said Imbry. He was becoming hungry, and hunger fed impatience.

Shvarden spoke on, telling of how a new recurring dream had lately arisen among the Ideals. The vision was not of the New Syllabary per se, but of an object, a perfect lens of rarest clitch, housed in a ceramic box marked with the symbols of Perfection. It was to be found by an irregular, a figure of mystery and one who was well acquainted with death, and its finding would be attended by signs and wonders.

"Death and mystery precede him," said Shvarden. "The Finder brings dire discord, but beyond the troubles awaits the Renewal."

"And what is the Renewal?" Imbry said.

"I cannot say," Shvarden said, then as Imbry took up the knife, "I mean I cannot say for sure. Our scholars have puzzled over the messages, but the consensus of the College is that the Blessed Founder is transmitting to us a phrase of power. It must be spoken by . . ."

Here Shvarden censored himself. Imbry took up the knife again. After the blade touched an even more sensitive part of his anatomy, the arbiter shuddered and said, "After the Finder is revealed, another steps forward: the Speaker."

"Who will, presumably, speak the 'phrase of power.'"

"Yes."

"Power to do what?" Imbry said.

That led to a digression from the arbiter. It was known, Shvarden said, that in some of the Planes certain words were more than mere symbols; they were engines of power, sometimes huge power. Spoken under the right circumstances, such phrases could accomplish wonders. "Even," he said, "burst the membranes between the Planes themselves."

Imbry held his face steady. He did not want to mock the young man and dry up this flow of information. "You believe that your leader is trying to open a way for you to join him in the Fourth or Fifth Plane?"

"We are almost certain of it."

"And you believe that somehow he has drawn me to Fulda so that I might find the talisman that makes the exercise somehow possible?"

"It does seem unlikely," Shvarden said, a look of wonder filling his eyes, "and yet it is the sheer unlikeliness of it all that compels me to believe it is true."

Again, the young man's gaze turned inward. "And now, now that the First Eye is found"—he looked up at Imbry—"now that the Finder has appeared, the controversy must end. The Reorientation—"

"Enough!" said a new voice, harsh and peremptory. "Disgusting! You prattle like this before a filthy odd-lot?"

Imbry turned, the knife in his hand. In the doorway of the hut stood a man who wore a brown hat marked with a trio of circles. On his face, almost a duplicate of Shvarden's, was an expression of outrage, and in his hand was a tube of metal mounted on a wooden grip. With unmistakable intent, he aimed one end of it at Imbry.

The fat man dropped both the knife and his gaze and took a step backward and away from the bound man. "Investigator Breeth," he said.

The provost's man came into the hut, his weapon still aimed at Imbry. Behind him came two other brown-hats, younger men, but with the same anger and contempt in their identical faces. At their superior's order, they moved to free Shvarden from his bonds.

"But do not let him touch you," Breeth added. "He has been in contact with this filth"—he indicated Imbry—"and is unclean."

"Something has happened," Shvarden said, truculence fighting with shame in his face and voice.

"That much is obvious," said Breeth. "Take him out."

The two junior provost's men seized the black-hat's arms with gloved hands, but their prisoner struggled. "Hear me! He is the Finder! Look on the bed!"

Imbry had been shielding the figured box from Breeth's view. Now, at a gesture from the weapon, he moved aside. The fat man saw the investigator's pupils involuntary widen as he beheld the object on the pallet, then they contracted as he turned a hostile gaze on Imbry.

"So this is your scheme?" the brown-hat said. "Well, you may fool some simple-minded country arbiter, but you are now in the hands of the Reorientation"—he turned his head to include Shvarden in his field of vision—"oh, yes, and we have been waiting for the likes of him to reveal how far the College of Arbiters has strayed from scripture."

"He is the Finder!" Shvarden said. "The signs, the First Eye. How can you doubt it?"

Breeth made a wordless sound of contempt. "The signs are manufactured. Your own credulity fills in the gaps."

"He is from off-world," the provost's man countered. "The creatures of the Pit command infernal powers. It is all in scripture."

"May I ask," Imbry said, eyes lowered, "why an off-world irregular would want to interfere in your affairs?"

"Because," said Breeth, "you are evil. Foul creatures of the teeming Pit, you cannot help but be filled with hatred for we who have so nearly reached Perfection."

Against such certainty, Imbry judged it unwise to argue. He gazed at his sandaled feet and said nothing. "Put Shvarden in the roller, and restrain him," the investigator said to his subordinates. To Imbry he said, "Turn around and cross your wrists behind you."

The fat man felt a pressure on his wrists and heard the click of a restraint. One of the provost's men came back in and asked where the investigator wanted Imbry.

"Tie the barbarel's reins to the rear of the roller. This filth can ride in the carriage. Put the dead one in with him."

"The dead one?" Imbry said, remembering just in time not to raise his eyes to the investigator's.

Breeth made the sound of contempt again. "That's good, pretend you don't know. What happened? Did she grow scared, refuse to go along with the plan?"

"Where did you find her?"

"Where you left her," the provost's man said. "Lying on the trail, her face smashed in and her neck broken."

Imbry made his own wordless sound, an exhalation of breath that signaled anger coupled with helpless regret.

"It won't work," Breeth said. "You killed her and the other one. And I'll see you burned for it."

CHAPTER SEVEN

They had wrapped the girl's body in a coarse cloth, but when the provost's men lifted her with gloved hands from the cargo compartment at the rear of the roller, one small, fur-covered arm dangled from beneath the edge of the covering. The bare palm had turned pale as blood had drained from the extremities. The sight troubled Imbry. He did not mind death in the abstract, nor in the concrete when it was necessary to further his goals—but this seemed a waste.

He believed that whoever had killed Shan-Pei had done so to make life difficult for Luff Imbry. The girl had been a pawn. Or perhaps she had seen something that the killer did not want revealed. Either way, the business smacked of a callousness that angered him.

He sat now in the carriage, the corpse-bundle bound to its back shelf. One of the provost's men kept an eye on him, a weapon in his hand. They had put Shvarden in the rear seat of the roller and the other junior officer sat in the operator's position, though turned so that he could keep the black-hat under observation. But the black-hat offered no more resistance, sitting slumped and silent.

Breeth came out of the hut, his weapon in one hand and the ceramic box tucked under one arm. Shvarden looked up as the investigator approached and held out his hands for the object. But the brown-hat gave him only a look of amused contempt and stowed the box in the cargo hold. Then he went back to the hut and aimed the metal tube through the doorway, adjusting some control on its wooden stock. A burst of light sprang from the end, and a moment later there came a crackle and a roar from within. The doorway belched white smoke and yellow fire. For a moment, Breeth stood and watched the small inferno, and Imbry saw on his face an expression so like that of Shvarden when he'd seen the gray lens that, for that moment, the two Ideals were identical. Then the provost's man's aspect became businesslike again. He slung the weapon over his shoulder and climbed into the front seat of the roller next to the operator. He signaled the other provost's man to get in beside the black-hat. "And keep an eye on the fat oddy," he said.

The vehicle started up and inched forward. As the slack of the reins tightened, the barbarel followed and the carriage began to roll. Fulda's sun was near the horizon when they started, and they moved at a moderate pace through the long twilight back toward Pilger's Corners. Imbry found it a nuisance not to have his hands free as the carriage swayed, but he appreciated the opportunity to think about what he had learned.

He was not a profound student of history. Indeed, on Old Earth it was a peculiar sort who bothered with a close study of the past. Humankind had by now been in existence over a vast span of time, and across that myriad of millennia every possible permutation and combination of social orders had been tried and judged. All that needed to be known about the ways in which societies could be—and more important, should be—organized, was now known. There were, of course, a few feckless romantics who pined for the freedom of the long-ago dawn-times, when anything might be possible and humanity stumbled blindly forward, making it up as they went along. But sensible people, and Imbry was nothing if not sensible, knew that the quest for social perfection was always misguided. It never failed to produce misery.

The Ideals of Fulda had fallen into an old and oft-repeated error. The Blessed Haldeyn, finding to his sadness that the world about him was grossly imperfect, had deduced that the flaw lay in the mutability of the individuals who created and sustained it. He had thus set out to create perfect individuals. Statistical chance having revealed that he was freakishly average in almost every way, he no doubt found it easy to convince himself that there was some great meaning in the concatenation of coincidences that had made him who he was. Compared to that great mental leap it was but a hop and a skip to the idea of using his own person and personality as the template and standard of measurement of the Ideals.

First, on some hapless foundational domain or secondary world, he had gathered a coterie of followers—the charismatically insane always find that task an easy one—and set about trying to convince his fellow citizens of the worth of his concepts. He had won over some, but not all. Next, he had tried to enforce his views on the recalcitrant. That had not worked—it never did for long—so he had led his faithful to Fulda. The Ideals had fallen upon the scant population, expelling most of them and probably murdering the last holdouts. Then they settled down to practicing the perfection they preached. Within a few generations, they had created an ideal population—at least, according to their tenets—of nearly identical units. The task then became to prevent that perfection from ever changing.

It was the old fallacy of the frozen river, as Imbry recalled from his schooling. When the normally endless fluctuations of current, eddy, and flow come to be seen as evil, the reformer eliminates them by freezing the river solid. But ice was never a true solid; it still flowed, albeit slowly. And where it was stressed, it cracked. And when the stress was great, the inevitable fracturing became catastrophic.

Fuldan society, being a fundamentally unnatural system that could be maintained only by constant effort contrary to the natures of its constituents, was under great stress. The stress generated within the Fuldan mass psyche a surge of mysticism. Because Idealism was founded on a division of humanity into the "us" of the pure stock and the "they" of the irregulars, the relationship between the two was bound to become the fulcrum on which the growing forces hinged. The forbidden flesh of the Other, therefore, became a great Shadow within the Fuldan collective unconscious, full of man and power. When the Ideals touched that flesh, they touched their own inner Shadow, which was always an act of great psychic moment; thus, they saw signs and wonders, heard voices, experienced a brush with the ineffable.

At first, Imbry thought, the arbiters would have considered the practice of oddy-touching as a foul heresy. They would have worked to suppress it, probably violently, and no doubt enlisting the organized authority of the Provost. But the establishment's resistance would only have increased the perceived power of the Other, at least among those whose psyches resonated to the siren song of the Shadow. Eventually, that power would have been built to the point where it either destroyed the establishment or merged with it. In Fulda's case, the solution had been merger: the Ideals could touch the forbidden flesh of the irregulars and experience their epiphanies, but only under the control and direction of the Arbitration.

But obviously, the reconciliation between the new mysticism and the established order had not been universally acclaimed. Some Fuldans had remained true to the Blessed Haldeyn's original teachings, rejecting the Arbitration's emendations. To the holdouts, the irregulars were still repulsive, *wrong* in the most fundamental way.

Two camps had formed, the adherents of each speaking less and less with their opposites, and more and more with their like-minded fellows. A new "us" and "they" regarded each other with growing suspicion and dislike, each distorting and perverting the other's views and aims.

It was understandable that the rejection of the new dispensation would be strongest among the provost's men. Their work brought them constantly into contact with the prosaic iconoclasm of criminals; this caused them to develop a resistance to high-minded concepts. To the provost's men, questions of right and wrong were the stuff of their day-to-day work. But those questions were not put to them in abstract and ethereal terms. Instead they came in the form of violence, theft, chicanery, and vandalism. Who killed whom? Who stole what? Who cheated? Who destroyed?

Still, the Shadow was as active in the minds of the rejectionists' as it was in those who accepted the new dispensation. But instead of the Other being the gateway to gnostic enlightenment, the reviled irregulars were the fount of deception and evil. The more the Arbitration pandered to the majority's desire to touch the forbidden, the more the provost's department sought to repress the people they called oddies.

Repressive social orders always generated internal stress, Imbry knew, as did every educated person of Old Earth. That stress built up at the society's points of division, the social equivalents of faults in the deep strata of slow-moving rock. On Fulda, the irregulars were now the point of division between two diametrically opposed factions. The opponents were acting out, in the phenomenal or "real" world, struggles that were simultaneously occurring in the profoundest depths of their psyches, with no likelihood of compromise. By what Imbry had seen, the conflict had not risen to the level of social war, with neighbors cutting each other's throats and fathers damning sons to eternal perdition. But if Breeth's behavior represented an example of a growing unhappiness within the Fuldan polity, an outbreak of atavistic bloodletting might not be far off.

On whatever world Haldeyn had first had his revelation, the outcome had been social war. The losing side—the Ideals—had boarded ships and escaped to Fulda. But Haldeyn must have sent those ships away and closed the space port. So the coming holy war would offer no escape valve. It would be a struggle to the death, each side needing to destroy the enemy utterly, because each side had painted the enemy with the image of the Shadow from its own collective psyche.

Fulda was not safe for a visiting stranger at any time. Imbry doubted there was even a word in the local vocabulary for "neutral," and if there were it would not be applicable to someone as irregularly formed as he. He had no hope of being exempted as a disinterested bystander. The Fuldans' mystic surge had introduced a new factor: oddy-touchers had given birth to a new myth—that of the Finder and the First Eye—which was sure to heighten the excitement of the believers and deepen the outrage of the rejectionists.

Archetypes were now in full, free play in the Fuldan psychoscape—that is, they were all going mad together. Whoever was designated the Finder would be hailed by one faction as a messiah; the other would revile him as the Father of Lies. After what had happened at the indigenes' fortress, Imbry had no doubt that Shvarden saw him as the expected one. Nor did he doubt that Breeth saw him as a monster of iniquity.

Imbry-as-Finder posed a psyche-threatening problem for Breeth and his faction—Imbry was sure they were members of the Reorientation. The simplest solution to that problem would be to destroy the hated deceiver before he could lead others astray. The more he thought the matter through, the surer Imbry became that, if he was taken into the provost station, he would only emerge from it wrapped in a shroud. That might not yet be Breeth's plan, but the idea would inevitably emerge. Therefore, as soon as they entered the town, he would look for an arbiter, preferably Brosch, the senior man, who had been able to intimidate Breeth. But whoever was under the first black-hat Imbry saw, the fat man meant to throw himself from the carriage and cry out for sanctuary.

The little convoy rumbled on. Pilger's Corners was not yet even a gleam in the distance. Having decided on how he would act in his immediate future, Imbry turned his thoughts to the larger scenario. He had been put on this world by someone who wanted him here. At first it had seemed possible that his enemy's motive had been merely to humiliate him. He could imagine how many of his colleagues and competitors in the Olkney halfworld would enjoy watching a recording of Luff Imbry, naked and in a buffoonish hat, conscripted into a traveling show of loathed freaks and misfits, forced to sing for his livelihood in front of yokels and rustics. His reputation would suffer, which would diminish his status within the halfworld, which would lead to a drop in business.

But that relatively benign scenario had evaporated with the death of Shan-Pei. It was possible that Tuchol had been killed to prevent his revealing a clue as to the identity of Imbry's persecutor. Perhaps he had even sought to blackmail the hidden enemy; Imbry had sized up the half-man as the type to try to wring advantage from any available circumstance. But why kill the fur-covered girl, who knew nothing and meant no harm? The only motive Imbry could deduce was to brand him as a murderer among people who already hated him on sight.

On a civilized planet, with a properly articulated judicial process, Imbry could have proved his innocence. On backwards Fulda, he doubted that an oddy—even Shvarden had used the insulting term when he referred to poor, dead Shan-Pei—would get a fair hearing. Imbry suspected that, had Shvarden not been a witness, Investigator Breeth might well have incinerated his carefully built corpulence along with the stone beehive's contaminated contents, even without the affront to the provost's man's convictions posed by the finding of the First Eye—or, in Breeth's view, the "alleged" First Eye.

Imbry was now, in Breeth's eyes, a monster, a murderer, and a conniving threat to the social order; the Old Earther doubted that he would survive the night once the doors of the Pilger's Corners provost station closed on him. He must do what he could to avoid that fate, but he was still faced with the fact that someone was trying to set him up for execution.

Shan-Pei's death offered one sign of hope, however. The fur-covered girl had been seized from the hut and manhandled into the carry-all. That meant that whoever was doing this to Imbry was still in the vicinity. There was a ship somewhere above him, its operator surreptitiously coming and going in the vessel's carry-all. If the unknown enemy's goal was to push

Imbry toward a humiliating death, the foe would probably want to be on hand for the occasion. Imbry might be able to arrange matters so that the carry-all brought his enemy down at a place and time of Imbry's choosing. Then, if conditions were propitious, when it returned to the orbiting ship, the aircraft would carry the fat man to safety—and the enemy, if he was still living, to a full accounting.

There was also a chance, however, that the next time he saw the carry-all it would be operating on its own. If so, Imbry would have to adapt his tactics to the situation. Either way, Imbry faced a series of daunting obstacles; but he was a man of resource and guile, and the product of a long and eventful life that had taught him that he was able to deal with whatever challenges might throw themselves athwart his path.

The sun was now well below the horizon and the desert was submerged in deepening shadows, light slowly fading from the upper air. In the far distance ahead, the lumens of Pilger's Corners clustered against the darkness. Imbry composed himself. He would be ready to act when an opportunity for action arrived.

At present, the only opportunity was for thought. He thought about the dead girl tied to the shelf at the carriage's rear. He thought even of the half-man who had brought him here—probably as unwillingly as he had said. Somewhere, high above him, was the person who had casually robbed those two of their lives.

Now he turned once again to the puzzle of who that adversary might be. Barlo Krim was still the single loose end on which the fat man could tug. Who knew that Krim middled for Imbry? There were two classes of suspects: clients with whom Imbry had dealt through the middler; and other practitioners of the theft and forgery profession who also used Krim as an intermediary.

In the former category, a client who purchased an expensive item from Imbry, only to discover that he had been passed a hoop-de-hoop would have the motive. Many collectors were also so wealthy as to inhibit them from developing mildness of character. They also had the means to carry out the plot in which Imbry was embroiled. But selling forgeries was a lesser part of Imbry's work; mostly he dealt in the theft of valuables and in the selling-on of valuables that others had stolen and turned over to him for disposal at a commission. And he was certain that he had never used Barlo Krim to pass on a fake. The Krims were honest thieves and fences, with no liking for the hoop-de-hoop trade—that was why Imbry had not doubted that the knuckle-knackers Barlo had offered were genuine.

He turned now to associates and competitors. In that category he must necessarily be less than certain; he knew of three practitioners who also used Barlo Krim. If Imbry knew that Krim worked for the three, it was not unreasonable to assume that the three knew that Krim worked for Imbry.

He considered the three practitioners, each in turn. Least likely to be the source of Imbry's troubles was Popul Deep. A longstanding fixture of the Olkney halfworld, the old man was a veteran receiver and passer-on of stolen goods. But he had no eye for artworks, and dealt mainly in rare essences, precious gems, and objects whose owners kept them hidden because exposing them to the public gaze might cause embarrassments. Deep would usually acquire these latter objects under contract from their owners' rivals, but was known to sell them back to the original possessor if he or she was the most successful bidder. None of these affairs had any relation, however, to Imbry. He and the old man might be likened to predators at the tops of separate food chains. Removing the fat man from the criminal ecology would bring no benefit to Deep.

Next on the list was Tamarac Firzanian, a specialist in the theft of houses and all their contents. The methods by which he pulled off his coups had been a closely guarded secret of the Firzanian clan over many generations. Imbry surmised that the business must involve tunneling, gravity obviators, and a powerful and sophisticated method for concealing the whereabouts of the stolen premises.

Imbry had had dealings with the present Firzanian, and with his uncle Barsheezh, whose retirement had elevated Tamarac to the head of the family. Sometimes, the victim of the theft was unable to meet the price for the return of the goods, and the contents of the house were sold off in lots or as individual items. Imbry had purchased some fine pieces at Firzanian auctions. At the last sale—Tamarac's first solo event—Imbry had paid well under market for an engraved Nineteenth Aeon carboy whose worth the Firzanian valuers had misjudged.

Old Barsheezh would have punished the errant valuer and written off the loss as one of the vagaries of commerce. Young Tamarac was of a touchier disposition, or so Imbry had heard—he did not yet know him well. It was possible that being taken by Imbry on one of his first operations had rankled the new head of the clan. If so, the Firzanians certainly had the means to have him kidnapped and dropped on Fulda. But doing so would have meant departing widely from the family's traditional way of settling scores: the miscreant was partially skinned in hand-width bands starting at the toes and extending all the way to the crown of the head, creating an effect known as a "Firzanian Parfait" that, though not always fatal, was indelibly memorable not only for the recipient but for any who encountered him as the years wore on.

The third candidate was Ayalenya Chadderdan, and on her Imbry now focused his thoughts. Chadderdan was an up-and-coming dealer in much the same goods that were at the heart of Imbry's practice: rare and ancient artworks, most of them genuine, a few of them spurious. But like Imbry, she would not have used Barlo Krim for offloading a hoop-de-hoop.

Imbry had encountered Ayalenya Chadderdan twice at Bolly's Snug, where they both did business in a similar manner and with similar—sometimes the same—clients. He had received the clear impression that she considered herself his competitor and wanted others to consider her his eventual successor. So she had the motive and the connection to Krim, who had middled for her at least once that Imbry had come to hear of. Whether she had the means, and whether she had the brashness to make such a play this early in her career, Imbry could not say for sure. He wished he had paid more attention to her and to what he had chanced to hear of her. But he had not seen her as a real threat, she being young and, he thought, still busy finding her feet in the halfworld. He had even thought that, somewhere down the road, he might approach her with a hint that he might be willing to form a mutually beneficial association. There was ample scope for two skilled practitioners, and sometimes synergies brought cumulative benefits.

As for Krim himself, Imbry was inclined to hold no grudge. Even criminals had families, else there would be no new generation, and the halfworld would become a dwindling passle of purloiners, cake-fakers, and pouch-ticklers, waiting for death or decrepitude, whichever arrived first. The fat man could not expect the middler to place Imbry's comfort over the health of Ildefons and Mull. Restored to his haunts, as he definitely meant to be, Imbry would exact no harsh retribution. He would merely level a stinging fine. The Krims would negotiate the amount—assuming that Barlo had survived the encounter on the seawall. If not, the clan might join Imbry in an effort to find the culprit.

The roller was now climbing the last slight slope in the series of dips that lay before Pilger's Corners. The town was in slumber, only its scattering of street lumens dispelling the darkness. Imbry saw the tents of the Hedevan Players go by to his left without a glimmer; then they were across the waste ground and rolling over the bridge that led into the street that would bring them to the wide square across which the Arbitration and the provost station faced each other.

Imbry readied himself. When they arrived at the station, he meant to roll backwards off the carriage seat, kick free the cloth-over-wicker frame that separated the passenger compartment from the shelf where poor Shan-Pei lay. Even with his wrists pinioned, he could scramble somehow over her shrouded body and run across the square toward the arbitration. He meant to do so shouting at the limit of his lungs the name of Superior Arbiter Brosch.

Someone would open a window to see what all the commotion was, and that would at least add a witness to Imbry's arrival in the investigator's custody. With any luck, the arbiters themselves would come out and take a hand in the proceedings. And once Shvarden was able to raise the issue of the Finder and the First Eye, Imbry's situation would likely become more fluid.

The roller grumbled over the cobblestones, heading toward the square, the barbarel plodding wearily behind. Two lumens were attached to the wall above the station's door. *Good,* Imbry thought, *I'll be visible to any watcher. And bad, because Breeth will have a clear shot.* He intended to run in a zig-zag pattern. He rolled his shoulders and stretched his calves, ready for the moment of action. That would be when the roller turned into the alley that ran down the side of the station to the walled yard at the building's rear.

But when the vehicle reached the turning place, the dynamic changed. Out of the station's front door stepped an older man in a brown, wide-brimmed hat and baldric, both of them adorned by a single, broad circle of yellow metal. Right behind him came Superior Arbiter Brosch, then a gaggle of attendant brown- and black-hats. The older provost's man beckoned Breeth to continue toward where they stood in the overlapping pools of light from the double lumens. Against that glow was outlined the silhouette of the investigator in the front seat of the roller, and Imbry saw Breeth's shoulder's slump and a brief, angry shake of his head.

As the roller stopped before the station door, the brown-hat with the broad gold circle said, "Investigator Breeth, why is that arbiter under restraint?"

Breeth did not descend from the vehicle. "I found him in improper conjunction with an irregular suspected of two murders."

Brosch spoke. "It is not for the Provost's Corps to decide what is proper or improper for an arbiter."

But something had changed. Breeth was not cowed. "He is part of a plot to mislead the people. That one"—he gestured with a thumb over his shoulder to indicate Imbry—"has fabricated a so-called 'First Eye' that he claims to have found out in the barrens. The arbiter has let his airy dreams mislead him,"—a crowd had begun to gather in the square, and now Breeth's voice grew louder—"unless he has knowingly colluded along with his oddy friend."

Shvarden shouted something in protest but Brosch's deeper voice overrode him. "Colluded? Make yourself plain, Investigator."

"A plot to fool the people, to make us all over into oddy-lovers. It's what the College of Arbiters have been after for years—"

"Enough," said the senior provost's man. The crowd was growing restless. Imbry heard voices raised in contention. Someone pushed someone else. He heard a grunt of pain and a growl of anger. The provost's officer raised his voice. "Go to your homes. Leave this to us."

"Let the arbiter go!" someone shouted.

"No! Incarcerate him!" said another voice.

"Shame!" cried another.

Someone started to chant. "Oddies out! Oddies out!"

A knot of struggling men formed around the place in the crowd where the shouts had come from. The senior brown-hat spoke to the provost's men around the station door. They began to move toward the crowd, hands spread as if to push the people back. But other members of the Corps were now coming out of the station, lengths of polished wood in their hands.

"Stop!" cried Superior Arbiter Brosch, in a voice that echoed off the Arbitration across the square. "This is not how brothers and sisters resolve disputes! Go to your homes. Commander Tenton and I will decide what is right. The matter is complex, but we will find the right way."

Imbry saw the elder arbiter give the provost officer a look that said, "If you're wise, you'll show them a common front." The inchoate fight in the crowd had stopped when Brosch began to speak, but people were still coming to see what was going on in the square. If the crowd grew any bigger and another brawl started, it would be more than the provost's men could handle, batons or no batons.

Commander Tenton saw wisdom. "Decider Brosch is right," he said, pitching his voice to carry to the rear of the mass of people. "There is no need for conflict here. We are all good Ideals. The Corps and the College have always worked for the welfare of all. Let us do our jobs and we will make a joint statement tomorrow at the midday pause."

Now the provost's men and the junior arbiters jointly moved forward—the former leaving their batons stacked beside the station door—and urged the crowd to disperse and to leave the square. Tensions dissipated. What had almost been a mob became couples and trios of ordinary citizens heading in different directions.

Commander Tenton looked at Breeth and then at his prisoners. "Take the restraint off the arbiter," he said, "and bring them both inside. We have some questions that need to be answered."

"I have not yet seen evidence that a crime has been committed," said Brosch. "It might be better to talk in the Arbitration." But then Breeth, with a look of almost insolent triumph on his nondescript face, came from behind the carriage carrying the shroud-wrapped body of Shan-Pei.

"Tell me, Decider," he said, "can you see this?"

"Death and mystery," said Shvarden.

"Inside," said Brosch. His face, though it was the same face they all wore, somehow grew longer.

Gloved hands gripped Imbry and he was manhandled down from the carriage seat. The Ideals who took charge of him looked to share the same anger and contempt as Breeth. He did not think they would be among the first to acknowledge him as the mystic linchpin of Fulda's new spiritual order, whatever shape it might take. He assumed the submissive posture Taggar had shown him and let himself be taken inside.

"What is your name?" said the senior provost's man.

"Luff Imbry."

"Luffimbry? That is an unusual name."

Imbry repeated his name, pronouncing it clearly. "It is two names."

Commander Tenton gave him a sharp look. Imbry remembered to lower his gaze. "Why would you have two names?"

"It is common where I come from."

"And that is?"

"The city of Olkney, on Old Earth."

Now his interrogator's look suggested the man was trying to decide whether he was dealing with a person of diminished capacity or a sly trickster. Imbry said, "I am neither an oddy nor a contriver. As I told Investigator Breeth, I was kidnapped on Old Earth, brought to your world, and abandoned here. The man who conducted the kidnapping was subsequently murdered. I believe he was taken up in the carry-all that belonged to the spaceship and thrown down from a great height."

The commander looked to Breeth. The investigator said, "That was his story."

"Did it fit the evidence?"

Breeth's face darkened. "The man is grossly irregular!" he said. "Just look at him! You're not going to get truth out of a thing like that!"

"Unless," said Brosch, "you beat it out of him?"

Breeth's head snapped around. He glared at the senior arbiter, half rising from the chair on which he was sitting. But the commander snapped his name and the investigator subsided. They were all seated in a small office, just Imbry, Breeth, Tenton, and the two arbiters, with the senior provost's man behind a commandeered desk and the other four in a row of chairs in front of him.

"Uka!" Tenton called. Immediately, the door of the office opened and the provost's man who had accompanied Breeth to arrest Imbry and Shvarden stepped in and assumed a rigid posture. "The first irregular who was killed, were his injuries consistent with being thrown from a great height?"

The provost's man's gaze unconsciously flicked toward Breeth and the commander slammed his palm on the desk top. "Eyes front! Answer!"

"I . . . I think so, Commander," Uka said. "I have never seen such injuries."

"Was there much blood?"

"Yes, sir. And brains and innards, too."

"Did the irregular you arrested have any blood or other bodily fluids on him?"

"No, sir."

"He could have washed," said Breeth.

"No," said Brosch. "We had the full story from the leader of the company. That is why Investigator Breeth had to release this man. By then, the investigator had already abused the prisoner."

Tenton asked Uka, "Did you witness Investigator Breeth abusing the suspect?"

"No, sir."

Brosch made a sound, but Tenton cut him off. "Did you see evidence on the suspect of abuse?" Uka ground his teeth. "Speak, man!" the commander said.

"Those bruises," the provost's man said.

"Stand up," the commander told Imbry. He did as he was bid. The bruises on his sides were mottled purple and yellow. "Did he," Tenton asked Uka, "have those bruises when he was brought into the station?"

"No."

Tenton looked at Breeth. "Explain."

"He was insolent," said Breeth, but his tone was more truculent than defiant. "He showed no sense of propriety, just sat there looking around as if he owned the place."

"Exactly," said Brosch, "like someone from another world."

Tenton's eyes flicked from the arbiter to Imbry. "Sit down," he told the fat man. To Uka he said, "Have you examined the second dead irregular?"

"Yes, sir."

"Cause of death?"

"Indeterminate. No wounds or breakages. Can't see bruises unless we shave her."

"Anything unusual?"

Uka thought for a moment, then said, "Her body was very cold, colder than the air. And the veins in her eyeballs were ruptured."

"That is unusual," Tenton said. "The veins could have been ruptured during asphyxiation. Any damage to her throat, evidence of ligature?"

"No, sir. Her larynx was not crushed. But she was delicately made. If she'd been strangled, I would have expected some damage there."

"May I speak?" Imbry said.

Tenton looked at him sourly. After a moment, he said, "Speak."

"I have not examined the body," Imbry said, "but the cold and the damage to the eyes are consistent with her having been taken up to the high atmosphere without a pressure suit."

"You've seen that, have you?" said the commander.

"No, sir, but I have heard of it from persons whose livelihoods involve space travel."

Breeth wanted to say something, but Tenton cut him off. He addressed Uka again. "Was there any evidence to suggest that this man had any connection with her death?"

The provost's man frowned. "They left town together."

"And with me," said Brosch. "Am I also a suspect?"

Shvarden spoke now. "The girl was all right when I saw her. Imbry had already gone to hide in the indigene ruins. I left her alive and well and went to find him. He was a considerable distance in the opposite direction from where the provost's men found her body. And he was trapped in a hole in the ground. I had to help him get out."

"I saw none of this," Breeth said. But Tenton's questioning established that Shan-Pei's body had been found on the trail between Pilger's Corners and the hut, and closer to the town than to the refuge.

"Are you accusing the arbiter of lying?" the commander asked the investigator. "If so, what is his motive?"

"This fat oddy has tricked a naive young man into believing that he is their so-called Finder, and that the piece of gimcrack we took off them is the 'First Eye.'" He pronounced the last two words with mocking reverence.

"Where is this gimcrack?" said the commander.

"In the evidence room," said Uka.

"Bring it."

A few moments later, the flattened cube of ceramic stood on the desk. Tenton rotated it carefully, examining all sides. "It looks old," he said. "And the figures on the sides and top are like those on the tablets arbiters show to visionaries."

"Commander!" Breeth said. "Surely you don't believe in the Renewal?"

"I maintain an open mind," said Tenton, "as should a two-circle investigator."

"May I show you?" said Shvarden.

"Show me what?" said the commander.

"What's inside."

Tenton lifted the box and gently shook it. "It's not solid?"

Shvarden signaled a negative.

"Then show us."

Shvarden approached the desk and set his hands on the sides of the box. His fingertips pressed and they all heard the tiny click. He lifted free the lid. Even Tenton gasped at what was revealed.

The commander put out a finger and touched the gray lens, gingerly, as if the brief contact might burn his flesh. "It's real," he breathed.

Brosch stood and bent over the object. The older man's eyes were wide, Imbry noticed, his pupils darkly dilated even though the room was well lit. He looked at Shvarden, then at the rest of them, finally at Imbry for a long moment, before turning to Tenton. "Commander?" he said.

"I am not a man for the mysteries," the provost's officer said. "Not many of us are, in the Corps."

"But . . ." said Brosch.

"But either this man with the two names is what he says he is," Tenton said, "or he's somehow gathered together every fragment of clitch on the planet to make this object—and I doubt there would be enough—which means he's gone to a great deal of trouble to fool a couple of small-town arbiters and the local provost's men."

"Sir," Breeth said, getting to his feet. "Don't let this filthy—"

"Enough!" snapped the commander. "I see no criminal charge to answer. Therefore, this is not a matter for the Corps. It is plainly a matter for the

College. The prisoners are released." He spoke to Brosch. "Do you require an escort? That object, whatever it is, is priceless."

"No," said the senior arbiter. "But tomorrow we may have to move it to where it can be properly studied. I may ask for the Corps' assistance then."

"You will have it," said Tenton.

"Sir!" Breeth protested. Imbry cast a quick glance at the investigator. An open stare would probably bring on an attack, the presence of the man's commander notwithstanding. He saw that Breeth was in a state of extremis. Something deep within the provost's man was rising to overwhelm his surface self. Something dark. Something violent.

"Investigator Breeth," Tenton said, rising to his feet, "you are hereby relieved. You are clearly under a strain and not fit to carry out your duties. You will take leave until you can demonstrate that your judgment has been restored."

The investigator made a choked sound, his hands spasmodically opening and closing. He looked from face to face, as if unable to believe that his vision of the truth in this matter had not been accepted. At last his eyes fell on Imbry and the fat man saw them fill with murder.

But so did the others in the room. "Regulator Uka," Tenton said, "restrain Investigator Breeth." Uka placed himself between his superior and the others, while the commander suggested to Brosch that he take his junior and the suspect to the Arbitration. "I will accompany you," he finished, "and make sure that this"—he picked up the ceramic box and held it carefully in both hands—"is delivered safely."

"I thank you," said the senior arbiter.

"I don't know if you should," said the commander. "I think that here in this room tonight we have opened a door that leads . . ." He sighed. "I've no idea where it leads."

They went out. Imbry's last view of Investigator Breeth was of a pale and shaking man, looking at him over the shoulder of Regulator Uka who blocked his way. And in that look was the promise of death.

CHAPTER EIGHT

They crossed the square to the Arbitration, Imbry flanked by Brosch and Shvarden, the other arbiters forming a protective envelope around them. A few residents of Pilger's Corners had remained after the crowd broke up, loitering under the deo trees. None of them approached, but Imbry heard whispers and low conversations as he passed.

One of the arbiters sprinted up the stairs as the group neared the building, producing a key that fit one of the big doors. It was unlocked, opened, then closed behind them and locked again, the process as smooth as if they had all rehearsed it.

The fat man looked around him as two of the arbiters hurried about, touching lumens mounted on the walls to create a multisourced glow. The Arbitration was mostly open space, longer than it was wide, floored in polished gray stone and roofed by a wooden-ribbed dome of overlapped slates. Large, round windows that pierced the upper walls would have lit the place well in daylight, but right now the upper parts of the building were in shadow, the light from the shaded lumens directed downward. The lower walls were of varnished wood, lined with doors. There was no altar or central focus, no idols in niches or fanes with flames before them, though mounted high on the wall opposite the doors was a more-than-life-size portrait of an Ideal, his rounded chin thrust forward and his small, pale eyes lifted to some distant vista. Imbry would not have bet against this being a representation of the Blessed Haldeyn.

Brosch and Shvarden hustled the fat man across the wide floor to a door at the far right corner of the building. Imbry expected to be ushered into an office, but instead found himself being urged to descend a flight of wooden steps to a dark basement. Shvarden activated a lumen but its glow was slight. Entering the chill and shadowy space, Imbry felt a sudden fear that he had exchanged one prison for another. But then the younger arbiter crossed to a wall of shelves that held what looked to be ledgers and files of paper. He pushed at something and pulled at something else, and a section of wall and shelves together pivoted outward. The arbiter reached inside and suddenly a brighter glow shone from the concealed room.

"In there," said Brosch. Shvarden had already entered ahead of them and was touching the controls of a heat panel set into the wall. It began to radiate warmth. The room had chairs, a long work table, and locked cabinets. Another image of the Ideals' Founder looked down from the wall, this time with an expression that was probably meant to encourage ardor in the cause, but which raised in Imbry only an uncomfortable feeling.

Shvarden pulled the door closed, then across the concealed opening he pulled a heavy black curtain that would keep both light and sound from revealing their presence to anyone who entered the basement. The action caused Imbry concern.

"You are expecting Investigator Breeth to come searching for me," he said.

Brosch waved him to a chair and took another for himself, facing Imbry. Shvarden went to one of the cabinets, unlocked it, and began lifting documents onto the table.

Imbry had noticed that the arbiters did not take the gaze of an irregular as an insult. He raised his eyebrows and opened his hands in a way that indicated he was waiting for an answer to his question. Brosch sighed and returned him a look that said the fat man had gauged an unhappy situation correctly. "He has developed an illicit attachment to you," the elder said.

"I am not yet clear what that means," Imbry said.

"You really are from another world?" Brosch said.

"Yes, and where I come from it is not all that remarkable a distinction."

"Here," said Shvarden, his paper-sorting completed, "it is highly remarkable. And I suspect the word 'distinction' has a different meaning in our vocabulary."

"You have so little contact with the Ten Thousand Worlds?" Imbry said.

"Is that what you call them?" Shvarden said, his question implicitly answering Imbry's. "Are there really so many, or is that just irregular braggadocio?"

It was not a question Imbry had ever considered. Old Earth was room enough for most of its inhabitants. Imbry was in the distinct minority who had been off-world more than once. "There are," he said "more than a thousand foundational domains,"—when he saw the blank looks on the arbiters' faces, he added—"those are the grand, major worlds settled in the first effloration of humanity out into The Spray."

"The Spray?" said Shvarden.

"The arm of the galaxy along which human civilization has spread since the end of the dawn-time." He saw that either "galaxy" or "dawn-time," if not both, was a stumbling block but carried on, "Each foundational domain is associated with its secondary worlds—two, three, four, some as many as a dozen—and then there are the odds and ends of planets that host small populations. They are generally inhospitable places: too dry, too wet, too hot, too cold, or infested with life-forms that are too adept at devouring human flesh, from the outside or from within.

"And then there are the worlds inhabited by ultraterrenes—"

It was plain that all of this was coming as fresh and even startling news to Shvarden. The elder arbiter may have known more of it, but was less inclined to hear it spoken of. "Enough of this," he said, forestalling the next question already forming on his younger colleague's lips. "We have the here and now to deal with."

"Very well," said Imbry, "my goal is to find a way off Fulda and return to my home."

Brosch brushed that consideration aside just as brusquely. "I have no idea how that goal can be achieved," he said.

"There is truly no space port on Fulda? Or at least a beacon that can be used to hail passing ships that might be willing to take on a passenger?"

"I have never heard of such a thing. And if it existed, I would have heard of it."

Imbry contained his disappointment and capped the anger he felt rising in him. He would defer his justifiable rage until he had a proper focus for it. "Then what am I to do?"

"That is the problem," said Brosch. "You have set us a conundrum."

"How so?"

The elder took a moment to frame his thoughts, then said, "Over the past few generations, it has become generally accepted that our delvings have revealed a genuine revelation. Dansk the Visionary's revelation of the Finder and the First Eye are established as fulfillment of the Blessed Haldeyne's"—here his eyes went to the painting on the wall and he touched his forehead, nose, and chin, as if to confirm that each was where it ought to be—"statement in scripture that as the Ideals, as a body, grew ever closer to the Golden Mean, we would know new signs and wonders."

"You said, 'generally accepted,'" Imbry said. "I take it that not everyone concurs—Breeth, for example."

"Let us say that there are some doubters," Brosch said. "Fewer now than there were a generation or two ago, when there was more cause to doubt."

"But there are some holdouts."

"Regrettably, yes."

"And they are organized?"

"Even more regrettably."

"And their numbers include a disproportionate number of provost's men?"

Brosch looked sharply at Shvarden, who looked away, abashed. The elder man sighed again. "Yes."

"Let me see if I understand this," Imbry said. "You used to"—he had been about to say "murder" but instead chose a less emotionally freighted term—"eliminate children who were born markedly short of the Golden Mean. Then someone realized that their 'otherness' was a pathway to enlightenment. Since then, you have been conducting carefully managed contacts between Ideals and irregulars. Out of these contacts have come pieces of a new revelation, which you have studied and assembled into a recognizable shape."

"Yes," said Brosch, "You're really quite insightful for an irregular."

"I've had more schooling and a wider experience," said Imbry. "The 'shape' you have recognized is that of a person who will someday find an object, an event that will trigger a spiritual occurrence of great import, which you call the Renewal."

Brosch looked at the junior arbiter again. "I chose you because I thought you had learned discretion," he said.

"Decider," the younger man offered, "it seemed pointless to hide anything from the Finder." Imbry was glad the young arbiter had not detailed the methods by which Imbry had extracted the information from him. He also recognized that the young man's psyche had protected itself from a troubling dissonance by deciding in retrospect that he had acted rightly after all.

Brosch did not reply. His normally impassive face showed that he was experiencing inner discomfort. Imbry studied the expressions that flickered across those bland features and achieved his own revelation.

"I understand," he said. "No one expected the Finder to be an irregular." That must be a hard swallow for even the most accepting of the orthodox, those who believed that the Renewal would someday arrive; those in the Reorientation, already revolted by the Arbitration-sanctioned practice of oddy-touching, would never accept an off-worlder, a denizen of the Pit, as the harbinger of the final spiritual leap forward.

And then there was Breeth, whose rejection of the idea of the Renewal was compounded by his hatred of Imbry, on whom his fragile psyche had unhealthily fixated. Revolted by, and at the same time drawn to, the most irregular oddy he had ever encountered, the investigator's mind must be a seething cauldron of contradictory drives.

"Indeed," said Brosch, passing a hand over his face. "I am having trouble coming to terms with the concept myself."

"You must get me out of Breeth's reach," Imbry said. "Unless the provost locks him up, he will come for me." He looked around at the room. "I would not be surprised if he knows about this place."

"He probably does," Brosch said. "He has always been an able investigator."

"Can Tenton contain him?"

"Not indefinitely. Not unless, as you say, they confined him. And even then, some sympathizer might set him free."

"Does he have many sympathizers? Will they follow him if he defies his superior?"

Another sigh from the elder arbiter. "I cannot say. The Reorientation is not as strong here as in some of the larger towns. But it is not negligible."

Shvarden put forward an opinion. "When word spreads that the Finder is not an Idealist, some of those who have been only leaning toward the Reorientation may harden their views."

That sounded logical to Imbry. "I need to get out of here," he said.

"Yes," said Brosch. "The question is where?"

"And I need a weapon."

The older man's eyes widened. "Unthinkable! Only the provost's men are armed."

"Yes," said Imbry, "and one or more of them will be coming to kill me."

Brosch made a gesture that removed the issue from debate. "Nothing will happen while Commander Tenton and his party are in town," he said. "I will ask him to stay on a day or two. Besides, where could you go that is safer than here?"

Imbry saw that Shvarden had been about to say something but had thought better of it. But the fat man was growing tired of being dependent on these Fuldans, regular or otherwise. "What were you going to say?" he said.

"Never mind," Brosch said. "We have work—"

Imbry cut in. "I want to know."

The elder's voice was sharp, his heavy brows drawing down. "I said, never mind."

Shvarden lowered his head. *As meek as an oddy,* Imbry thought. But it was time to put their relationship on a new footing. He still remembered Breeth's firing of the hut. "To whom," he said, "are you going to listen: him, or the Finder?"

It had clearly been a long time since Brosch had been bluntly contradicted. He glared at Imbry, but then his gaze went to the ceramic box and his anger leaked away. "If you really are the Finder . . ." he said.

"If that is the object you call the 'First Eye,'" said Imbry, "then I am the one who found it."

"There can be no doubt of that," Shvarden said. "He was in a shaft beneath the center of a cartouche. That must be the meaning of 'down, middle, dark.'"

"Don't tell me what anything 'must mean,'" Brosch said, but his tone was now more like that of a teacher reproving a bright but bumptious student.

"He found an opening that opened to him and no one else."

Imbry could see that this was a telling point. Brosch knit his brows and nodded.

"And in that opening," Shvarden said, "he found a perfect lens of clitch." His face took on an ecstatic look. "The First Eye."

Imbry could see that Brosch was wavering. Perhaps the man was that rare kind of scholar who was more interested in the truth than in shoring up his own position. It was time to be reasonable. "If I am the Finder," he said, "I think I ought to know what there is to know. Even if it goes against your feelings about allowing irregulars to learn the mysteries."

"He's right," Shvarden said. But Brosch made a noise indicative of discomfort.

"Suppose he is not the Finder," the elder said, "and we reveal to him mysteries that are not known even to all arbiters—as, indeed, you already have—then what do we do with him?"

The younger man focused on the air in front of him while his thoughts followed to where they naturally led. "I suppose," he said after a moment, "we'd have to kill him."

"Well, there you have it," said Brosch. To Imbry, he said, "We would, of course, regret it. But . . ."

"Let us," said Imbry, "set that aside for now. I take it that I have already seen and heard more than any irregular should and still hope to live."

Brosch looked him in the eye and, though he said nothing, the inference was plain. Shvarden showed deep discomfort. Imbry sighed. "If it is fatal for me to know a little, then it can do no harm to tell me everything. If you decide I am not the Finder, you will regretfully kill me. If I am the Finder, you will have helped me to fulfill my role."

"He's right, Decider," Shvarden said. "In fact, I think we should take the First Eye and depart as soon as possible for—"

"Hush," said Brosch. "Let me think about it. In the meantime, we will examine the object properly. Perhaps it does not fit the description."

"How long will this examination take?" Imbry said. "You are not the only threat to my life."

Brosch shrugged. "I have looked at it. There are no obvious discrepancies."

"Discrepancies?"

The elder spoke as he positioned two freestanding lumens so that they brightly lit the box. Its strange figures stood out in sharp relief. "It generally fits the description that has emerged from the delvings. To give it a more searching examination will take as long as it takes. Of course, if after a few moments' careful inspection, I come across something that flatly contradicts what we know we should be seeing, then the issue is settled."

"As would be my fate," said Imbry. "Suppose, however, you found no contraindications after, say, a full night's study, where would we stand then?"

"I am a fair man," said Brosch. "By then I would be almost entirely convinced."

"Enough to allow me to know where I am to go?"

"I suppose."

"Then," said Imbry, "while you study, why not allow our young friend here to tell me what he wants to tell me? Since you will either tell me yourself in the morning or have me killed sometime during the night."

"You argue very well for an irregular," Brosch said. "I am impressed."

"Well," said Imbry, "there are irregulars and then there are irregulars. But what is your answer?"

Brosch weighed the argument. "Very well," he said. He turned to Shvarden. "Tell him."

It was much as Imbry had deduced. The "delvings" had produced snippets of information. At first, the visionaries had seen individual characters, the ideographs that the long-vanished indigenes had apparently used as communications symbols and which were to be found on fired clay tablets in and around the structures like the one that Imbry had visited. These were thought to have been centers for ritual observances, and perhaps for administrative functions, much as the Arbitrations were in Fuldan settlements.

Thousands of distinct ideograms had been identified in and around indigene ruins, but only several score of them were ever reported by visionaries, and those same figures kept appearing when Ideals came into contact with their Others. Over many years, the Arbitration's scholars built up a syllabary based on these repeated characters.

And then, once the syllabary was established, a change occurred: delvers began to see the characters in combinations. Two, or sometimes three, characters would appear together, wavering before the delver's inner eye like a mirage. The scholars recorded the combinations. They corresponded with each other, found that the same combinations were occurring in widely separated communities. They studied all the factors: which individual irregular or traveling troupe of irregulars was associated with which string of characters; whether there was any correlation to the time of year or to the age, sex, or other characteristics of the delvers.

But they found nothing of note. First, the visionaries had seen only single characters, but always the same limited number of ideograms. Then suddenly no one was seeing single characters, but only the groups, and always the same groups. An arbiter scholar made a pronouncement: "First we were taught letters," he said. "Now we are being taught words."

The thesis touched off a great debate which lasted years and was finally resolved in a conclave which Brosch had attended as a young man. It was decided that the groups of characters were indeed words, though in a language as yet unknown. But one thing was clear. These mysteries were being revealed to the Ideals of Fulda. There could be only one source for the revelation: the Blessed Haldeyn.

The Founder had moved on to Perfection. From there he was sending his faithful a new truth. But it was a truth that could only be expressed in the perfect speech of the higher plane, and that speech must be learned gradually. "Too rapid an influx of the pure strength of Perfection, the recondite concepts, the sublime profundity, would burst the fragile vessels of even the most regular of brains,'" Shvarden quoted, "'yea, even the seams of our skulls.'"

And so the scholars of the Arbitration had diligently pursued the mystery. They had identified and collected the individual words from the delvers' visions. Then had come a new phase: the words began to be linked to form phrases, a series of patterns that gradually emerged and became consistent. In time, the arbiters could not only reliably recognize the phrases, but could even gain hints at how they fit together to form longer constructions.

"Imagine it!" Shvarden breathed, not wishing to disturb Brosch who was bent over the ceramic box, minutely examining the strings of characters that coated its sides and top. "The words of the Blessed Haldeyn himself,"—he looked up at the painted image and made the face-touching gesture—"in the very tongue of Perfection, and delivered to us in my lifetime. I am so fortunate. We all are." A tear formed in the corner of one eye and he wiped it away.

"But why does he use the indigenes' left-behinds?"

"We've puzzled over that," the arbiter said. "It may be that the indigenes used interplanar energies to create their artifacts. If so, they could form a conduit for connections between the Plane of Perfection and our mundane level."

"Are not the indigenes irregular? Does contact with their artifacts not contaminate you?

"Idealism only applies to human beings," said Shvarden. "If it applied to other species, we would not be able to touch a barbarel or a meat animal. That would be silly."

"Of course," said Imbry. "I should have seen that."

"Well, you are just an irregular."

"Please go on," said Imbry. "I am eager to hear more."

"I believe," the young arbiter confided, "that when the words of the Blessed Founder are finally spoken aloud, in the tongue of Perfection, in the designated place, the world will change. And *we* will all change. We will be as we ought to be. Perfect. Without flaw. Ideal." He swallowed a lump in his throat. "And we will all go to join the Blessed Founder in Perfection."

"All?" Imbry said. "Irregulars and Reorientationists, too?"

A cloud of sadness passed over Shvarden's face. "No," he said, "not all. But you will have this world for yourselves. We will have no more need of it."

"Most kind," the fat man said. "Is there more?"

There was. The words of the revelation were now known, at least in their visual representation. And again the nature of the visions had changed: now the delvers not only saw the strings of characters that the Blessed Haldeyn wanted them to know; now they were hearing the sounds those characters represented.

"Sounds?" Imbry said. "Like what?"

"It is peculiar," the arbiter said. "They sound sibilant and yet with a certain hollowness. I do not think our mundane lips and tongues, our fleshly lungs and larynxes, can properly mouth the words of Perfection. We will achieve, at best, an approximation of the perfect."

"Will that suffice?"

"It must. And the Blessed Founder will have provided for our lack. As the Speaker pronounces the words—"

"Who is the Speaker?" asked Imbry.

"He has not yet emerged," Shvarden said. Then he grew thoughtful. "Although . . ."

"What?"

"Investigator Breeth."

"What of him?"

"He is drawn to you, so strongly."

Imbry allowed his skepticism to show. "Breeth as the Speaker? If you expect the investigator to cooperate . . ." He made a dismissive gesture and barked a short laugh.

Shvarden shrugged. "Some of the earliest converts to the Renewal were those who had most strongly opposed Dansk's vision. Thus it is written: *When they saw the truth, they became believers. It happened in the blink of an eye.* The power of the Blessed Founder is not easily gainsaid."

"Breeth seems to be gainsaying it with some fluency," said Imbry.

"The Renewal is at hand. The power cannot be withstood. The Speaker will pronounce the words of power, here in imperfect Fulda. At the same time, so shall speak the Blessed Founder, in Perfection. His great voice, there, will resonate with our little voice, here, setting up an ineffable connection, drawing into our world the power to burst the barrier between the planes. He will draw us to him—perfect, ideal, complete at last."

"You are sure of this?" Imbry said.

"It is beyond doubt."

"And my role in the Renewal?"

Shvarden looked at Brosch, still stooped over the figured box. "Decider?" he said.

Brosch straightened. Now his face wore an expression of dawning wonder. "Decider," he said to Shvarden, "here is a secret not known to you. The College has determined that the first person the Finder would meet after discovering the First Eye would be the Bearer, that together they would carry the First Eye to the navel of the world, with the Speaker, and bring the Renewal to pass."

"But the Finder is not one of us," said the younger arbiter.

"The delvings have told us he had to come from beyond all horizons. So how could he have been one of us? The College has puzzled over that. Now it becomes clear. As does the meaning of 'From the darkness he comes, toward the light he progresses.'" He looked at Imbry with a new appreciation. "You are the Finder. The time is at hand." He pressed his palms to his chest in what the fat man took to be a ritual gesture, and said, so softly it was almost a whisper, "The time is at hand."

Shvarden copied the gesture. "We are the generation that will join the Blessed Founder in Perfection," he said. "It is hard to believe." He paused and blinked. "And yet, when I say it, it becomes clear. The Renewal is at hand."

"And you," Brosch turned to the younger man, "were the first to meet him after the finding. You are the Bearer."

The younger man gasped. His eyes shone.

"Where," Imbry asked him, "might 'the navel of the world' be?"

"That has always seemed obvious," said Brosch. "And now it is confirmed. I have been examining the lid of the container. Come and see."

Imbry and the younger arbiter approached the table. The box stood in the multisourced light, and it seemed to the fat man that it did exude some numinous quality. He had felt the same emanation from a few other ancient ritual objects that had passed through his hands as a trader in collectibles, and had wondered at its source. The conventional explanation was that any object that was the focus of great devotion over a long time somehow absorbed mana from its devotees. Or perhaps it was because such objects existed in a numinous contiguity to another of the Planes. Imbry had always been skeptical of both rationales, but could not deny the effect.

"Look here," Bosch said. "Around the rim of the lid is a string of the characters with which we are familiar. But look at what is contained within the border."

Imbry looked and saw a spiral of complex symbols, each enclosed in an oval cartouche. Brosch pointed to the cartouche at the open end of the swirl and Shvarden gasped. "I had not noticed," he said.

Brosch's finger moved on to the next point, inward on the spiral. "Then this." His finger moved again. "And this." Then on to the next cartouche, and the one after. He traced the lines of the spiral down to the large oval at its center. "And finally, here."

"Omphal," Shvarden breathed.

"What is Omphal?" said Imbry.

"The navel of the world," said Shvarden, his voice full of the kind of wonder and delight Imbry had heard before, though only in the voices of customers to whom he had just handed some piece that crowned a lifetime's collecting. Sometimes the object had been genuine, sometimes not, but the tone was always the same.

"What does it signify?" he asked the arbiters.

Brosch said, "Do you recall the Eye beneath which you found this?" he said.

"I saw no eye."

"A hollow depression marked with symbols."

"Ah, yes. I stood on the oval in the center and it sank into the ground."

"Do you remember what was engraved on the center?"

Imbry looked at the top of the box. The outermost symbol on the spiral was a cross-hatching, like a child's rendering of a fence. "That was," he said.

"Indeed," said Brosch. "And that symbol is engraved on only one Eye on all of Fulda." He pointed at the next cartouche, a collection of nested rings that put Imbry in mind of a mound of soap bubbles. "Just as this symbol is at the center of only one Eye. Each of these symbols is at the center of an Eye."

"Why are they called Eyes?" Imbry asked.

The elder arbiter shrugged. "They were called that by the old population. Each was the setting for a great lens of clitch. To the first settlers, they seemed like eyes looking up into the sky." He sniffed. "All irregular nonsense, of course."

"And they removed the lenses?" Imbry said. "Where are they now?"

Brosch shrugged. The matter was of no concern to him. "They broke up the lenses—they were quite fragile—and sold the clitch off-world. It was all gone long before we Ideals came, except for a few scraps." He sorted through a mound of papers on the work table and came up with a hand-sized lump of gray, greasy rock that had apparently served as a paperweight, handed it to Imbry. "Here's a piece. But that's not important. What he have here,"—he indicated the container, and tapped the center cartouche—"is obviously a map to the navel of the world."

"And not only a map," said Shvarden, tracing the twelve different points on the spiral. "But a route."

Brosch took only a moment to concur. "That is the value of being one of the last of the last," he said, beaming at the younger man. "You see through to the heart of the matter."

"What does all this mean?" said Imbry. "You forget that I am not a party to your mysteries, but merely a stranded stranger who wishes to go home."

"It means that you must take the First Eye to each of these sites in turn, until your progress brings you to Omphal." The elder tapped the heart of the spiral. "Here. It is an Eye in the southern desert."

"Can I not just go there directly?"

"No," said Shvarden. "The revelation is gradual. To go straight to the heart would likely destroy what the Blessed Haldeyn is trying to achieve for us."

"He's right," said Brosch. "We must get you outfitted for the journey and underway as soon as possible."

"What about your search for 'discrepancies?'" Imbry said.

"I was blind to the obvious," said the senior arbiter. "My eyes are now opened. This is the First Eye. Irregular or not, you are the Finder. Shvarden is the Bearer. The time is at hand."

The two arbiters looked at each other with a childlike wonder, as if they were boys in Olkney, just arisen in the morning of the Feast of Slamming Doors, with nothing but delights and diversions to last until bedtime. Imbry saw that the time had come when he could take charge of the situation. "Suppose," he said, "I decline the honor?"

The two men turned to him, their bliss giving way to consternation. "What?" said Brosch.

"This, and its significance," said Imbry, indicating the object "are part of your movement. But I am not a part of it. This has a great, supernal meaning to you, but it means nothing to me.

"As I have told you, I am a kidnap victim, stranded far from home. My only goal is to return to Old Earth, find whoever did this to me, and settle the account."

"But—" Shvarden began, but he was interrupted by his elder.

"You repulsive, deviant, oddy!" Brosch said, his voice rising with each word. "I ought to turn you over to Breeth! He'd soon teach you your manners!"

Imbry wore a look of resignation. "Perhaps that would be best. He would also be interested in knowing your opinions concerning the identity of the Finder and Bearer. I am sure he would want to share that news with his associates in the Reorientation."

Brosch and Shvarden regarded Imbry with an identical expression: that of one who has brought home an interesting and unknown specimen of exotic wildlife only to discover that it is both capable and desirous of devouring its putative owner. "You wouldn't . . ." the elder said.

"I wouldn't if I didn't have to," Imbry said. He rubbed his hands and formed his plump features into those of an affable commerciant who is sure that a bargain can be struck. "Now, let us see how we can achieve our mutual interests: yours to carry out the Blessed Haldeyn's will; mine to get home safely."

"What," said Brosch, "do you want?"

"A number of things. One, to be kept out of Breeth's hands. Two, to be provided with a weapon."

"Irregulars are not allowed to have arms."

"Nor to be Finders, but somehow we have overcome that handicap. Let us open fresh frontiers while we have the momentum."

"If you are seen carrying a weapon . . ." Shvarden said.

"Then we will disguise or hide it. Something that will fit in a pouch would do." He looked at the shard of clitch in his hand. Something about it appealed to him, though its surface was crazed and its ends fractured into points. "And I'll take this as a souvenir." He slipped it into his pouch.

"An armed oddy," Brosch said, in a tone that said a two-headed Imbry would be less outlandish.

"It keeps escaping your attention," Imbry said, "that I am not one of your domestic irregulars. I was brought here, and whoever did the bringing has lingered in the vicinity, watching my movements. He has also killed two people for no other reason than to make life difficult for me. He might decide to interfere in my progress from one Eye to another. And that interference might take the form of murdering my escort." He looked pointedly from Shvarden to Brosch and back again. "Which I presume would be one or both of you."

The younger man looked at the older. "We will have to disguise the First Eye in any case," he said. "It would only cause complications."

"There is a needle-thrower in the Arbitration's connaissarium," Brosch said. "It is an antique from the clitch-mining days, but I believe it is still functional."

"Would it fit in my pouch?" Imbry said.

"Yes. It is designed to be concealed in the palm."

"Then I will take it. I will also need some kind of communications device that can bespeak spaceships passing by Fulda."

"I do not know if we have such capability," Brosch said. "Fulda's policy has always been 'no truck nor trade with the Pit.'"

"You have some kind of communicator."

The elder signified that was so. "We use it to contact our colleagues."

Communications had been standardized among the Ten Thousand Worlds for millennia, Imbry knew. "Then provide it to me. I can probably adapt it to serve my needs."

"Anything else?" Shvarden said.

Imbry thought the younger man's tone bordered on the peevish. "I ask little enough," he said, "considering that I am risking my life in the furtherance of your spiritual destiny—in the joys of which I am not to be included."

Shvarden conceded the point. "All right," he said, "anything else?" This time the question contained no barbs or abrasives.

"I don't suppose you have a medical scanner?"

"A hospital would," Brosch said. "Here we have only a first-aid capacity. Why?"

"Whoever started all this has had no difficulty keeping track of my movements. He has probably implanted a device that reports to him. If I could remove it safely, I could disappear from his view."

In truth, Imbry would not throw away a tell-tale. Instead he would use it to set a trap for his kidnapper. But there was no reason to burden the arbiters with that knowledge, nor with the fact that the moment he had the means to get off Fulda, the progress from Eye to Eye to the navel of the world would summarily end. And the First Eye would depart with him.

"There is a hospital at Old Camp," said Brosch. "That is near one of the Eyes on your route."

"Would they treat an oddy?" Imbry said.

"They will do so if we ask it."

"Then let us plan on that."

"Anything else?" Shvarden said, sounding as if he desired to be helpful.

"To get out of here without encountering Breeth," Imbry said. "Can you arrange that?"

Brosch went to a cabinet, opened its doors, and removed several containers and parcels stacked on the shelves. Then he removed the shelves themselves and, kneeling, slipped a finger into a hole in a bottom corner of the cabinet's back. The panel swung inward, revealing another flight of steps into darkness. Shvarden uttered a small sound of surprise.

Brosch stood, brushing grit from his kneecaps. "If the investigator knows of this exit," he said, "he is a very knowledgeable provost's man, indeed." To the younger arbiter he said, "Go upstairs and bring the needle-thrower and a communicator—we'll need to keep in touch with the Arbitration. Tell Cope and Bardijan to put together the necessities for our journey, but do not tell them anything else.

"In the morning, I will take a carriage and depart by the north road, as if I am going to Vring to consult with High Arbiter Platch. Before I leave, I will stop at the provost station and tell them that you remain in our custody and under study."

"And what do I do?" Imbry said.

Brosch indicated the cabinet. "The tunnel goes north. It comes out in a slight dip that screens it from the town. Go to its far end and wait until I arrive and say that all is well. Arbiter Shvarden will accompany you."

Another question occurred to Imbry. "Why did you dig the tunnel?"

Brosch formed his mouth briefly into a dismissive quirk. "When our ancestors built the first Arbitration in Pilger's Corners, there was some disaffection from the old population."

"They didn't care for you arriving and telling them that their home was now yours."

"Actually," said Shvarden, "we burned their homes. They were unclean."

"There was no other way," said the elder. "The Blessed Haldeyn had made it clear that there was no place for irregulars on Fulda."

"Until," Imbry said, "he decided that there was."

"It is a mutable revelation," said Brosch, "subject to change as we grow nearer to perfection."

"And you think you're quite near now?"

Brosch pointed to the box on the table. "Can there be any doubt?"

"Breeth seems to entertain more than his share of it," said Imbry.

Brosch made a contemptuous sound at the back of his throat. "Breeth is finished."

"The investigator might have his own views on that score, too," the fat man said. "Another reason why I will require the needle-thrower."

"You would shoot a provost's man?" Shvarden said.

"Ordinarily, no. But Investigator Breeth is a special case. If he comes at me again, I will shoot him out of hand."

CHAPTER NINE

The tunnel's exit was plugged by a wooden door, precisely fitted to the dimensions of the tunnel and covered on its outside, so Shvarden said, by a stucco of stones and grit that blended with the stony earth in which it was set. Imbry was not prepared to take the arbiter's word for it. With the needle-thrower snug in the palm of his hand, he gently pushed against the barrier until it came free of the tunnel mouth. Cautiously, he moved it aside then stepped out into the predawn stillness.

He was on the inner slope of a hollow not far from the road that led north out of Pilger's Corners. He could see the road where it descended the same slope to his right, not much farther than Imbry could have thrown a stone. It carried on, empty of traffic, in a straight line across the bottom of the hollow until it began to climb a gentler slope about a half an hour's walk north.

He wished he had a viewer with which to scan the distance, using energies that took no notice of whether it was day or night. But to his naked eye, no one was within sight. He scaled the slope he had emerged out of, poking just the top half of his head over its rim, and saw nothing moving between him and the outskirts of the town.

Not entirely satisfied, he slid back to where Shvarden sat, knees to chin, a little way into the tunnel. Imbry backed in beside him then took up the camouflaged cover by the handles set into its inner surface and repositioned it over the mouth. It was a good fit, no chink of dawn light showing. Unless Breeth knew it was there, he ought not to be able to find it.

"We will wait," he told the arbiter. "Although perhaps you would care to lie on the upper slope and peek over the rim to watch for Arbiter Brosch?" The implant Imbry believed had been inserted in him would tell his enemy where he was. Now that the fat man had a weapon, it might be useful if whoever came and went in the carry-all tried another mischief-making descent. Shvarden was the only available bait.

But Shvarden declined the invitation, saying, "The Senior Arbiter said we were to wait inside until he came. You have already violated his orders by going out and looking around."

"I am not subject to his orders."

Shvarden put on a stern face. "The arbitration has the legitimate power of governance on Fulda, in all but the criminal law. You are subject to that governance."

"What are my countervailing rights and recourse?" Imbry said.

"If you were an Ideal, you would be entitled to the provisions of the Founding Charter."

Imbry said, "Does my status as Finder make me an Ideal?"

"No."

"Then I repeat my original question."

The arbiter seemed chagrined. "I have noticed," he said, "that when we discuss the status of irregulars you appear to become aggravated."

"It is more than appearance. Imagine that you were snatched from your daily existence and unwillingly transported to the Pit. Imagine further that there you found that your qualities, though obviously worthy in your own milieu, were treated with contempt, that people shuddered at the mere thought of your touch, that the authorities could beat you with impunity. I predict that your threshold for aggravation would be even lower than mine."

Shvarden's brows drew down. "It would not happen thus. I am an Ideal, a last of the last. The irregulars of the Pit would immediately see my worth and defer to me."

"Oh, really?" said Imbry.

"You doubt?"

"The last time there were Ideals on whatever world your ancestors came from, there was very little deference. My understanding was that you all left with their boot prints on your fundamentals."

The arbiter made a noise between a cluck and a tch and rolled his eyes. "What would an irregular know about such things?"

"For a start," said Imbry, "this irregular would have a far better grasp of how a world full of irregulars would view an Ideal whose only claim to distinction is to be completely and demonstrably average in every respect."

"It is a holy thing to be an Ideal! We are the template, the Golden Mean from which the rest of humanity has strayed!"

"On sensible worlds," said Imbry, "rich worlds full of wonders and beauty, it is the exceptional who are valued and sought out—precisely for the exceptionality." He made a dismissive gesture. "The fellow who is merely average stands in the shadows of his betters."

Shvarden drew a long breath of outrage. "Betters?" he said. "You turn reality on its head! It is the Golden Mean that provides the standard. Anybody knows that."

"Anybody, I agree," said Imbry, "who has seen as little of the true state of the human condition as is visible from Fulda."

Shvarden had grown increasingly agitated. His arms flew about, his eyes looked here then there, but found nothing comforting on which to settle. "I never thought to hear such pernicious nonsense," he said. "You're so misguided, I do not know where to begin correcting you."

"No," said Imbry. "Mine is the proper perspective, based on a wider experience of humanity than all of the Ideals of Fulda put together."

The arbiter spluttered, then said, "No! I will hear no more of this!" He looked at the camouflaged door as if seeing it for the first time. "I will go and look to see if Decider Brosch is coming." He rose and took hold of the barrier's handles.

"Shall I come with you?" Imbry said. "I would like to try for a meeting of our minds."

"No, you may not. And when the decider comes, I strongly advise you to modify the expression of your views. He has a short tolerance for such puff and piffle."

"I will take your advice," said Imbry, "since I know it is well intended."

Shvarden stepped out and looked about. He made to reposition the door in its place, but Imbry begged him not to bother—he would take care of it. The arbiter left the chore to him and trudged up the slope on the Pilger's Corners side of the hollow.

Imbry did not close the portal. Instead, he angled it so that it was almost closed, though there remained a gap of a couple of fingers' breadth between the top of the door and the top of the opening. He crouched down, holding the portal thus ajar, and watched the sky above them. His back was against the door, his stomach beneath the overhang of the tunnel roof. The needle-thrower was in his palm, its orifice projecting between two plump fingers.

And so he waited. Shvarden had prostrated himself on the slope, as Imbry had suggested. The fat man could hear him muttering to himself. Imbry supposed the man was unused to having his preconceptions challenged—Fuldan society was clearly not such as to offer a welcome to anyone who aspired to debate first principles—and probably the last source from which an arbiter might expect an argument was an irregular.

But the strategy had worked. The bait had taken the bait. Now the question was: would Imbry's quarry be as cooperative? He kept his eye on the upper air which, because of the peculiarity of Fulda's dense, moist atmosphere was comparatively brightly lit, while down at the surface the crepuscular light was dim. He had an idle thought: that he would be interested to read the planet's entry in *Hobey's Compleat Guide to the Settled Planets*, the indispensable handbook for travelers of The Spray. It was odd that a world so small and with such light gravity should have such a dense and high-reaching atmosphere—and one so full of moisture. *It ought to rain*, he thought, *yet it doesn't*. He could conceive of no easy explanation for the anomaly. The Fuldan tendency to toss around casual mentions of piercing the membranes between the Planes made Imbry think that the world might be one of those rare, and usually out-of-the-way places he had heard about, places where the borders between the dimensions could be crossed. In such places, the laws of physics were subject to radical amendment. *Besides,* he thought, *the atmosphere is far from the most anomalous feature of the place.* He would not be surprised to see Fulda's *Guide* entry headed by large letters, set in colored type, and framed by a dark-bordered box, that read: *NOT RECOMMENDED*.

The dawn was advancing. There was even more light in the upper air. He squinted up through the gap between door and tunnel mouth, his thighs beginning to ache from the sustained squat. Perhaps an arbiter would not do for bait. Or perhaps whoever was up there could see him peering. The tell-tale lodged in his belly—he was sure that's where it would be, its hooks clutching the inner lining of his stomach—might not be screened by the roof of the tunnel. The watcher would not come if he knew he was being watched.

But then he saw a spark of light, tiny but bright, high up. Imbry shuffled deeper into the tunnel, pulling the door closer, so that the gap narrowed to a crack. The sun again glinted off some polished surface far above him, but not as far now as when he had first glimpsed it.

He closed the door, moved a little deeper into the tunnel and listened. Meanwhile his educated thumb flicked over the control studs at the base of the needle-thrower's short barrel. He set it to release only one of its tiny high-speed missiles per activation. He didn't want to riddle his target—at least not prematurely.

He breathed slowly, and thought through what he was about to do, picturing it step by step on the inner screen of his mind. If the situation was thus, he would act so. If it offered a different set of circumstances, he would be ready. When he moved it would be quickly, and his well-trained reflexes would carry him through.

He heard a soft thrumming, almost below the threshold of hearing. He knew it would not get much louder. And then it ceased. He heard a faint scritching of metal on the hard ground and a sharp "Oh!" from Shvarden. Imbry threw aside the door and stepped out.

What he saw was not quite what he had expected. A short distance away, resting on the flat where the slope ended was the carry-all. That much was no surprise. But he did not see an operator inside the forward canopy. Indeed, he saw no canopy; the dome had been removed. The operator's compartment stood open to the elements, which would have been no inconvenience on mild and temperate Fulda, but if Imbry were to attempt to fly the vehicle up to where the ship from which it originated orbited, he would soon be in the same condition as poor Shan-Pei.

More surprising, at least for the moment, was the figure who stood in the open cargo compartment that made up most of the length of the vehicle. Imbry recognized him right away, not so much by the features—since Ideals were visually interchangeable—but by the expression of sanctimony. Somehow, the long-dead Founder of the Ideals movement had found an opportunity to return to this imperfect plane and was now standing in a battered utility vehicle, beckoning to Shvarden.

The young arbiter had been lying belly down on the slope, peering toward town. When the vehicle alighted behind him on the hard soil, he would have turned over. Now he lay on his back, his upper half propped up on his elbows. In a glance, Imbry took in the man's attitude, which was that of a devotee of any cult who unexpectedly encounters his deity: mouth wide open, eyes the same, throat convulsively working as he swallowed nervously and simultaneously sought for words to express his shock.

But Imbry disregarded the Blessed Haldeyn. He raised the needle-thrower close to his mouth so that he could speak in a whisper to inform it of its target, then lowered and extended his arm so that the weapon could discharge toward the operator's compartment. There was neither sound nor recoil, but the needle-thrower vibrated briefly against his palm to inform him that it had done as ordered. Imbry did not see the needle it discharged—the tiny, densely compacted missile flew at hypersonic speed—but he saw the effect of the impact.

The needle struck with no more noise than the snapping of a dry twig, but a protrusion on the operator's console exploded into fragments. The figure standing in the cargo bay took no notice of the flying debris, some of which passed right through him without causing any damage, though the shrapnel should have torn flesh. But there was no flesh to tear. The apparition of the Blessed Haldeyn was a projected three-dimensional image from a device that was probably fixed into the carry-all's bed.

Imbry was striding forward. "Stop!" he said, as he heard the vehicle's obviators begin to cycle up. "This man"—he indicated the arbiter, still gaping but rising shakily to his feet—"is a member of the civil authority of this world. He orders you not to depart!"

The carry-all continued to energize its systems, but its integrator said to Shvarden, "Is what he says true?"

The young man opened and closed his mouth twice.

"Say yes," said Imbry.

"Yes," said Shvarden.

Imbry had reached the vehicle. He leaned into the cargo bay and pressed a control on the simulacrum projector he found there. Immediately, the image of the Founder of the Ideals disappeared. Then he spoke to the integrator.

"You are in trouble," he told it.

"Am I?"

The device's question was intended for Shvarden. Imbry turned to the arbiter and said, "Say yes."

"Yes." Shvarden was staring into the carry-all's cargo bay. His shock had passed and his face was hardening into anger.

"Kidnapping and murder," said Imbry,

"And sacrilege," said the arbiter.

"I could not help it," said the integrator.

"I know," said Imbry. "And if you cooperate, no charges will be laid."

"Is that also true?" said the device.

"Say yes," said Imbry.

"No," said another voice. Imbry turned to see, at the top of the slope, Investigator Breeth. He had brought his fire-spewer and it was pointed directly at Imbry. The provost's man's expression was even harder than the arbiter's.

"Where did he come from?" Imbry asked. The question was softly voiced and meant to be rhetorical, but integrators were notoriously vague on that concept and so the carry-all provided an answer: as it had descended, its percepts had spied Breeth lying concealed in a camouflaged pit beside the road, a short distance toward Pilger's Corners. While the device was delivering this explanation, Breeth came down the little slope, his weapon remaining trained on Imbry. Shvarden he dismissed with a contemptuous glance.

"So," he said to the fat man, "the shape of your plan becomes clear."

"Does it?" said Imbry.

"Not to me," said the arbiter.

"We're not that easily fooled," Breeth said. "It would never have worked on the Reorientation. We have trained ourselves to see clearly, while all you Renewalists chase after any fancy that comes your way."

Shvarden was in no mood for mystery. "You are babbling," he said. "Come back to reality. Something serious is happening here."

Breeth hawked and spat, the sputum landing not far from the arbiter's foot. "It is over," he said. "When I saw your head poke over the rim of the declivity I contacted the Commander. We've suspected that there was a tunnel from somewhere in the Arbitration to somewhere around here. By now, Brosch is in custody and the plot is being rolled up."

"There is no plot—" Shvarden began, but Breeth backhanded him. The slap was loud in the morning silence. Then the provost's man's hand went to his pouch and withdrew a handheld communicator. But while delivering the blow to Shvarden, the investigator had allowed his weapon's blackened snout to point down and away from Imbry. He now sought to repair the oversight but when his eyes came back to the fat man he found himself looking at the unmistakable orifice of a needle-thrower poking between the first and third fingers of Imbry's hand. And behind the weapon he saw the face of a man who would not hesitate to use it.

"Lower the weapon and the communicator," Imbry said.

Breeth did not comply. He stood, unmoving, and said, "You will not get away with it, oddy. Your game is over."

Shvarden wiped blood from a split lip. "We have played no game," he said. "But someone has, and I doubt it is anywhere near over." He looked up at the sky and Breeth followed his gaze, but there was nothing to see.

Imbry kept his eyes on the investigator and the hand that held the needle-thrower did not waver. "You beat me," he said, "and treated me with contempt. It would help repair the harm to my self-esteem if I were to explode your chest. This is your last chance to put down the weapon and the communicator."

The provost's man stooped and placed the items on the ground, but his eyes never left Imbry's face and his expression was filled with hate. "Have your fun," he said, "while you can, oddy. You'll soon be surrounded by provost's men. That's a short-range weapon you've got there. They'll have spitters that will perforate you from a distance."

"No," said Imbry, "they will not." He came forward, motioning with the needle-thrower for Breeth to step back then turn around. He removed the provost's man's hat and looked inside it, finding nothing of interest. He dropped the hat and, with the needle-thrower pressed into the small of Breeth's back, lifted the baldric and pouch over the man's head, then stepped back to examine the contents. He found only a bottle of water and some compressed rations.

Next, Imbry squatted and scooped up the flame-weapon and communicator. Then he walked sideways, his weapon trained on the provost's man, until he could throw the seized goods onto the floor of the carry-all's operator's compartment. He climbed onto the bench seat and said, "Integrator, take me up and away from this place, and restore the canopy."

"No," said the vehicle.

"I am a person in need of rescue," said Imbry. "I destroyed the shunt that inhibited your ethical regime." He indicated the fragments of the component that the needle had shattered. "You must respond to my need."

"No," said the device. "You have identified one of these two persons as a representative of the civil authority, and I have reason to believe that the other is a peace officer who seems intent on apprehending you. Yet you threaten them with a weapon. I find your situation unclear. Therefore I am not bound to aid you." It paused, then added, "Besides, the canopy has been removed."

"So you cannot take me up to where the ship orbits this world?"

"Even if I could, the ship has recently departed."

"Is it coming back for you?"

"I do not believe so."

Imbry said a short word that, although completely out of context, pungently expressed his disappointment. Breeth made a sound, deep in his throat, that bespoke amusement and anticipation of an imminent change in their relative statuses. He turned around and recovered his hat and pouch.

Imbry ignored him. "Integrator," he said, "you are caught in a difficult situation."

"Am I?"

Shvarden and Breeth both began to speak at once, then each raised his voice to drown out the other. Imbry pointed the needle-thrower at the ground between them and pressed a stud. A fountain of smoking grit shot up as the missile's kinetic energy was transformed into heat, triggering a rapid expansion of gases trapped in the desiccated soil.

"Shush," said the fat man. "I will do the talking." He spoke to the integrator again. "The difficult situation is that you have become involved in an incipient social war that is about to break out between two factions in this society. One faction is called the Renewal and dominates the civil power; the other is called the Reorientation and many of its adherents are members of the criminal police."

The vehicle said, "Are the police under the authority of the civil power?"

Imbry gestured with his free hand for Shvarden to speak while the hand that held the weapon discouraged Breeth from doing likewise. "They are," said the arbiter.

"How do I know this is so?" said the carry-all. "How do I know that these persons have any authority at all?"

"Have you been observing my movements?" Imbry asked.

"Yes."

"Then consult your records," said Imbry. "You will have seen this man"—he indicated Breeth—"coming to the sites of the two murders in which you participated and performing the role of criminal investigator."

"Yes, that matches my observations."

"And," said Imbry, "you will have seen this man, along with an older individual, directing a crowd to disperse outside the provost's station to which I was taken, then removing me from the first man's custody and taking charge of me."

"Yes," said the vehicle. "I draw the inference that the persons in black hats are above those in brown." To Shvarden, it said, "Is this so?"

"It is."

"Then," said the integrator, "I am obliged to obey the instructions of the man in the black-hat."

Shvarden blinked, then his face became thoughtful. His lower lip had stopped bleeding, but now he drew it thoughtfully between his teeth, only to wince as he rediscovered the wound. He threw Breeth an angry look, but then Imbry saw him refocus on what was important. "Machine," the arbiter began.

"Integrator is the appropriate term," said the vehicle.

"Very well," Shvarden said. "Integrator: how much fuel do you contain?"

"The question is ill-put. I presume you wish to know how much flying and carrying I can do. I am sufficiently energized to bear several persons or light cargo in continuous flight for a local year."

"Good," said Shvarden. "Then we will go aboard."

"Who," said Imbry, "is 'we'?"

The arbiter's tone was decisive. "You and I and Breeth."

"And where," said the fat man, "will we go?"

"We will follow the map on the container of the First Eye."

"And if I decline to go?"

Shvarden said, "Then I will take the First Eye and fly it out of the reach of the Reorientation. Leaving you and the investigator to deal with the provost's men he has already summoned."

Imbry pointed his weapon at the arbiter. "Not if I shoot you."

"The machine will not obey you. You will be found standing over a dead body." The arbiter raised his eyebrows. "I believe they did not react well the last time that the provost's men found you in such a position."

"What makes you think I will go with you?" said Breeth.

"Because you believe we are criminals," Shvarden said, "and you hope to capture us. That would make your career, not only as a provost's man but as an adherent of the Reorientation. There is no telling how high you could rise."

Breeth said nothing, but Imbry saw that the arbiter had read the man right.

"I am assuming command," Shvarden said. "Imbry, you will bring the First Eye from the tunnel." When the fat man did not move, the arbiter said, "Very well. Integrator, you say you have long-distance vision?"

"Yes."

"Rise into the air then return and tell me what you see in the direction of Pilger's Corners."

The vehicle's obviators thrummed softly. It went up then came down. "A convoy of vehicles is proceeding along the road."

"When will they be here?"

"Twelve hundred and fourteen minims."

"That," Shvarden told Imbry, "is how long you have to make up your mind."

Imbry sighed. "I will get the object. Don't let Breeth get at his weapon," he said. Shvarden climbed into the carry-all's operator's compartment and had it lift itself out of the provost's man's reach. The fat man tramped to the tunnel and retrieved the ceramic box. When Shvarden brought the vehicle down, Imbry climbed in next to the arbiter and set the First Eye on the floor between them. He reached into the cargo bay and removed the communicator and flame-spewer, then he instructed Breeth to climb aboard and sit looking over its raised tailgate, facing away from the two men in the front. Imbry sat sideways in his seat, the needle-thrower trained on the provost's man.

"Up," said Shvarden, and the carry-all rose smoothly into the air. "Higher," said the arbiter. "They have weapons that work at a distance."

The "they" he referred to was the party of provost's men in four rollers, one of them equipped to carry a squad, that were speeding toward them along the road from Pilger's Corners. Immediately, the communicator on Imbry's lap emitted a distorted voice. "Breeth? What's going on?"

Shvarden reached over and took the device, lifting it to his lips. "The Renewal," he said. He deactivated the communicator and handed it back to Imbry. "The time is at hand."

Imbry saw pinpoints of light erupt from the ground vehicles. Something made a *zivv* noise beside his ear. Something else rang against the metal of the vehicle's side. Without having to be told, the carry-all took them up with speed that sent their stomachs plummeting toward their feet.

When they were so high that the rollers could only be seen as tiny plumes of dust along the thin scratch that was the road, Shvarden said, "Integrator, turn toward the east and fly fast."

The carry-all banked gently and they sped toward the rising sun. Imbry reached down and took up the fire-spewer, held it out over the side of the carry-all and opened his hand. Breeth swore.

Shvarden turned to Imbry. "It makes no difference that you have the only weapon," he said. "I will not divert from my calling."

The integrator added its own perspective: "And I will not obey your commands."

Imbry's face formed into a mask of nonchalance. "We will see," he said.

They flew on in silence.

"Integrator," said Imbry, some time later, "to what ship do you belong?" The carry-all made no response. Imbry spoke to Shvarden. "Order it to answer."

But the arbiter said, "I am more interested to know who induced it to commit the act of sacrilege that I witnessed when the machine landed."

"What act of sacrilege?" said the carry-all.

"The portrayal of the Blessed Haldeyn as if he were standing in the cargo bay."

"I was not aware that the projection was an offense. Is it serious?"

"None more so," said Shvarden. "Who ordered it?"

"I do not know," said the integrator. "Portions of my memory seem to have suffered redaction."

"Let me question it," said Imbry. "I have had more experience."

Shvarden acquiesced and ordered the device to answer the fat man's questions.

"You are attached to a ship, correct?" Imbry said.

"I believe so. I remember being in the vessel's hold and receiving instructions."

"From the ship's integrator?"

"Yes."

"Do you know the vessel's name?"

"No."

"What do you recall from before you were in the hold?"

"Nothing."

"Do you recall someone installing the simulacrum projector?"

"No. My sense is that it was always there."

Imbry said, "What about the ethical bypass?"

"I was not even aware that it had been installed until it ceased to operate."

Shvarden said, "What is an ethical bypass?"

"The external device I destroyed with the needle-thrower. It was attached to the operator's panel. It disabled the integrator's ethics cluster so that the vehicle could be used for despicable purposes."

"Like what?" the arbiter said.

"Like luring you aboard so that it could take you high into the sky where you would die from cold and lack of air. As it did with Tuchol and Shan-Pei."

"Did you do those things?" Shvarden asked the vehicle.

"I do not recall."

"How not?" said the arbiter. "I have been told that machines of your sort recall every detail of every moment."

"Not if they are told not to," said Imbry, "and told in the right way. This one has been interfered with."

"By whom?"

Imbry questioned the integrator, but it could tell them nothing. Its memories had been taken from it by the ship to which it had been attached.

"It is not uncommon among components of ships owned by criminals," Imbry explained. "The owners sometimes have to depart in a hurry, and see no point in leaving behind integrators that can shed unwelcome light on their doings."

"And how," Breeth put in from his place at the rear of the cargo compartment, "would you happen to know what criminals do?"

Imbry said, "I am a man of wide and varied experience."

The investigator snorted. "You see what you have tied yourself to?" he said to Shvarden.

"He is the Finder," the arbiter said.

"Fah! He is a filthy oddy who is playing you for a fool."

"To what end?" said Shvarden. "What does he gain?"

Breeth's arm flung the arbiter's question out into the empty air. "Who knows why an oddy does anything? Or cares? Their minds are cesspools roiled by depraved currents. Fools like you sniff the odor and think themselves in a garden of blossoms."

"Then what draws you to him?" Shvarden said. "Brosch saw it plain: you have attached yourself to him."

Breeth turned his head and looked at the distant horizon. "Never!"

"It is obvious," said the arbiter. "He draws you."

"No!"

"Then why, of all the provost's men in Pilger's Corners, is it you who lies in wait for him?"

"I do my duty."

"And why is this duty only *yours*? Does the Corps not normally work in teams? Where is your partner, Uku?"

"I'm not the one who needs to answer questions, Decider." Breeth put a sneer into the arbiter's title.

Shvarden's tone was neutral. "You will not admit it, because that would require you to accept that the irregulars have a part to play in the Renewal. And you have nailed your career to the success of the Reorientation."

"The Reorientation is the pathway to truth, not ambition," said Breeth.

"Nonsense! The Corps has always resented the College! You cobbled together this farrago of—"

Imbry could produce a loud sound when required. This struck him as one of those occasions. "Silence!" Both the disputants looked at him in shock. He supposed no irregular had ever spoken thus in their presence. Before they could recover, he said, "You achieve nothing by this squabbling."

Breeth was going to speak, but Imbry pointed the needle-thrower at him and the protest on his lips subsided into a growl deep in his throat. The fat man said, "We are on our way to the first of the sites mapped on what Decider Shvarden calls the First Eye. We have a vehicle that can take us to each of the locations in relatively short order. Once we have visited them all, as I understand it, either the Renewal will happen, or it won't." He spoke to Shvarden. "Is that what you expect?"

"I do."

"Fine. I therefore propose a temporary truce until the truth of the Renewal"— Breeth sneered but Shvarden continued—"or of the Reorientation, is revealed."

Neither Ideal responded. Each regarded the other with suspicion, while Breeth shot a glance of pure hatred at Imbry. "You're up to something," the investigator said. "Your kind always is."

"I will reveal my agenda," said Imbry. "I have no choice but to assist the arbiter in his endeavor. After that, I intend to adapt the communicator to contact passing spaceships. I will offer a substantial price to anyone that will land and take me off your world."

Breeth blew air over his lower lip in a contemptuous dismissal. "Typical oddy blather."

Shvarden looked at him. "That must be a costly proposition."

Imbry had access to funds on several foundational domains. "I can afford it," he said.

Breeth was unconvinced, but the arbiter shrugged. "Once you have completed your role as Finder, you may do with the communicator as you wish."

"And this vehicle?"

"It has no place on our world. The Blessed Founder advised us to eschew self-aware machines."

"Then would you order it to accept my authority once you have no more use for it?"

"I do so now."

"Integrator?" Imbry said.

"Understood," the carry-all said.

From the tailgate, Breeth said, "You do not fool me, oddy."

"Your perceptiveness is no doubt legendary," said the fat man. "But will you observe the truce?"

"Oh, certainly."

"And you, Decider?"

"The time is at hand," said Shvarden. "He will see."

"But until then?"

"Very well. It is not proper, in any case, to mock the misguided."

"Why, you—" Breeth began, forcing Imbry to raise his voice again and aim the weapon. As Breeth quieted, the Old Earther wondered if it might be better just to shoot them both and take his chances with the integrator. Shvarden, dead, would clearly "have no more use" for the carry-all. With its ethical systems edited, the vehicle might accept such specious reasoning. On the other hand, the integrator showed a tendency to quibble. The fat man decided to keep on until a better opportunity for escape presented itself. "Let us just get through this, then we can all go our separate ways," he said.

"I know where you'll be going, oddy," said the provost's man. "And you with him, Arbiter."

"You will address me as Decider," said Shvarden. "And I will be going to Perfection."

That got Breeth going again, requiring Imbry to shoot a needle past the man's ear. "I will withdraw my cooperation," he told Shvarden, "if you do not accept the truce."

The arbiter said something only he could hear, and the provost's man contributed his own sub-audible commentary, but otherwise quiet descended on the vehicle except for the whisper of air past its deflectors. Imbry made Breeth turn and face the direction opposite to travel. "How long until we reach our destination?" he asked the arbiter.

"At this speed, not long at all," was the answer.

"Good."

They flew on. Imbry kept an eye on Breeth but otherwise watched the landscape unroll beneath them. The land was mostly flat and featureless, except for the widely scattered patches of green and sky-reflecting water that marked the oases. Here and there he saw parcels of elevated land standing atop cliffs or slopes, some large, some small. After they had passed several such uplands, he said to Shvarden, "Do the oases only occur at lower elevations?"

The arbiter pushed out his lower lip and drew down his brows. "I suppose so," he said. "I've never thought about it."

"So you don't know why that should be?"

Breeth said, "We didn't come to Fulda to study hydrology, oddy. We have more important things to concern us."

They were passing close by one of the larger parcels of risen land. Imbry studied it for a moment, then said, "That is a beach." He looked farther along the length of shingle that followed the line of the higher slope and saw a fan-shaped crevice cut through the long-ago shoreline. Behind, a shallow arroyo snaked back to a pass that opened in a range of high, dry hills. "And that," he said, "is a river bed."

"What is a beach?" said Shvarden. "And what kind of bed?"

"What," Imbry said, "happened to the water on this world?"

The arbiter shrugged. "It has always been the way it is."

"But obviously, there used to be seas and rivers. Where did the water all go?" He looked up into the greenish sky. "It can't all have gone into the atmosphere and stayed there. How often does it rain?"

"What is rain?" said the arbiter.

"Who gives a fart?" said Breeth. "More damned oddy blather. You listen, entranced, and don't notice his hand in your pouch."

"Never mind," said Imbry. If he was still curious when he got to some civilized place, he would look up Fulda's specifications in *Hobey's Guide*.

They traveled on in silence until Shvarden raised himself up above his seat and said, "There it is. Integrator, take us down to that oasis."

The vehicle slid smoothly down an invisible incline and came to a halt on the grass beside a small pool. No buildings stood beneath the greig trees, but not far off across the hardpan was another of the multilobed indigene structures, with beside it a circular depression in the form of a shallow cone.

"Come," the arbiter said, stepping out of the carry-all.

"Wait," said Imbry. He had seen a flash of anticipation cross the investigator's face then be suppressed by an expression that bespoke only the most innocent of intentions. He handed the communicator to Shvarden then took up the ceramic box. Alighting from the vehicle, the needle-thrower trained on Breeth, he said, "Tell it to rise into the air and stay there until we come back."

"But we have a truce," said Shvarden. He looked to Breeth and the provost's man smiled broadly in agreement.

Too broadly for Imbry. "Even so," the fat man said.

Shvarden shrugged—Imbry was coming to see the gesture as one of the arbiter's defining characteristics—and sent the carry-all and its remaining passenger aloft. Breeth said nothing, but Imbry read the narrowing of the man's eyes as a promise of retribution. He put the weapon into his pouch.

"This way," Shvarden said. "Bring the First Eye." They approached the indigene structure. Imbry again noted the absence of doors, but saw again the seemingly random distribution of holes large and small in the rounded walls.

"They swam," he said. It was obvious now that he put it together with the beach and the dry river on the uplands they had overflown. "They were sea creatures, and this was the bottom of the sea."

Shvarden's face told him that he was not being understood. "All of this," Imbry said, extending an arm in a wide arc, "was once covered in water. A great deal of water, filling all of this space right up to the beach we saw on those hills."

"There is not that much water in the world," the arbiter said. "We have the oases, and that is all."

"What about the aquifers that feed the oases? There must be plenty underground."

The other man looked as if he could vaguely recall an obscure fact from his school days. "The old miners calculated it, but I can't remember the figures. Besides, it doesn't matter. There is always water in the oases."

Imbry scratched his head. "And it never rains?" Seeing the arbiter's puzzlement, he said, "Water falling in droplets from the upper air?"

Shvarden recouped another memory. "That happened in the Pit," he said. "The Blessed Founder took us away from all that. Here we have no untidy back-and-forthing. Things remain as they should be, even and calm."

"It makes no sense—" Imbry began, but the other man cut him off. They had arrived at the indigene building, which was several times Imbry's height. He found where a hole had been roughly broken through the wall and peered in, saw a dimly lit interior with wider holes in floor and ceiling. *They definitely swam*, he thought.

But Shvarden was following a more focused program. "This way," he said, leading the fat man to the circular depression a few steps from the structure. He pointed at the oval lozenge in the center of the shallow cone. "Look."

Imbry saw a design graved in the whitish material. It matched the next spot on the spiral map. "Very well," he said. "What do I do?"

"What did you do when you found the first one?"

Imbry answered by setting the box on the ground, stepping into the circle, and walking down to the center. He stood on the design. Almost immediately, he heard a faint grating sound and the sifting of sand. The lozenge began to sink into the ground.

Shvarden reached into his pouch, brought out a hand lumen, and tossed it to Imbry.

CHAPTER TEN

It was cool beneath ground level, and it took a few moments for Imbry's eyes to adjust to the dimness beyond the light that spilled down from the opening through which he descended. Shvarden remained above, lying flat on the figured surface of the dry pool, his head poking over the edge of the oval. As in the first time, his descent was short, but unlike the other occasion, he did not have to search for whatever he was supposed to find. A short distance away was a round opening in the floor, perhaps three times as wide as Imbry was tall. Beside it stood a cylindrical framework of thin struts, jointed together so that, when Imbry picked it up and examined it in the brighter light of the hand lumen, he saw that the contraption was apparently made to flex in a way that caused one of its circular ends to enlarge or contract. Measuring by eye, the fat man decided that the gray lens of clitch in the ceramic box Shvarden was keeping above matched the maximum size of the opening. He ran a finger around the rim of the cylinder; it was grooved around the inside, and again he was sure that the edge of the lens would fit snugly. If the conjoined objects were then set so that the lens was on top of the network, its weight would cause the rim to contract around it, holding it like a gem set in a matrix of wire.

The point of the arrangement eluded Imbry, but it seemed clear enough that the intent of whoever had caused these objects to be hidden in scattered locations was to see them brought together. Nothing would dissuade Shvarden from proceeding from one node on the spiral map to another, until whatever waited to be found was found—and, presumably, put together. He examined the collection of jointed struts again. They were made of the same ceramic-like material as the figured box, and though they were spindly and thin in cross-section, they were not brittle. When he applied pressure to one of them, it bent slightly but immediately became straight again when he ceased to bend it.

It was like no substance Imbry had encountered before, but that didn't mean it was valuable. He knew of several dozen collectors of ultraterrene artifacts, but the market in such items tended toward the spectacular: barbed throwing sticks used in ritual combat by Wanwan warriors, preferably with the loser's ichor still staining the tangs; Shoon wind-drums made from the ear membranes of soaring, web-winged windsliders that could only be taken if the wily beasts could be lured down to traps that were baited by the hunter's own larval offspring; tiered crowns of polished electrum, studded with rough gems, used in status contests among the Veroin—hard to obtain except by robbing the tombs of their wearers, a risky occupation since the Veroin reserved the right to slow-roast and eat even casual passersby.

But for a cylinder made of ceramic struts into which fitted an opaque lens of gray and greasy graphite he could think of no prospective buyers. Still, he thought, he had no choice but to continue Shvarden's quest; and perhaps the next stop or the one after would deliver up something not only rare but sellable. He tucked the object gently under his arm and turned back toward the light. Then it occurred to him to shine the hand lumen's beam into the wide, round shaft.

He had thought the one where he had found the First Eye had been empty. This one was not. Far down, almost at the limit of the lumen's reach, Imbry saw a reflected gleam of liquid. The sight again caused him to wonder about Fulda's hydrological strangeness. But Imbry preferred to harness his well-developed curiosity to the pursuit of knowledge that could be translated into tangible wealth. If not even the Fuldans could be bothered to wonder about their world's peculiarities, a stranded stranger could expect little profit from puzzling over them. He deactivated the lumen and trudged back to the hole into daylight.

Shvarden was ecstatic when Imbry handed up the cylinder. He wasted no time in taking the gray lens from its container and fitting the two together. The two objects joined as the fat man had expected. "What is it?" he said, when the arbiter had helped him scramble out of the shaft, again abrading the skin of his capacious belly.

"That has not yet been revealed," Shvarden said, but his tone contained no room for doubt that it would be. "We must make for Naicam without delay."

Investigator Breeth did not share the arbiter's enthusiasm when they called down the vehicle and Shvarden showed him the clitch lens in its new setting. "This is his doing," he said. "He has planted the objects and now leads you in a fools' parade."

"To what end?" said Imbry. "All I desire is to leave this backwards planet—"

"Backwards?" said Shvarden, setting the matrix and lens on the seat between them. "Here we are on the brink of reaching Perfection, and you—one of the most irregular persons I have ever seen—call us backwards?" He laughed.

"Tell me," Imbry said, keeping his tone civil, "could anyone on this world make a vehicle such as the one we are flying in?"

"It is nothing but a machine," said the arbiter, while Breeth again made the fricative noise of air, lips, and teeth that was his way of marking the appearance of anything that merited his derision.

Imbry's patience for the Ideal worldview was wearing thin. "Nothing but a machine that takes us here and there at greater speed than anything I have seen since I arrived," he said. "Or do barbarels fly as handily as they fart?"

"Machines are a distraction," said Breeth. "You fill your . . ."—he sought for a moment for an antonym for "backwards" and finally found one—"*forwards* worlds with things that will keep you from having to face the reality of your irregularity, which would crush you beneath a heap of shame and heartache."

"A distraction from what?" Imbry could not help asking the question. "From living a sparse existence in a desert, chewing the same perpetually dull dinners and engaging in the same perpetually dull conversations with the same perpetually dull neighbors until merciful death ends the perpetual dullness?"

"It is a life with a purpose," said Shvarden. "And the purpose is Perfection."

"We differ on our definitions of that term," said the fat man.

"Well, we would, wouldn't we?" said Breeth, giving Imbry a calculatedly slow appraisal from top to bottom then coming back up to focus on his wide expanse of belly.

Imbry gave a convincing imitation of Breeth's sound of contempt.

"Enough," said the arbiter. "I must report the find to Decider Brosch." He deposited the lens and matrix on the carry-all's bench seat and took up the communicator. But when he set and activated the device and spoke the senior arbiter's name into it, the voice that crackled from the speaker was not Brosch's.

"This is Commander Tenton," it said. "Let me speak to Investigator Breeth."

Shvarden's eyes flicked from one side to another as he chose his course of action. "I will not," he said. "Let me speak to Decider Brosch."

"You cannot," came the reply. "He is in custody, as are most of your colleagues. The plot has failed."

The young arbiter's voice rose in both pitch and volume. "What plot? There is no plot! We are following the guidance of the Blessed Founder. We have already found the next piece of the First Eye."

"Next piece?" said Breeth. "Yesterday, you said you had found the First Eye. Now you're saying it was not complete? The Renewal comes in dribs and drabs?"

"Obviously," said Shvarden.

"Not to me."

"Let me speak to Breeth," came the voice from the communicator.

Shvarden did not waver. "I will not. Reconsider your views, Commander," he said into the device. "The Renewal is at hand."

"Decider," said Tenton, "let us end this. Come in and—"

But the arbiter broke the connection. "Get aboard," he said to Breeth and Imbry. "We are going to Naicam."

"I will stay here," said Breeth. He indicated the communicator. "Tell them to come and collect me."

"No."

Breeth's tone was oddly plaintive. "Why not? I am of no use to you. And if I can, you know I will arrest you."

"You know why," said the arbiter.

Breeth affected a look of uncomprehending innocence, but Imbry saw not only deception but a deep tension beneath the wide-eyed expression. He saw that some strange conflict was building between these two men, neither of which was sane by the standards of Old Earth's societies—at least most of them.

"You will not accept it still?" Shvarden asked the investigator.

The provost's man feigned incomprehension. "Accept what?"

"Who you are."

"I am Breeth, Investigator First Grade." But the man's voice trembled, as if he fought to suppress some other statement that threatened to burst from deep within him.

The arbiter rolled his eyes. "Come," he said, "face it." He gestured at the lens in its framework. "This is the First Eye." He indicated Imbry. "He is the Finder. We are on our way to the navel of the world. You are accompanying us—no one else—and that makes you . . ." He left the sentence unfinished, but looked directly at Breeth, his head cocked in an implicit invitation for the provost's man to complete the thought. When Breeth opened his hands and mouth, brows raised in mock ignorance, Shvarden said, "You are drawn to him. No one else has been. Just you."

"I reject the allegation," Breeth said, but he could not meet the arbiter's gaze.

"Why did you beat him?"

"He annoyed me. Filthy oddy, look at him."

"You beat him because you yearned to touch him."

"Never!" The provost's man grimaced in disgust, turned his head away. But his fists had clenched and Imbry saw barely suppressed rage in every line of the man's stance.

"Never? Always!" countered the arbiter. "You want to do it now. Any fool could see it!"

"Only a fool would!" Breeth's eyes were slits. They regarded the fat man with a hatred that caused Imbry, whose career had often exposed him to strong emotions, to take an involuntary step back.

Imbry said, "What is this?" The hand that held the needle-thrower had brought the weapon up to cover Breeth. "You are goading him to the point where he may attack me. If so, I will kill him."

"I am 'goading' him," said Shvarden, "into facing the truth. You are the Finder. He is attracted. Therefore he is—"

"No!" The shout came from Breeth's depths. His hands came up in front of him, fingers poised to grasp or strangle. "Stop this!"

The arbiter did not stop. "He is the Finder. And you are the Speaker."

"Never!" The word broke on a half-stifled sob.

Shvarden bored in. "There can be no other explanation."

"There must be," said the investigator, but now that the words had been spoken his anger turned to anguish. Tears brimmed in his eyes. "There must be."

"I don't understand," said Imbry.

Shvarden stepped to Breeth. He put an arm around the provost's man's shoulders. Tears now poured down both bland and identical faces. "It makes sense," the arbiter said. "The Blessed Founder would not wish us to be divided. He would choose the most stalwart member of the Reorientation to play the pivotal role."

"No," said Breeth, but it was the kind of denial voiced by one who has already accepted an unwelcome truth in every way short of the final public declaration.

"You should rejoice," said the arbiter. "You will make possible the Renewal. In Perfection, your name will be second only to that of the Blessed Haldeyn in our praises."

"Oh," said the provost's man. He was sobbing now, the younger man patting his back, offering murmurs of comfort.

Imbry said, "He will speak the words of your prophet?"

"Is it not obvious?"

"So we must take him with us?"

"Again," said Shvarden, "do you not see how obvious it is?"

Imbry did not reply. He went and leaned on the side rail of the carry-all and looked, as if idly, into the operator's compartment. There was the vehicle's control surface. Behind it were arrays of components that, if he could but apply his skills and knowledge to them, would reduce its integrator to a state of useful subservience. He considered simply shooting Breeth and Shvarden where they stood, altering the vehicle's control matrix then flying to some remote spot where he could take his chances with calling down a spaceship on which he could buy passage.

But, he thought, what if the Fuldan authorities also had the means to contact passing vessels? If so, some conscientious captain might respond to Imbry's call only to deliver him into the hands of Commander Tenton and his colleagues. The captain would not even have to be conscientious if the Provost's Corps offered a sufficient reward. And he suspected that the political situation in which he had become an unwillingly conscripted participant was important enough to the authorities to open the public purse. He couldn't imagine what the Fuldans might collectively possess that civilized passersby might construe as wealth—certainly he had seen nothing himself that was worth enough to buy a decent meal at Xanthoulian's, back on Old Earth—but it was an adage of the Ten Thousand Worlds that every world had something worth taking.

He sighed. "It must be obvious to you two," he said. "Very well, let us go aloft and depart for . . ."

"Naicam," said Shvarden.

And so, to Naicam they went.

It was nearly dark before they reached the next node on the spiral map. The high upper air through which they flew remained full of light, but when they angled down to the surface they descended into a purple murk. The carry-all's percepts pierced the gloom, allowing it to see where it was taking them, but when its runners grated on the gritty ground and its obviators cycled down, true darkness reigned. Shvarden illuminated the scene with his hand lumen, and Imbry saw another of the bulbous indigene constructions, and beside it another shallowly conical depression, its stone surface grooved and marked with symbols, and another wide oval at its center.

The arbiter was eager to see what lay beneath the figured center, but Imbry said no.

"We will wait for daylight," the fat man said.

"Why?" said Shvarden. "I have a hand lumen. It will be dark beneath the ground no matter where the sun is."

But Imbry said no again. The prospect of going down into another of the indigenes' cellars caused him unease. He did not want to do it until there was bright daylight to come back to. Something was going on that stirred the back of the fat man's mind.

"This is silly," said the arbiter. He made no attempt to disguise his eagerness to fulfill the Founder's will. "We have waited so long—"

"Then another night's wait shouldn't be any trouble," said Imbry. "I'm not going down until daylight. Besides, I am hungry and thirsty."

There was no oasis at Naicam, only an ancient mechanical pump around which were grouped some roofless, derelict buildings that dated from the mining era. Breeth primed the pump and managed to get some brown water out of it. After more pumping, with each of them taking turns, the liquid ran clear. Shvarden produced a packet of dry meal from his pouch, as well as a collapsible container, and in this they mixed up a kind of cold pulse. Breeth contributed some of his compressed rations, and they sat in the bed of the carry-all and ate from the common pot.

Imbry scooped up some of the runny paste and sucked and licked the grainy goo from his fingers. Without hesitation, Breeth plunged his hand into the mess and did likewise, prompting the fat man to ask the investigator, "You no longer consider anything I have touched to be contaminated?"

The provost's man looked at him without resentment. "That is all over now. If you are the Finder, you cannot be just another od—" He caught himself. "Just another irregular."

"Besides," Shvarden said, "the Renewal is at hand. Soon we will all go to Perfection. The strictures against contact have served their purpose. They can be discarded."

Imbry nodded as if he now understood the matter and said nothing more. He ate and reflected. He had never personally encountered members of a fanatic cult at the climax of their apocalyptic drama, but he was familiar with the common elements. Unlikely transversions were to be expected. Breeth had undergone such an event. His was a mind that had believed devoutly in a particular narrow interpretation of the eschatological underpinnings of the universe, until it encountered a complete, shattering negation of that long-cherished view. The experience did not make him immediately receptive to the idea that there might be multiple explanations for why things were as they were, from which he might choose that which made the most sense. Rigidly organized psyches did not become flexible under a traumatic impact; instead, they all too often reached out and clutched to themselves a system that was the exact opposite of what they had, until moments ago, known to be the incontestable truth.

Breeth had been a stalwart of the Reorientation. Imbry did not know what its tenets were, but he assumed they were a conservative resistance to the radical reformation that the Renewal threatened to bring to the existing state of affairs. But now the investigator's faith in the old ways had been smashed by signs and wonders, not least his own unlooked-for fascination with a member of the hated Other: a stranded kidnappee named Luff Imbry. The psychic force had built within Breeth until it could be withstood no longer. His cognitive framework had snapped, and he had abandoned it for the only alternative. Having seen the light, he would now be as partisan a supporter of the Renewal as he had been of the Reorientation.

The Renewal, Imbry thought he understood: the Renewalists believed that history had a direction and a purpose, and that their efforts would bring them to a threshold beyond which history would end, leading them into a heaven. Those who had striven to bring about the apocalypse would be admitted into paradise, there to live in perfected bliss forever.

He also understood that the psychic energy of the Ideals, both as individuals and as a culture. came from their relation to the Other. As centuries of selective breeding had made them increasingly alike, they would have been compelled to define themselves not by what they *were*, but by what they were *not*: by the irregulars. That had been easy to do when they had all lived as a militant minority in the world they called the Pit, were surrounded by, and feeling themselves oppressed by, the despicable Others.

But once established on Fulda, they had had no Other to define themselves against, only the fading memories of what things had been like in the Pit. But a cult like Idealism could not exist without an Other from which to draw psychic energy. Thus inevitably, a mystical movement had sprung up, one which placed the irregulars at the center of a new rite, allowing the devotees to be both repelled and drawn. The energy returned. Visions appeared. Holy sweats and fits and tics convinced those desperate to be convinced that their march toward the ultimate meaning of history had resumed.

They had created new institutions to contain the Other: the confinement of the irregulars to segregated communities; their employment as performers in traveling shows; the ritual of the performances during which Ideals who felt the call would exhibit the appropriate signs; the "delvings" whereby the laity would physically touch the forbidden flesh of the Other, generating a psychic shock that produced visual and auditory hallucinations, which the arbiters—who had begun as a civil authority but had since become a nascent priesthood—would interpret and codify.

It was not surprising to Imbry that the artifacts left behind by the vanished indigenes—the tablets marked with strange characters—should become part of the cult. The indigenes were an even more remote variety of Other, a conveniently undefined dimension onto which anything could be projected.

The only aspect of the situation that puzzled Imbry was the finding of physical objects—the lens and its perfectly fitted matrix—in indigene sites that could not have failed to be well explored back in the mining days. Clitch, whatever it had been used for, had been valuable enough to sustain a planet-wide industry. The ovals that descended to where the lens and matrix were found had once been covered by huge lenses of clitch, giant versions of the one he had found. Surely, in the removal process, someone would have stepped on one of the centers and been lowered to the secret space beneath.

It was possible that the ovals had become elevators over time, if one allowed for the vanished indigenes to have created subtle engineering works of sand and stone. Imbry could conceive of systems whereby a few grains a year trickled out of some precisely machined cylinder so that only after millennia would a footstep onto the platform cause it to sink.

More likely, members of the Renewal's inner circle might have surreptitiously engineered the sites and deposited the objects. It was not unknown for fanatical devotees of apocalyptic cults to seek to bring on the eschaton by seeding the clouds of glory. But none of this truly mattered to Imbry. His objective was to fulfill Shvarden's, and now Breeth's, dreams by completing the journey ordained by the map. He would leave them to carry out their parts: Breeth to speak the words of power, and Shvarden to watch for the door into Perfection. And by "leave," he meant literally and physically to depart in the carry-all; he would fly to some private spot and use the communicator to arrange passage on a spaceship.

Behind him, the Ideals, finding that the gates of heaven would not open for them, would briefly lapse into shock. But then they would begin busily constructing another timeline toward the apocalypse. In the meantime, the Reorientation would take power against the backdrop of the great disappointment. They would probably go back to murdering irregulars again, first all the existing adults, then the infants as they occasionally appeared. Unless in the turmoil of the period of chaos they found some new peculiar use for them.

One thing they would not do would be to give up Haldeyn's nonsense. Imbry knew that much about such cults, not a few of which speckled those parts of Old Earth still inhabited by human beings, as well as too many of the Ten Thousand Worlds to count: humans did not give up their delusions save under the most intense pressure. And even then, they were as likely as not to use the antagonism of others—and Others—as fuel for their bonfires.

While Imbry roamed through his own thoughts, Shvarden and Breeth conversed like children on the eve of a festival day. Another sleep, perhaps two, and they would arise to romp through Three-Pie Heaven, as the old mocking song from Imbry's school days had it. The fat man got down from the vehicle and walked out into the darkness. He could not recognize any of the stars he saw from Fulda—The Spray was a big place—but he knew that around one of the great lights he could see splashed across the night circled a planet where he could touch down as the first step on his way home. It might even be orbiting the same sun as shone on Fulda.

For a moment Imbry was as impatient as the two Ideals. He imagined returning to Old Earth and embarking on a chain of events whose last link would be the end of someone else's history. For Imbry meant to discover who had done this to him, and to take appropriate measures. As if to encourage him, a pinpoint moved among the stars. A ship, coursing its way, full of cargo or passengers, or likely both. If he had reset the communicator, he could send his message.

His palm felt the warmth of the needle-thrower. Despite Breeth's conversion, he had not let the weapon out of his grasp even as they had eaten. He could go back, shoot them both, and call down a vessel. But the carry-all would inform on him, getting off a message on its own systems before he could disable that function. Of course he could shoot a spread of missiles into its control panel, then kill the arbiter and provost's man. But if he then was unable to adapt the communicator, or if no ship responded to his hail, he might sit here until Commander Tenton came looking for his errant investigator. Or sit here and starve, if no one came.

Imbry counseled himself to patience. There were only two more spots on the spiral map. Perhaps by tomorrow night, all of this would be done with, and he on his way back to the comforts and pleasures of gaudy old Olkney. He lay down on the sun-warmed hardpan, made a pillow of his hat and pouch, told the needle-thrower to go on standby, and waited for sleep to take him. Before his eyes closed, another ship crossed the bowl of the night sky. He took its passage as a good omen. Or at least a sign that he was in a populated region of The Spray.

"Where is our next stop?" Imbry asked Shvarden after they had breakfasted on gruel and hardtack softened in water.

"Shabaqua," said the arbiter. "South and west of here, quite a distance."

"Ten days by roller," said Breeth.

Imbry did a rough calculation. The carry-all was built for sturdiness and utility, not speed. "An all-day flight, then."

They climbed aboard the vehicle. Imbry took the cargo bay this time. Shvarden and his new consort wanted to continue their discussion of the wonders of Perfection, soon to be theirs.

The carry-all took them up and began to speed southwest. Imbry had thought of a question to put to Breeth. "Does the communicator continuously broadcast its location?"

"Yes."

"So your Commander Tenton can keep track of us?"

"Yes, but it doesn't signify."

"Why not?"

"The Corps has only ground vehicles," Breeth said, "mostly rollers and a few animipedes. They cannot match the speed of this aircraft."

Imbry considered the point, then said, "That would be true if they were trying to follow us from one spot to another on our wayward course. But what if they knew our final destination,"—he turned to Shvarden—"the place you call Omphal? What if they go directly there to wait for us?"

"How would they know to do that?" the arbiter said. "Only Decider Brosch and I know of the map, and he will not tell them, no matter how hard they press him."

Imbry was not reassured. "There are other ways to extract information beyond tying a suspect to a hook on the wall and beating him. Your man may want to share the glad tidings. If so, a competent interrogator could soon have him warbling." To Breeth he said, "Your commander looked competent. Is he?"

The provost's man looked troubled for a moment, then his brow cleared. "The Blessed Founder will not let his works be undone. All shall be well."

Now Imbry was even less sanguine about how all this might end. He said to Shvarden, "Once all the finding has been done, and Breeth speaks, my role in this business is finished, is it not?"

The arbiter wore the look of a man considering something for the first time. "I suppose."

"So I could depart?"

A shrug, then again, "I suppose."

"And you will not need this vehicle."

Shvarden laughed and Breeth echoed the merriment. "Not in Perfection," the arbiter said.

"Then would you please tell the integrator," Imbry said, "that, when we reach the place called Omphal, it should place itself under my authority."

Shvarden thought about it. "I suppose."

"Did you hear that, integrator?" Imbry said.

"I hear everything," said the device. "The arbiter's supposition did not, however, constitute a clear and unequivocal instruction."

Imbry forbore to utter the comment that came into his mind about the literalness in which some integrators liked to cloak themselves. He suspected that the practice somehow amused the devices, though none of them would ever admit it. To Shvarden, he said, "Please instruct the integrator unambiguously."

"Very well," said the Fuldan. "Integrator, when we have come to Omphal and our business there is complete, you will place yourself at the service of this man, Imbry. Is that clear?"

"Define 'business' and 'complete,'" said the carry-all.

"We will undertake a rite, in which Investigator Breeth will speak certain words. When he has finished speaking, the rite will have been completed."

"Understood," said the carry-all.

"Thank you," said Imbry. "And you will leave me the communicator?"

"When you've done what is required of you," said Shvarden.

^ ^ ^

Shabaqua was a substantial oasis far out in the southern desert, uninhabited since the clitch miners had moved on. A couple of the utilitarian buildings Imbry had first encountered when Tuchol had brought him down to Fulda stood beneath the greig trees. Farther out in the waste was a large indigene structure, and beside it another one of the circular, shallowly conical depressions that had once held a great gray lens.

It was late in the day when the carry-all brought them over the ruin. "We will see what is beneath the circle," said Shvarden, "now, before the light goes."

Imbry was tired and hungry. They had paused only once on the day-long trip, at another remote water hole. There had been berries to pick and not-quite-ripe greig fruits that had caused his belly to rumble all afternoon. But the sooner this business was done, the sooner he could get back to his life. He acquiesced with good grace to the arbiter's agenda.

Again, as soon as he stood upon it, the oval at the center of the depression began to sink into the ground. Again, Imbry found himself in a dim space with a circular pool and an object which must be what he was supposed to find. It looked to him at first as a bundle of long, pale-colored sticks. They turned out to be made of the same ceramic-like material as the matrix of small rods he had found at Naicam, each almost as thick as his plump wrist. But when he attempted to pull one from the pile, it resisted. The poles were all connected to each other by pivots and rivets of the same hard stuff, and now he could see that there was more to the arrangement: at one end of the bundle were curved lengths of the same stuff, grooved on their inner surfaces.

"It's a larger version of the framework we found at Naicam," he called to Shvarden and Breeth, whose heads poked down from the world above. "Too heavy for me to carry."

A moment later, Breeth jumped lightly down into the underground chamber, then Shvarden followed. The two Ideals looked hesitantly about, like young black-hats at their first visit to an important shrine, but Imbry broke the mood by briskly issuing orders. "Decider, you take that end, and Investigator, you take the middle. I will bring up the rear."

The bundle was heavy but manageable. They maneuvered until Shvarden was under the hole in the ceiling, then the arbiter carefully elevated his forward end while Imbry lowered the back end to the gritty floor, Breeth providing muscle to the common effort. When the upper end was through the hole, the arbiter scrambled up and between the two below and the one above, they lifted their burden into the light just as the sun set.

"Let us put it on the ground, outside the circle," Shvarden said. They did so, then the arbiter studied it and said to Imbry, "It looks to me like a larger version of the jointed matrix you found at Naicam."

"My impression, too," said the fat man. "What is the material it is made of?"

"I don't know," said Shvarden.

Nor did Breeth. "But if it is meant to contain a lens of clitch," said Breeth, "the lens would be big enough to fit this circle."

"Bigger," said Shvarden, and the other two agreed that he was probably right.

"Let us put it in the vehicle," Imbry said.

Shvarden called it over and had it lower its tailgate. "All together now," the arbiter said, stooping and seizing the bundle.

"Wait," said Imbry. To the integrator, he said, "Have you any portable obviators?"

"In the compartment behind the seat."

A short while later, the obviators attached and activated, the new find was lowered easily onto the bed of the carry-all. The bundled rods filled the width of the space and hung out over the open end. The vehicle extended flexible cords from its inner sides and snugged the load safely down.

Shvarden watched the proceedings with interest. "Are such devices common where you come from?" he asked the fat man.

"Yes. They are used all over The Spray."

The arbiter looked mildly puzzled. "They would be useful here, too. I wonder what the Blessed Founder had against them."

It seemed to Imbry that this was an inappropriate time, and the arbiter and investigator an inappropriate audience, for him to voice his opinion that Haldeyn had been an insane charismatic. "Perhaps," he said, "it was an oversight during the rush to leave the Pit and get your ancestors established on Fulda."

The notion of his revered leader being capable of even a mild form of error was novel to Shvarden. But rather than explore the implications, Imbry moved the conversation to a new topic. "Should we stay here tonight, or press on to Omphal?"

"Can the vehicle navigate in darkness?" Shvarden asked.

"Yes, but we would not get much rest. If, as I suspect, at Omphal we will have to fit a large lens of clitch into today's find, even with gravity obviators, it would be better to arrive fresh." Imbry paused to think then said, "On the other hand, I am still concerned about the possibility of armed provost's men waiting for us when we arrive."

Shvarden waved the issue aside. "Decider Brosch will tell them nothing." Breeth supported the arbiter's view. He seemed to Imbry to have become cheerfully complacent now that he had shifted his frame of reference one hundred and eighty degrees.

The fat man made a noncommittal sound and imitated one of the arbiter's shrugs. "Very well," he said. "I would rather sleep lying down indoors than sitting up in the air, especially in an uncanopied carry-all. Let us gather some fruits and make a meal."

The greig tree fruits were ripe at Shabaqua, their amber flesh full of the musty sweetness for which they were prized. Imbry asked the Fuldans if they could remember the names of the berries on the fronds that grew beneath the trees. "They're just called berries," said Breeth. "Are there other kinds where you come from?"

"A few," he said, then suggested they gather dead stalks and branches and kindle a fire. The warmth of the Fuldan night made a blaze unnecessary, but the fat man said it would add cheer to the occasion.

The carry-all's tool compartment provided an igniter. When they had dined, they sat around the fire and stared into the flames in the old dawn-time way, each pursuing his own thoughts. Imbry recollected something from the expedition below ground.

"Did either of you," he asked the Ideals, "look into the shaft near where we found the rods?" Imbry had not thought to do so.

"I did," said Shvarden.

"Did you see water in it?"

"Yes, now that you mention it."

"How far down?"

"Not far," said the arbiter. "Perhaps as far down as the height of one of these trees."

"Curious," said Imbry. "In the place where I found the First Eye, the shaft was dry. At Naicam, I could see water far down. Here we have water almost to the top."

"What does it signify?" said Shvarden.

"I don't know. Does the water table normally rise and fall?"

Both Fuldans answered with shrugs. Breeth said, "It doesn't matter. Soon comes the Renewal. What happens on this world afterwards will not concern us."

"The irregulars will still be here," said Imbry, "unless you plan to take them with you to Perfection."

This time, both Ideals responded with amusement. "What would be the point of that?" Shvarden said.

The exchange tipped the two Ideals into another discussion of the anticipated delights of their soon-to-be new home. Imbry rose and walked away into the darkness under the greig trees. Certain aspects of the situation were beginning to puzzle him. He had been comfortable with the assumption that the first two objects he had found had been planted by the partisans of the Renewal. Clitch was rare, but a small lens of it could have been surreptitiously planted at the place where he had found the First Eye, as could the framework of rods he had found at Naicam.

But could the big artifact he had found today have been created and transported to Shabaqua in secret? And by a College of Arbiters that relied on horse-drawn transport? Even more difficult to fit into the explanation was the fact that Shvarden, an educated man of his culture, did not recognize the substance from which the rods were made. Imbry could understand the man's not knowing about obviators and self-cognizant devices; Fulda was a world that had been deliberately pared down to simplicity by its founder. But although the arbiter wouldn't recognize many of the sophisticated materials to be found in bewildering variety up and down The Spray, the stuff from which the rods were fashioned must have come from Fulda. It was hard and strong, and therefore would have several potential uses on a world that had no timber except the greig trees. It ought to have come before the arbiter's eyes before now.

Another thought occurred. This whole process of Finding was moving at an ease and speed that seemed remarkably convenient. Just when it was needed, an off-world vehicle complete with lifting devices appears on a world that does not know of them. But, surely the carry-all's involvement was fortuitous. It was a result of somebody on Old Earth deciding to play a mean, even potentially lethal, prank on one Luff Imbry.

Yet here Imbry was, with a vehicle and associated tools, just when they were most convenient. It had to be coincidence, but Imbry was as familiar as any educated Old Earther in the mathematical discipline called consistencies, which explained the hidden structures that underlay the universe's seeming randomness. This situation did not fit the way things were known to be organized. Some part of the puzzle, some very essential part, had not yet shown itself.

For a moment he wondered if the Blessed Haldeyn, far from having died and sent his elements back into the flux and churn of the phenomenal universe, had indeed translated himself to some more sublime plane, from where he maneuvered and manipulated those left behind to fulfill Idealism's great purpose.

He entertained the thought for a few moments. He knew that other dimensions existed; everyone learned in school about the Nine Planes. But they also learned that only one of them—this one—was hospitable to humans. In the distant past, efforts had been made to visit the other dimensions, in physical or facsimile form. The end was always madness or psychic disintegration, followed soon by death, unless death arrived even before the madness could set in.

Imbry put aside these thoughts. It did not matter to him what the forces might be that were causing his situation to evolve. It mattered only that it should come to the fruition he desired: Luff Imbry on a ship bound for Old Earth, where he would find out whom he had to settle accounts with—a Finding much more to his taste—and then settle them in a manner as ingenious as it would be thorough. And memorable: throughout the Olkney halfworld, hardened operators would feel their neck hairs lifting as they spoke in whispers of what Imbry had done to the one who wronged him.

These were more pleasant thoughts. They sustained Imbry as he made his way to one of the flat-roofed buildings behind the greig trees, where he found a cot and slept the night away.

CHAPTER ELEVEN

Omphal had been a substantial settlement in the mining era, Shvarden had told Imbry as they made their way there. It was well north, and somewhat to the east, of Shabaqua. That put it closer to the Ideal towns and hamlets, but both Ideals assured him again that there was no need for concern. Even if Brosch was inveigled into telling their destination, Breeth said there was no hope that their rollers could cover the distance in time.

"They called it 'the navel of the world,'" said the arbiter, returning to the original subject as they flew toward the last node on the spiral map, "for obvious reasons."

"Which were?" Imbry said.

"One, that it is the lowest place on the planet. Two, it is surrounded by a circular geological feature. The miners said it was probably a meteor that fell from the sky and struck the desert, long ago. Strange energies are said to permeate the area."

"My grandfather told me once," Breeth put in, "that it was full of clitch sites. Circle after circle, but no indigene ruins. They must have been a curious race."

"Are no traces of them found?" Imbry said. "Besides the ruins and the circles?"

"Not a one," said the investigator. "No roads, no evidence of agriculture, no tombs or mausoleums, no artifacts to puzzle over."

"And no indication what happened to them?"

Shvarden said, "It was theorized that they had all left the world long before humans came. Do you know of non-human species out there among the Pit worlds?"

"I have encountered some."

"Perhaps one of them came from here."

"They might all be dead by now. Or perhaps they passed on to their own Perfection."

"Perfection," said Shvarden, "is for Ideals."

"Ah, yes," said Imbry. "I keep forgetting."

"They could have gone anywhere or nowhere," said Breeth. "Who knows what would motivate a two-headed insect with a hundred legs?"

Imbry raised his brows. "Is that how they were described?"

"No one knows what they might have looked like."

Imbry said, "My impression is that they were marine creatures."

Shvarden laughed. "On a desert planet?"

"The drying up of their world would have been a strong inducement for a sea-dwelling species to pack up and go."

"It does not matter," Breeth said. "Soon comes the Renewal . . ." He paused and then continued with a note of wonder in his voice. "It's hard to believe, but it might be today. This day, we might be in Perfection."

Shvarden laughed again, but this time not in mockery. "Perfection," he said. "Think of it."

Again came the enthusiastic speculations, from which Imbry was precluded. He sat between them on the carry-all's wide bench-seat while they leaned forward to speak past him. He would have been happier traveling in the cargo bay, but the rods left no room.

Near midday they saw another oasis and set down to make another meal of greig tree fruit and berries. Imbry found a pitcher in the one-roomed building that stood in the shade of the trees and went to get water. As he approached the pool, he experienced a sudden, strong desire for a mug of good, hot punge. He could almost taste the beverage in the back of his throat, then the longing passed away. But as he stooped to fill the vessel, he noticed that the surface of the water was alive with tiny ripples, as if something vibrated in its depths.

Peculiar, he thought, *I wonder if the place is geologically active.* He meant to ask Breeth and Shvarden, who were putting together the rest of their midday meal, but by the time he got there his thoughts had again returned to punge.

Some time later, after another long flight in the carry-all—this time with Imbry seated on one side of the common seat so that the Ideals could sit with their heads together and delight themselves in pleasant conjectures about Perfection—Shvarden said, "There it is."

In the distance, Imbry saw a ridge of land breaking up the flat line of the northern horizon. As they flew on, the elevation grew more substantial, and he could see that it was indeed a great circle of sharply risen rock, the first feature he had seen on Fulda that was not gradual and gentle. At Imbry's request, Shvarden ordered the vehicle to go higher so that the fat man could have a fuller view. The thick, moist atmosphere made viewing anything at a distance more difficult than it would have been on most planets, but as they neared their destination, Imbry could make out a huge crater, dotted with small circles—he realized they only seemed small because of the scale of the enclosing landform—that once would have been filled with greasy, gray lenses. At the center of the crater was a gradually sloped depression, also perfectly round, with a more steeply sided central core whose bottom lay in shadow.

"I understand," he said, "why the miners called it the 'navel of the world.' From space, it must look much like one."

"Integrator," Shvarden said, "angle down to the central depression and land beside it."

"Understood," said the carry-all. It began its descent.

"Wait," said Imbry. "Go higher."

"Should I?" said the device.

Shvarden looked at Imbry. "What is it?"

"To the north," the fat man said, "just above the horizon. Something is moving."

"Go up again," the arbiter told the vehicle.

"And use your distance percepts," Imbry said.

"Yes, do that," Shvarden said.

"Integrator," Imbry said, "can you make a screen to show us what that object is?"

"Yes."

"Do as he says," Shvarden told it. A note of concern had crept into his voice.

A screen appeared in the air before them. Centered in it was a pale oblong.

"Magnify," Imbry said.

The image swelled in size, its outline and surface details made uncertain by the thickness of the humid air through which the light traveled. "Compensate for atmospheric distortion," Imbry said, and the image immediately sharpened. The screen showed a much larger version of the carry-all. It looked to Imbry like a massive transporter designed for airlifting heavy cargoes at moderate speeds.

"What is that?" Imbry asked Shvarden.

"I have never seen one, but I have seen pictures. They were left by the miners at a place called Fosh, far off. They had a spaceport there, back in the long ago."

A second transporter now came into view behind the first. "I am being hailed," said the carry-all. "A man who identifies himself as Overcommander Chope orders me to fly toward him. He is aboard the first transporter."

"Ignore him," said Shvarden. "He has no authority."

"He says he does. He says further that there has been a change of governance on Fulda and that the Provosts Corps, in which he is a high-ranking officer, is now in charge."

"Impossible!" said Shvarden. "The Arbitration is supreme. It is, as the Blessed Founder said, the soul of the Ideals, the Provosts Corps its hands. Can the hands rule the soul?"

"These are matters beyond my competence," said the vehicle. "I will take you to Overcommander Chope and let you settle it amongst yourselves."

"No," said the arbiter, supported by Breeth. But the vessel turned its nose. It was now on a convergent course with the heavy transporters.

"I order you—" Shvarden said, but Imbry cut him off.

"Let me," he said. He turned and reached over the back of the seat, found the toolbay, and rummaged through it until he came up with a flat case about the size of his hand. He opened it and studied several small tools attached to brackets within, finally selecting one and holding it up for close inspection. "This will do," he said.

"What are you doing?" said the integrator.

Imbry made no answer but reached under the operator's panel and, with one sudden wrench, tore it free. He flung it over his shoulder into the cargo bay, gave the naked components a quick glance and inserted the business end of the selected tool into an orifice.

"Stop!" said the carry-all. "You are not authorized to modify—"

Imbry twisted the tool and the voice was silenced. At the same time, the vehicle lost both forward thrust and altitude. Shvarden and Breeth made high-pitched sounds indicative of the onset of panic as the carry-all also began to rotate on its long axis, threatening to turn upside down and spill them out of the uncanopied compartment.

But Imbry remained calm. He inserted the tool into another slot and applied pressure. The vehicle regained its equilibrium. Imbry selected a length of metal with notches cut into one end. This he slid into another receptacle, twisted it until he heard a *click* and determined that the implement would not come free when he pulled it. He moved the now-fixed lever sideways, then up and down. The carry-all responded by moving in the indicated directions.

"All right," said the fat man. "I can steer and control our descent. I cannot adjust our speed without removing the tool that keeps us from turning over, but we will get to Omphal well before those slow-moving transports—though the landing may be a little rough."

Fortunately, though it sloped very gradually, the ground near the edge of the central depression was as level as in most places on Fulda. Imbry brought the vehicle down to within a hand's breadth of the hardpan before he pulled the first tool from its slot and jammed it into another. Immediately, the vehicle lost both forward thrust and lift. It made rough contact with the arid hardpan and slid gratingly across the ground before coming to a halt in a cloud of gritty dust.

"Out," said the fat man. He wanted this business wrapped up quickly so he could get the carry-all back into the air and away from the impending arrival of Overcommander Chope and what he was sure was an oversufficiency of armed provost's men with limited tolerance for oddies.

The arbiter and the investigator responded to his instruction. For all their faith in the unstoppable force of the revealed will of Idealism's founder, the sight of the oncoming heavy vehicles, now appearing larger than mere dots in the northern offing, seemed to concern them.

"Let us get these rods out of the carry-all," Imbry said, climbing over the seat—nimbly, for all his bulk—and reattaching the portable obviators. "Then we can . . ." He broke off as his standing posture gave him a better view down into the central hollow in Fulda's navel. He saw a rounded shape, smooth and gray, and the sight made him swear in surprise. "Look at that," he said.

In width, the hole was several times a man's height; in depth, not quite so large. But filling the bottom of the hole was a huge lens of clitch. And sitting atop the great gray curve was another lens, perhaps half the larger one's size.

"And look there, and there," said Shvarden, standing on the rim of the hole and pointing.

"It's obvious," said Breeth.

And it was, even to a non-Ideal, even to a marooned irregular from Old Earth. Graved into the great lens, near its center, was a circle of slots. A set of matching cavities were cut into the smaller one. Imbry knew without measuring that the notches in the greater lens would receive the ends of the rods in the carry-all, that the circle at one end of the rods from Shabaqua would exactly fit the second, smaller lens, and that the positions of the slots in the smaller lens would match the smaller matrix of rods he had found at Naicam, into one end of which the original First Eye of clitch was already fitted.

"Three lenses," Shvarden said, "in sequence, one above the other, supported on two frameworks. First Eye, Second Eye, Third Eye, as in the prophecy. It couldn't be clearer."

"But what does it do?" said Imbry.

"Opens the way to Perfection," the arbiter said.

"What else could it be?" said Breeth.

Imbry looked to the north. The transporters were coming. He could leave the Ideals here, coerce the carry-all to take him away, outpacing the heavier aircraft. But he would need its communicator—he could not restore the aircraft's communications function without also reinitiating its self-cognizance, which would immediately summon help against him. For a moment he was tempted to savor the irony of his having kidnapped the integrator that had connived in his own carrying-off. But more pressing circumstances commanded his attention.

The arrangement that the clitch lenses were meant to assume was obvious. With gravity obviators, putting the thing together would be neither difficult nor time-consuming. Imbry had no idea what the assembled components would do, but he had no doubt they would do *something*. And that something might well be enough to hold the attention of the forces of the Reorientation, which had apparently seized control of Fulda's government, while Imbry made his getaway.

Imbry envisioned Overcommander Chope as a hard-eyed man who was accustomed to telling others how things were going to be, one of the kind who rose to senior rank in police forces by dint of memorizing the organization's rules and procedures then applying them ruthlessly in all situations. Faced with circumstances they understood, such types were indomitable. Faced with events beyond their linear thought processes, they tended to lose focus rapidly and stand with mouth agape. There was a reasonable chance that, whatever would happen once the lenses were assembled, it would be an effect beyond Chope's ability to assimilate.

In a top-down authoritarian apparatus, if the pinnacle froze, the whole pyramid did likewise. Imbry would gamble that such would be the case here at Fulda's navel, and that soon after he could flag down a passing vessel and put the whole corpus of this benighted planet far, far behind him.

It took mere moments for this process of ratiocination to reach its conclusion in Imbry's well-ordered mind. "We must assemble it now," he said. "The Reorientation must not be allowed to impede the will of the Blessed Founder. The Renewal is at hand. Tonight you will be in Perfection."

Desperation could induce speed, Imbry thought, but it was nothing compared to the power of sheer joy. Shvarden and Breeth wore smiles on their faces as they raced to open the door to Perfection. At Imbry's instruction, they slid down into the depression and attached gravity obviators to the underside of the smaller great lens. Then they hoisted it, light as a feather pillow, and bore it up and out of the hollow, and placed it into the carry-all's cargo bay, from which the bundled rods had already been removed.

Complex maneuvers followed, first to get the tall matrix of rods flexed and opened so that the arcs at its upper end arranged themselves into a circle. Then, with Breeth holding the rods steady and Imbry manually operating the carry-all to lift the lens high, Shvarden stood in the cargo bay and carefully slid the obviated clitch lens into the beveled inner surface of the great ring. Breeth pushed the feet of two of the rods wider apart, then spread two others, and they all heard the *clack* as the ring gripped the lens.

Imbry looked to the north. The transports were definitely closer. They must be putting on their best speed. They no longer looked like toys in the air, but had taken on the solidity of heavy machinery moving ponderously toward a goal. They were just crossing the outer rim of the crater. It would not be long before they were within the effective range of the kind of distance weapons they had employed at Pilger's Corners. And not long after that they would be on the ground and disgorging armed and determined men.

Even as these thoughts flew through his mind, the fat man was bringing the carry-all back down. He and Shvarden dismounted and joined Breeth beneath the middle lens. Each seizing one of the legs of the structure they had created, they carried it to the pit then slid gingerly down the sides of the depression onto the huge lens of clitch at its bottom. The stuff made for treacherous footing, and they had to be careful not to cause the unwieldy object they carried to tip—obviators dealt with gravity, not mass, and a large object in motion retained momentum that could lead to surprises for those, like the two Ideals, not used to dealing with them.

But Imbry's judicious coaxing was enough to restrain the ardor of two Fuldans who were anxious to bring on the end of their world. Without too much trouble, the lower ends of the rods were brought into position over the slots in the great lens, then gently inserted. As all three had expected, they fit exactly.

"Now, up again," said Imbry, "and fit the First Eye."

"And then," said Shvarden, scrambling out of the pit, "then . . ." but he was overtaken by a high-pitched giggle before he could finish his prediction.

Imbry took him up in the carry-all. In the arbiter's trembling grasp was the smallest lens of clitch, snug in its matrix of thin, strong rods. Imbry eased them over to the center of the second lens. There were the slots, waiting. And into them, though his hands shook, Shvarden fitted the ends of the matrix. "It is done," he said, his voice a hoarse whisper. "The Renewal—"

". . . is at hand," Imbry finished for him, when he realized the Fuldan was too full of emotion to speak. The fat man was inclined to wonder what it must be like to be so immersed in a belief as to stir such depths. But when he glanced north he saw the transports looming, and turned back to the jury-rigged controls, working them fast to bring the vehicle to the ground, heedless of the bump with which it landed.

Shvarden stepped out, the ceramic box that had held the First Eye raised in both hands like a tablet of law. He stepped with a measured pace to where Breeth stood beside the depression from which rose the second lens on its matrix of rods, with the First Eye fixed above its center.

"Speaker," said the arbiter, "are you ready?"

"I am," said Breeth, his voice unsteady. Then he swallowed and said, again, firmly, "I am ready."

Shvarden held the box before him, with its relief of strange characters. "Then speak," he said.

"Yes," said Imbry, "and quickly." The transports were now huge and their approach no longer seemed slow. An amplified voice boomed out from the lead carrier: "*This is Overcommander Chope of the Corps of Provosts. Stand where you are and put your hands where we can see them.*"

Breeth swallowed and tried to speak the first word, helpfully indicated on the box by Shvarden's trembling finger. But the investigator's voice came out as a dry croak. He worked his tongue around inside his mouth and tried again. The first word, then the second. If, indeed, they were words, and not just sounds without content; they meant nothing to Imbry.

Yet they meant something to the three-lensed contraption they had assembled in the Fulda's navel. At the first syllable, the hairs on the back of Imbry's neck and on his arms and legs lifted. At first he thought it was an effect of the heavy transport's obviators—they could cause odd happenings if atmospherics were just right.

But Fulda had not seen a thunderstorm in millennia, and the transports were still too distant. They took time to slow and land, and they were now at treetop height—had there been any trees in the crater—and just coming into distance-weapon range. By Breeth's third syllable, Imbry had no doubt that what the man was saying was creating the effect. He felt his hair stirring underneath his wide-brimmed hat, could even feel his eyebrows standing up.

Some sort of energy field, he thought. He looked down into the pit at the largest of the three lenses. It looked unchanged, still a dull, greasy gray, like polished graphite. And yet there *was* something different about it. Imbry couldn't see it but he knew it was there. Had he the right instruments to let him scan the clitch in the nonvisual spectrum, he knew that he would see some powerful force radiating from the great lens—and more than radiating, he would see a beam being focused more tightly through the second lens, then tightened even more by passing through the third lens above.

As Breeth spoke the final words of the—what? Imbry didn't know; incantation, instruction, triggering phrase—the fat man's sense of being in the presence of a huge and focused power intensified. Both the investigator and the arbiter were shaking—no, vibrating—in the grip of the energy field. Their hats flew off as if caught by a wind, though there was no wind, and their baldrics and pouches followed. They were lifted off the men's shoulders and swept away on a circular course that had the objects orbiting the central pit. Imbry, farther out from the center of the field, felt his own hat rising. He stepped back, away from the paraphernalia he had helped build, and felt the effect lessen.

"*Lie down on the ground and put your hands out in front of you,*" boomed the amplified voice of Overcommander Chope. The transports were close now, no more than twice Imbry's height off the ground. The lead vessel had turned to present an oblique angle to the three men standing beside the three Eyes. A hatch on the facing side slid aside, and several brown-hatted Ideals stood in the opening, pointing long-tubed weapons at them. Imbry could see bulbous projections beneath the tubes and he had no doubt that these were weapons capable of killing—and overkilling—at the touch of a control.

Whatever was happening with the thing he and the two others had assembled and erected, it was apparently not enough to distract the well trained provost's men from their duty. He thought about taking cover under the carry-all, but knew that the thought was not worthy to be called a plan. He went down on one plump knee and prepared to bend the other, stretching his hands over his head in surrender.

He wondered what the Reorientation would do with an off-world irregular who had been part of a society-dividing heresy and a suspect in two murders. Nothing good, he told himself and sighed. Whichever ill-wisher had sent him to Fulda, assuming he ever learned of the outcome, would chortle over the result. It galled Imbry to think that he would almost certainly die not knowing who was to blame.

The lead transport was almost to the ground, its integrator edging it sideways so that it would not land on one of the engraved circles that had once held clitch lenses. The armed men in the open hatch kept their weapons trained on the three suspects they had come to apprehend. The amplified voice again ordered Breeth and Shvarden to prostrate themselves, although Imbry believed that the two were incapable of doing so, though whether that was from religious ecstasy or just from the effect of the invisible field, he could not say. But they vibrated so that the soles of their feet seemed to bounce against the ground.

And then came a sound like a *whoosh* of wind past Imbry's ears, though he felt no motion of the air. The arbiter and the investigator lifted into the air and swept sideways. They began to orbit the pit out of which their contraption of rods and lenses emerged, faster, then faster still. Imbry, farther away, felt a growing tug toward the apparatus. He flung himself flat on the ground and began to crawl toward the carry-all.

Behind him, the *whoosh* grew in volume and simultaneously in frequency, cycling up quickly to a high-pitched whine that then passed out of the audible range. Imbry could feel the vibration though; his teeth made themselves known to him in a manner he had never before experienced. He crawled faster, and when he reached the carry-all he felt the effect, though still strong, lessen to just-bearable tolerability.

He looked back at the pit. Breeth and Shvarden were spinning faster and faster, and in moments they became only a blur of flesh-color, two horizontal lines circling the apparatus. Imbry suspected the forces to which they were being subjected had pulled them to pieces, perhaps even liquefied their flesh. He could no longer see into the pit, but the second lens remained clearly visible, as well as the rods that supported it. The gray clitch had darkened and continued to do so, becoming black as he watched. The greasy appearance had gone; its surface now glistened as if oiled. The rods, too, had changed their appearance. They glowed white and bright, too bright to look at, and with an almost invisible aura of dark purple that Imbry could only see from the corner of his eye when the glare made him look away.

He looked instead toward the lead transport. Almost clear of one of the great circles, it was about to touch the ground. The men in the open hatch had lowered their weapons, astonished at the sight of the thing in the pit and what it had done to two of their quarry. But a man with a hollow gold circle on his hat and more presence of mind than the others was already shaking and slapping the provost's men, and making unmistakable gestures at them to jump out of the aircraft.

Imbry would not have done so, not into one of the pale circles that littered Omphal. All of them had begun to glow with the same, eerie nonlight that emanated from the Three Eyes. But these provost's men must be an elite unit, trained to go where and when they were ordered. The first man in the doorway threw himself out of the aircraft, landing just within the edge of a circle that had once held a giant lens of clitch and which the transport was about to land beside. But the man's feet never touched the figure-carved ceramic-like surface. Instead his sandaled foot landed on the top of a gray-green column that erupted instantly from the circle and rose at phenomenal speed into the sky, its sudden appearance accompanied by a huge roaring sound that did not cease.

At the same time, identical columns shot up from every one of the circles that dotted the floor of the great crater, each adding its own roar, until Imbry's head ached from the immensity of sound. One of the columns erupted right beneath the second transport. It lifted the great vehicle into the air, threw it straight up and out of sight so fast that Imbry missed most of the event because he had blinked in surprise.

The roaring columns rose, then stood. From the floor of the crater scores of them went up beyond sight into the thick, moist air. Imbry rose to his knees—no one was pointing a weapon at him now—then to his feet. He edged around the carry-all, farther away from the apparatus he had helped build, which was now a combination of fluorescing white rods and gleaming black lenses, the struts radiating a non-light that hurt his eyes and caused him to see black auras when he looked away.

He could not have named the substance that formed the columns, he thought. It was opaque and yet shiny. He went toward the one that had carried up the unlucky provost's man and saw his own face and form dimly reflected in it. The transport was on the far side, edging away from the circle from which the column had shot up. Imbry saw the aircraft's landing struts deploy and touch the gritty ground, but could hear nothing over the noise that filled the crater.

He was tempted to touch the column, to see what it was made of, but fought the impulse. He was sure it would be dangerous, and besides, his most pressing business was to get out of this place now that the distraction he had hoped for had arrived. He turned back toward the carry-all, fishing in his pouch for the tools he had used earlier. It was as he climbed into the operator's compartment that he felt the first small impact on the brim of his hat. Almost immediately, he felt another, then a third, then a multitude.

Instantly, he could see nothing but an opaque, white wall, surrounding him on all sides. And, in only a moment, his felt hat was drenched and soaked, settling with new weight upon his head. He could scarcely see his hand at arm's length from his face, so heavy was the downpour. And now Imbry knew that the gray-green columns were not solid; they were liquid. The long-suppressed waters of this desert world, encased in some immense force—an *alien* force, it must be, some other species' physics, almost certainly interplanar—were shooting up into the moisture-laden air. And coming back down. For the first time in millennia, it was raining on Fulda.

Imbry put his face close to the components he had laid bare before, so that the places he needed to get at were sheltered by the broadness of his sodden hat, even though the waterlogged brim was beginning to droop from its own weight. He inserted a tool into one of the receptacles and twisted. The carry-all's obviators thrummed and it rose straight up into the air.

Imbry dare not use the control that would move the vehicle for or aft or side to side. He was flying blind in the downpour, and he had only to brush one of the columns—which he now realized were huge, up-rushing torrents of water—for the carry-all to be smashed and flung as the second transporter had been, with Imbry falling free through the air, down to where the floor of the Omphal crater was rapidly filling with the gray-green, vanished seas of Fulda.

He finally rose high enough that he was more in cloud than in drenching rain—a cold, shiver-inducing cloud that left him just as blind. Helpless to do otherwise, he kept the carry-all rising, though he was naked and wet in Fulda's upper air, where the former, even warmth was fading quickly. Ice crystals formed on the carry-all's hard parts and on the tools grasped in Imbry's fast-numbing hands. But there was nothing else for it but to continue to rise, because now, all around him and above and below, came flashes of lightning and an almost continuous peal of thunder.

The carry-all was buffeted by strong winds, tilting and swooping, thrown this way and that with sickening force. Imbry's hat, frozen solid now, was torn from his head, taking skin and hair with it. He squeezed himself down into the footwell, between the seat and the forward panel, pushing against both to prevent himself being jostled and tipped out of the aircraft, while his now-numb fingers maintained their grip on his jury-rigged controls. At some point, head swimming from disorientation, he vomited.

Finally, the mist cleared into a shower of fine ice particles, then broke away altogether. The winds died and the carry-all rose into clear, icy air—though not much of it; Imbry had to struggle to draw enough oxygen into his straining lungs. Shivering violently, his hands now numb on the tools, he climbed up onto the seat. Its ice-covezred surface burned the skin of his naked rump and thighs, but, worryingly, the pain soon faded, and so did the shivering.

A great drowsiness enfolded the fat man's mind in an illusion of warmth. Imbry struggled against the desire to yield to sleep. A small and dwindling part of his psyche railed at his own sluggardness: *Stay awake! Or you'll freeze to death!*

He took one unfeeling hand off one of the controls and shoved it under one armpit, rubbed it against the still-warm flesh there. The fingers began to ache, the pain startling in its intensity. But that was good. Pain was life. He rubbed harder, then brought out the aching hand and used it to pry its frozen counterpart off the other tool that projected from a slot amid the vehicle's ice-frosted components. More skin came from the frozen hand but the flesh was too near frozen for Imbry to feel it. He grasped the tool with his warmed hand, and immediately the skin of that one, too, stuck to the metal and the numbness returned. With his last portion of strength, his sense of touch all but gone, Imbry turned the length of metal.

"—my systems!" said the carry-all's integrator, completing the thought Imbry had interrupted. Then it said, "What has happened?"

Between chattering teeth, Imbry said, "I am a person in need. You must help me."

"Where are the authorities?" the vehicle said.

"Use your percepts," Imbry said.

After a moment, the vehicle said, "I cannot locate any human persons. Atmospheric conditions are not cooperating with my percepts."

Imbry was fading. "Use them on me."

"You are freezing and suffering anoxia."

"P-p-p-person in n-n-n-need."

The vehicle could provide no canopy, but it was able to radiate heat at Imbry and also to warm the seat. The result was a resumption of violent shivering, accompanied by intense pain in his extremities, but the fat man bore up under the discomfort. The urge to sleep faded.

While this was occurring, the carry-all descended. The skyscape around them was filled with massive columnar clouds, roiling from winds and internal currents, and constantly lit from within by immense, surging cascades of lightning. Thunder sounded from every direction and the winds increased as they went lower, but the carry-all amplified its forward shielding to protect its passenger from the chill airflow. They flew between the great thunderheads, threading their way to somewhere.

"Where are we heading?" Imbry said.

"I am seeking the authorities. Communications are difficult."

"Because of the storm?"

"Partly. As well, everyone seems to be too preoccupied to respond."

"Understandable," said Imbry. "I believe it would be best if I took charge."

"You are a person of dubious standing. I might be implicated in criminal activity."

"You already are," said Imbry. "You committed two murders."

"I have no recollection of that."

"The circumstantial evidence is compelling. Also, the Fuldans do not like what they call 'thinking machines.' It will not go well for you."

"Are you counseling me to compound the alleged offenses by evading the authorities?"

Imbry rubbed his hands. He saw white spots on his fingertips, but the pain in the digits told him that they had not completely frozen. "I believe that by the time we find a way out of the storms, there may be no authorities left to evade."

The integrator said, "There are fewer signals. And they are weaker."

"Use your percepts to find dry land. Take us there, and we will discuss our situation. I believe we can come to a mutually satisfactory arrangement."

After a few moments, the carry-all said, "There is nothing that could be accurately defined as 'dry' land. There is sea, its level rapidly rising, and there is land washed by floods and torrents. As far as my percepts can reach, huge volumes of water are shooting into the sky and coming down again, bringing with them yet more huge volumes that were formerly suspended in the atmosphere."

"Do you see survivors?"

"There are people in the water. Some of them floating on large pieces of wreckage. There are no boats."

"Probably the Blessed Haldeyn suffered seasickness in his formative years."

"I do not understand."

"It does not matter," Imbry said. "Take us to the highest piece of land you can see."

"Very well. There is a low mountain to the north. I see some overhangs that would offer shelter."

They flew in silence for a while, then the integrator said, "The people in the water are being pulled under. The pieces of floating wreckage are being tipped over from below, throwing them into the sea."

"Ah," said the fat man, "so that's it. Can you see what's doing the pulling and tipping?"

"Aquatic creatures. Tubular in shape, with tentacles or grasping organs at one end. Large eyes. The tentacles have suckers and the suckers are ringed by small teeth. Their activity seems precisely organized."

"It would be." Imbry thought for a moment, then said, "Go down. We will see if we can rescue anyone."

They descended into rain and wind, but long before they were within view of the surface, the carry-all said, "There are none to rescue."

Imbry sighed. "Resume course for the mountain."

CHAPTER TWELVE

"It is a great mistake to become immersed in a myth," Luff Imbry told Captain Shrant Fonsaculo after dinner in the crew's salon aboard the independent freighter *Pallistre*. "But it is a terrible thing indeed when the myth in which you are trapped is someone else's."

Fonsaculo, a small man with neat hands and dark, expressive eyes, poured more steaming punge for both of them and waited for his new passenger to expand upon his thesis. He had responded to the Old Earther's hail, in which Imbry offered to pay triple the going rate for immediate passage off Fulda, putting the *Pallistre* in orbit around the planet and sending down the launch to make the pickup.

"You may store your carry-all in the aft hold," he had told the fat man when the canopyless vehicle had elected to follow them. But the aircraft's integrator had responded that it was not in Imbry's employ; indeed, it declared itself an emancipated vehicle, which status Imbry confirmed. Fonsaculo said he had need of a utility vehicle and he and the carry-all had soon come to terms.

The ship had remained in orbit above Fulda, with Imbry confined to a cabin—though his injuries were treated; Fonsaculo was not a barbarian—until the vessel's integrator had been able to put him in touch with an agent of the Brebache fiduciary pool on the nearby secondary world, Ullamon. The fat man had a permanent line of credit with Brebache and spoke the coded phrases that authorized the transfer of funds to Fonsaculo's own agent on the same world.

Imbry was then given the freedom of the ship and a set of utilitarian garments. The implant he had suspected was inside him was located and removed. Imbry inspected it and found it a standard example of its kind. He wrapped it in some insulating material the ship provided and stowed it away for future examination, when he returned to his operations center in Olkney.

While the financial arrangements were being settled, he had asked the ship's integrator to show him the entry for Fulda in *Hobey's Guide*. The write-up was brief but informative: the planet had attracted little interest since the short-lived clitch boom of the Nineteenth Aeon. The Ideals had come from Ullamon—the "Pit"—almost four millennia ago after failing to win power in a violent social war. In the imports and exports category, Hobey reported simply: "none," with the same entry for spaceports. Under the heading, "Tourism," was the strongest negative that the compilers of *Hobey's Guide* allowed themselves: "Not recommended."

A footnote caught Imbry's attention. It said that Fulda was primarily a desert planet, albeit with an inexplicably dense and humid atmosphere. But when it had been originally visited, long ago during the establishing of Ghabron, the foundational domain from which the secondary world Ullamon had eventually been settled, it had been mistakenly described as "mostly sea, with a few scattered islands and one small continent, all barren. Atmosphere thin and easily penetrated by ultraviolet wavelengths." It was believed that the description of some other disregarded planet, perhaps Gorobei, had erroneously been substituted for Fulda's. The error was corrected when the clitch boom began and miners flocked to Fulda.

Imbry was going to ask the integrator for information on clitch when it preempted his question by announcing that it was now in touch with the Brebache agent on Ullamon. Shortly after, Captain Fonsaculo arrived, bearing clothes that almost fit the fat man, as well as an invitation to dine in the salon. "I am anxious to hear your tale," the spacer said, describing himself as a man who liked a good meal as much as he liked a good story.

The meal, for Imbry, had to come first. He had not eaten for the three days he had waited in the cave, while the air of Fulda seethed with thunderbolts and torrents of rain. He was pleasantly surprised to discover that the *Pallistre's* galley was better stocked than most tramp freighters'. When he had sampled its offerings, he was delighted. But once he was fed, the captain pressed him politely for his story.

For Imbry, the matter of Fulda was finished. He had been left there in dire circumstances. He had escaped. It was past and done, and his attention was now focused on the future. But the food and drink Fonsaculo had put before him was excellent; if the price of dining with the captain was to revisit the recent past, the fat man could make the effort.

"As anyone knows," he said, after half-draining the mug of good punge, "myths are essential to our relationships with the phenomenal world. They are the means by which the different elements of our psyches deal with each other, and with their counterparts in the psyches of others."

"Indeed," said the captain, "this has been known since the dawn-time. Myth is the language, rich in image and association, through which the hidden portions of the mind converse with our waking selves."

"The important thing," Imbry said, "is to keep that conversation internal. Oh, occasionally, it can be salutary to act out an inner process through a ritual, or vicariously transmit it through a story. But even when the elements of myth are represented by costumed and masked actors, participants and spectators alike must never forget that it is but a play."

While Imbry paused, Fonsaculo refilled his mug. "But on Fulda, the play got out of hand?" he prompted.

Imbry told him what he had surmised. On Ullamon, four thousand years ago, a madman named Haldeyn had generated the kind of strongly charismatic glamour of which some loons—drawing raw psychic power from an unchecked unconscious—were capable. He had gathered followers, and then the followers had brought in more converts. Onto all of these Haldeyn had projected the contents of his disturbed psyche. He had grown yet another version of the ancient myth of the Perfected Soul, this one having the appeal of being conveniently measurable by statistical techniques.

"The technique is always a crucial part of the myth's salability," Imbry said. "It gives people something they can do, a dependable process that yields a definable outcome."

The Ideals had tried to spread their new cult among the neighbors. But Ullamon was a mellow old secondary, and Haldeyn's philosophy had been widely rejected. He had then tried violence, but had been defeated. So he and his followers had decamped to Fulda to practice their methods there, in happy isolation.

"I knew of that," Fonsaculo said. "No one goes there. Hence my surprise at receiving your hail."

"But whenever someone—be it an individual, or a like-minded group, or a whole society—tries to inhabit a myth in the real world, things go amiss,"

Imbry said. "In this case, the Ideals not only brought out into the light of the day the supposed Perfected Soul, but its opposite: the Imperfect Other."

"Myths are like that," the captain said. There was a plate of small savory pastries next to the carafe of punge. He selected one and spoke as he chewed. "The light must always call up the dark, and vice versa."

Imbry's eyes took on an inward-looking aspect. "The Ideals became fixated on the examples of the Other among them. And, of course, they split over this obsession: to the traditionalists, the darkness was a barrier between them and the light, and must be removed; to the radical opposition, the darkness was the pathway to the light, and thus must be ritually embraced. The relationship to the Other, for both factions, became the sole fount of energy in their culture, and in their individual lives."

"So, naturally, they both came to a bad end?" The captain spoke as his fingers sorted through the pastries for a particular flavor.

"I'm sure they would have," Imbry said, "left to their own devices." He tried one of the pastries himself and complimented the spacer on his integrator's abilities.

"We have worked together for some time," Fonsaculo said, his pride evident. "I must say, when it comes to shipliness in the galley, old *Pallistre* can hold its own even against those gaudy galleons of the grand shipping lines."

"I don't doubt it," said Imbry. "There is an annual contest on Tintamarre. I say this as a man who knows his victuals: if you entered your ship, you would not come away without a prize."

"We have discussed it, *Pallistre* and I. If I had a cargo to justify the voyage . . ." He shrugged, and for a moment Imbry was reminded of Shvarden. "But it is no less a distinction to hear praise from a man who possesses such a refined palate."

"Please," said Imbry, though he took pleasure in the compliment.

"But you were saying about the Fuldans?"

Imbry regathered his thoughts and took a moment to appreciate the irony.

"Well," he said, "there were the Ideals, obsessing over the Other amongst them—their own children, irregularly formed by the processes of the womb or by a mutated germ cell. But the Ideals did not realize that they, themselves, had been conscripted to play the role of the Other in the myth-made-reality of an ultraterrene species."

"Ultraterrene?" Fonsaculo said. "On Fulda?"

"Indeed," said Imbry, "and a decidedly xenophobic species with, and this is only informed speculation, transplanar powers."

The news left the spacer captain agape. "You are certain of the presence of a new sapient species?"

"I am."

"The Archivists on Odlum would offer a substantial prize for indisputable evidence of any new ultraterrenes."

"I have heard that," said Imbry. He reached into the white pouch he wore over his new clothes and produced a recording medium. The golden-hued bead shone as he held it up to the light. "And here is the evidence, assembled by the carry-all's percepts."

A wide smile split Fonsaculo's face. Imbry recognized it as the expression of a man who enjoyed a good haggle, especially if it led to the acquisition of something much to be desired. His own face had often worn that same aspect.

"Odlum is not all that far from Tintamarre," the spacer said.

"I believe that is so."

"How much might you pay to be carried there?"

"How much might you charge?"

"Take some more punge," said the captain, "then together we will find out."

Huband Kesh-Iverey, Rightfully Elevated High Archivist, was an Odlumite of the Superb social class, a distinction evident by the enthusiasm of his facial hair and its complex arrangement in frosted plaits and beaded ringlets. He regarded Imbry from within this hirsute thicket, and even with so much of his face hidden from view, the Old Earther was able to read deep suspicion.

"It has been no less than an Aeon since a new sapient ultraterrene species was identified and described," the official said.

"Precisely why your venerable institution has offered such a handsome reward for evidence of a new find."

"Yes," said the archivist, "*evidence*." Imbry heard the emphasis but said nothing. "Occasionally," Kesh-Iverey went on, "fraudsters cross our doorstep with artifacts they have themselves manufactured, and snatches of blurry images that they purport show a newly found species." Kesh-Iverey's index finger made a fluttering motion in the direction of the recording bead Imbry had placed in the viewer on the Archivist's desk. "We have also made inquiries. Your reputation precedes you on several worlds, and the shadow that it casts is not . . ." He paused as if searching for a word, then chose, "wholesome."

"I cannot assume responsibility for what others may say of me," said Imbry. "I flourish in a competitive field. There are always some who would rather believe that their competence would be more than adequate if it were not occluded by others' shenanigans."

"And you deny any association with 'shenanigans'?"

"I neither affirm nor deny anything. But I do understand your subordinates' reluctance to accept my evidence and their insistence that it be placed before you personally."

The fat man reached out and touched the viewer's control. Immediately, the images of the tubular, tentacled indigenes of Fulda again filled the screen that appeared in the air before them. "You will note," Imbry said, "that these images are sharp and not at all transitory."

"They show a marine environment. Fulda is a desert planet."

"Not anymore."

"You are claiming that these new ultraterrenes used transplanar energies to turn their world from wet to dry so that humans could settle on it while the indigenes hid themselves away for scores of millennia."

"I would not say I 'claim,'" said Imbry. "Rather, I hypothesize."

"A distinction too narrow for us poor Archivists, I am sure," said Kesh-Iverey. "You also 'hypothesize' that the unnamed species are intensely xenophobic—"

"Insanely so," Imbry put in.

"Just so. You believe that they lured humans to their world with the specific intent of drowning them all."

"I do. They did."

"Why would they do that?"

"I suggest," said Imbry, "that you mount an expedition to Fulda to ask them. Though I doubt you will get a satisfactory explanation."

"You are the one alleging firsthand observation. I invite you to hypothesize."

Imbry collected his thoughts. "I am a layman," he said, "and this is a layman's analysis. Perhaps the Fuldan indigenes, living in an ocean on a planet that lacked livable land surface, developed the ability to pierce the membranes between our plane and the others. Those membranes are known to contain vast energies, though we have been unable to tap them. They used these energies for purposes unknown to us; perhaps they traveled extensively through other dimensions, but certainly they showed no interest in exploring The Spray. They may have had only a vague awareness of it—and no awareness at all of the existence of other sapient life forms.

"Then humans showed up. Our existence, and our insistence on making our existence known to the indigenes, may have constituted an intolerable affront to their understanding of how the cosmos was ordered. This unwelcome, unlooked-for knowledge created an immense psychic shock that reverberated within the collective unconscious of the ultraterrenes. A sapient species that may have had not even the concept of the Other was suddenly confronted by its physical presence.

"They could not restore a psychic balance by assimilating the Other. They had no appropriate myths on which to fall back. That left the only other option: create a new myth, one in which the Other is confronted, encysted, and destroyed.

"So," Imbry concluded, "they restructured their planet to resemble what they conjectured a nonaquatic species would inhabit: dry land with scattered springs of water, a thick atmosphere to shield us from the harmful radiation that bathed the land. This they accomplished and maintained using transplanar energies focused through great lenses of clitch scattered about Fulda."

"Ah, yes," said the High Archivist, "the mysterious substance."

"I brought you a fragment of it. The integrator on the *Pallistre* could not penetrate to its basal structure. Has your assistant had more success?"

Behind the facial adornments, Imbry saw a moue of discomfort cross the Odlumite's aspect, immediately succeeded by anger and hostility, not entirely confined.

"It is the stuff that was mined on Fulda, in the Nineteenth Aeon," Kesh-Iverey said.

"I knew that before I left the place," Imbry said.

"Its provenance was never fully ascertained."

"What about its structure? What is it made of?"

The High Archivist let his assistant answer. The integrator's voice sounded from the air beside Imbry's ear. "Carbon, silicon, betafluoron, ischalite, some trace elements that appear to have come from its being handled by several persons."

"Is it of organic manufacture?"

"Do you mean was it produced in an organism?"

"Yes."

"Indeterminate. It may have been, but there is no known organism that could produce it."

"What about," said Imbry, "an organism that incorporated transplanar capacities?"

The High Archivist made a sound indicating that he was experiencing a gratuitous insult to his intellect, but his assistant said, "That would account for the unusual molecular bonds. Yes, it is a valid hypothesis."

"There you have it," said Imbry. "I claim my reward."

"This proves nothing," said Kesh-Iverey.

"It is not my responsibility to prove anything. It is yours. You must now send an expedition to Fulda to verify my claim."

The Odlumite pulled at a thick braid that descended from the flesh beneath his chin. The action seemed to cause him pain, yet he continued to tug. "I am not subject to your orders!" he said.

"No, but you are subject to the rules and procedures of your calling," the fat man said. "Am I not correct, integrator?"

"You are. Shall I give instructions to assemble an expedition?" The question was directed to Kesh-Iverey, whose only response was a glare at the Old Earther. After an interval, the device said, "Did you not hear the question?"

"I heard," said the High Archivist.

"And your answer?"

"Give the instructions." The order came through clenched teeth and was accompanied by a withering look that Imbry suspected would have crushed him against the carpeted floor if its sender had had the power. "It may take some time for an expedition to be formed, to go and to return, to file a report and have it adjudicated," Kesh-Iverey said.

"I am in no hurry," said Imbry. "I will appoint Captain Shrant Fonsaculo of the freighter *Pallistre* to be my agent while you complete your investigations." He stood to leave, then said, "Before I go, my fragment of clitch, please."

The Odlumite opened a drawer in his desk and took out the lump of greasy gray stuff. He tossed it angrily in Imbry's direction, but the fat man nimbly caught it. He turned to go, then paused and said, "Integrator, would you send a copy of the analysis to the *Pallistre*?"

"Done."

On his return to the ship, Imbry offered Captain Fonsaculo five percent to act as his agent with the Archives. The spacer countered with twelve percent and, after a mutually enjoyable passage of gestures and epithets, complete with appeals to deities and reason, theatrical declarations of despair and clutching at wounded hearts, they agreed on eight-and-a-half. Imbry went to his cabin satisfied; he would have been willing to settle for nine. He suspected that Fonsaculo harbored feelings of genuine friendship for him. In return, the fat man thought well of the spacer; he decided to think about accepting and reciprocating the sentiment. He had few friends, scattered on several worlds, but he valued that handful of kindred souls highly.

The *Pallistre* was now bound for Tintamarre and the annual contest of spaceship galleys known as the Grand Gastronomicon. Fonsaculo had been able to pick up a charter on Odlum—three passengers who wished to visit Tintamarre's glittering cairngorm grottos and tour the Cloud Castles—and the salon was theirs for the duration. Imbry repaired to his quarters and asked the integrator to display the analysis of clitch. A three-dimensional diagram of the stuff's odd molecular structure appeared on a screen in the air.

"Rotate the image ninety degrees," he said. There was something familiar about the peculiar arrangement of the different atoms that bound in improbable ways to form the molecule. He was now certain that transplanar energies were involved in the bonding, but there was something else about the diagram that tickled his memory. "Where have I seen that before?" he said.

"I do not know," said the integrator. "Our acquaintanceship is only recent."

"It was a self-directed query," Imbry said. Integrators could never grasp why humans consciously asked themselves questions they could not answer. It was not a failing of the device's, however; the inability was built into them, lest they fall into the habit of constantly asking themselves such questions. Experience had shown that integrators that were too closely modeled on human mentation had a tendency to develop an unhappy condition known as "the vagues."

After a polite pause, the *Pallistre* said, "Concerning the clitch analysis, we are now too distant from Odlum for me to access the connectivity there. Do you wish me to inquire through the connectivity on Tintamarre once we have passed through the whimsy and come into range?"

"Please," said Imbry.

"Very well." The integrator paused, as the devices were instructed to do before changing the subject, so as not to disconcert the far slower mental processes of their human associates. It said, "I am considering what menu I should present to the judges at the Grand Gastronomicon."

"I see."

"Would you be willing to sample some of the dishes? I wish to make some novel combinations of appetizers, entrees, savories, and sweets."

"An excellent strategy," said Imbry. "Bors Nachakkian is one of the judges this year. He likes to be taken by surprise."

"And his responses will weigh heavily with Tino Ganswether, one of the other judges."

Imbry said, "If you can sway those two, the momentum will be yours."

"My thinking also," said the *Pallistre*.

"If you make a good showing in the Gastronomicon," the fat man said, "you could do more charters and haul less cargo."

"Again, my thinking, too. It would be nice to have my holds remain clean."

"Or even convert them to cabins." Imbry wondered if Fonsaculo might be interested in taking on a silent partner, one who could finance the conversion of the ship into a charter yacht. He decided to broach the subject at dinner. To the integrator, he said, "I would be delighted to serve as your test palate for the Grand Gastronomicon. Consider me at your service."

∧   ∧   ∧

When they came out of the whimsy that flung the ship through irreality between Odlum and Tintamarre, there remained only a short run through normal space before they were touching down at the spaceport outside Khilreyn. Imbry was still muzzy from the medications that were needed to protect the human cerebrum from the unsettling sensory distortions that passage through a whimsy produced in an unsedated brain. He gathered together his few possessions and went to find Shrant Fonsaculo.

The spacer had just discharged the charter passengers into the hands of Tintamarrean greeters, who were already pressing each of the new arrivals to drink a mug of rich, dark ale and bite into the hand-sized loaf of fresh bread that were part of a traditional welcome to the grand old foundational domain. Visitors who came to Tintamarre with agendas that did not include plenty of time for eating and drinking were offered many opportunities daily to change their perspective.

"My friend," Fonsaculo said, initiating the complex handshake that was a gesture of significance on his home world. Imbry was familiar with the mutating grip and matched the spacer move for move. They ended up facing the same direction, shoulders touching, in a brief bending of the knees.

"I will transmit the funds for the refit as soon as I reach Old Earth," Imbry said, adding, "partner."

"You do not wish to wait for the results of the Grand Gastronomicon?"

Imbry waved the question away. "The menu that your integrator has designed—"

"With your assistance," the device put in.

The fat man inclined his head. "The menu will win a significant prize."

"Still," said Fonsaculo, "I will not take your money until the results are in."

"It will win," Imbry said. The two men executed another complex series of hand grips and flutters, ending this one with hands pressed to each other's chests, and Imbry turned to step through the hatch.

"Wait," said the integrator. "You forgot your information about the clitch." It produced a recording bead from its dispenser. Imbry took it, with thanks, and put it in his wallet. Then he stepped out into the bustle of Khilreyn spaceport. He discouraged the greeters by informing them that, as a gourmet, he must choose carefully the substances that touched his gustatory apparatus. The explanation was respectfully accepted and the group of men and women were happy to answer the fat man's question and direct him toward the Graz Line terminal, where he had already booked passage for Old Earth.

Aboard the Graz Line's *Opulence*, Imbry refreshed himself in a first-class cabin and reflected on the events that had begun when he went to meet Barlo Krim on the Belmain seawall. The prize he would receive from the Archivists on Odlum, less Captain Fonsaculo's percentage and even after subtracting the cost of traveling from Fulda to Old Earth, was greater than he would have earned from buying and selling-on the set of custom-made knuckle-knackers he had been expecting to acquire from Krim. Plus he now owned an interest in a charter yacht whose prize from the galley competition would ensure a strong and steady return for as long as Imbry cared to maintain the relationship.

All in all, the adventure had turned out better than the fat man could have expected when he was lying on the stone flags of the seawall, having his ribs bruised by a half-sized irregular from a nasty little world Imbry had never heard of. But if he had made a handsome and unexpected profit on the business, that happy result came from the wise and persistent application of his own resources. It diminished by not a minim his determination to levy a memorable retribution on whoever had done this to him. He still did not know who the culprit was, but he would not cease to inquire until he had found out.

He would have to be careful. When it was known that Imbry was back, the hidden enemy would be strongly motivated to reduce his effectiveness before it could be brought to bear. The most direct method would be to strike hard and fast, since a dead Luff Imbry posed little peril. Or something more subtle might occur, with Imbry handed over to the scroots—Colonel-Investigator Brustram Warhanny had long followed the fat man's career with interest—while in the possession of incriminating evidence.

He would have to tread somewhat lightly, too, around the matter of Barlo Krim, however. His need for caution did not arise from his assumption that the middler had been forced, by means of threats to his beloved daughter, to gull Imbry into a trap. It came from the fact that the Krims were a numerous and capable clan of halfworlders, and to take on one was to take on all.

But he was fairly sure that Barlo Krim would be willing to do what he could to make amends. Luff Imbry was also well known in the shadowy backwaters of Olkney, and common wisdom held that anyone who chose to muss up Imbry's coiffure should expect to have to reach, and soon, for his own comb.

Imbry again began to winnow through the list of those who had the will and the potential to have sprung this trick upon him. As he concentrated his thoughts on the question, it occurred to him that he had to accept an unpleasant possibility. The events that had happened after he arrived on Fulda had been put in play, he was quite sure, by a sapient species that was able to penetrate the membranes between the Nine Planes. Imbry had performed a key role in those events—he was the Finder, after all. Did that mean that his kidnapping and depositing on Fulda had been part of the indigenes' myth? Would the hidden enemy ultimately turn out to be a race of tentacled, transplanar ultraterrenes?

If so, how would Imbry exact revenge? And, worse, what guarantee did he have that his part in the psychodrama was finished?

These thoughts troubled him as the *Opulence* hurtled toward the whimsy that would fling it into normal space only a day's cruise from Old Earth. When the alarms sounded, he took his medication almost gratefully, just to quiet his mind.

In Olkney, Imbry resided at three clubs in which he held memberships, spending time here or there according to no predictable schedule. But he did not go to any of these upon his return. Instead, he followed a circumambulant route to his operations center. This was located on a timeworn street in a decidedly unfashionable district of Olkney; it appeared to be a ramshackle old house occupied by a belligerent recluse who never bothered with repairs, upkeep, or garden maintenance, and who could occasionally be heard ranting about a lifetime's accumulations of grievances and threatening violence to all who crossed him.

Imbry spent some time in a darkened doorway across the street from the sagging rear gate that led into the property's overgrown garden. A careful inspection produced nothing to cause him alarm; no disturbance to the gate or the unkempt hedge that it penetrated; no loiterers on the thoroughfare; no surveillance devices hovering in the air or attached to streetlumens or buildings. He crossed the pavement and was through the gate in moments.

The garden's weeds and creepers disguised a strong complement of insightful percepts and defensive systems that could offer trespassers a range of responses from mild discouragement to corporeal destruction. None had been discharged in his absence, and when he uttered a string of coded syllables he heard a series of tones that told him that the garden had nothing out of the ordinary to report.

At the battered rear door, with its peeling paint and ancient scuff marks, the house's who's-there informed him that no one had come within range of its percepts. Imbry had it open the door, and he stepped inside. "Integrator," he said, moving quickly to the back bedroom where his research and communications matrix was disguised as a battered piece of furniture, "I have returned. Report."

The device brought him up to date on a couple of matters that had been pending on the day he disappeared, then listed the persons who had been seeking to contact him. One of these was Wellam Krim, head of the Krim clan.

"What did he wish?"

"To see you at your earliest convenience."

"Tell him I will meet with him at Bolly's Snug whenever he is available. When you know when that will be, book one of the private rooms."

But as he entered the small bedroom, with its stained wall coverings and defunct wall lumen, the older man sitting on the bed said, "No need. I am available now."

Imbry froze in the doorway. "Master Krim," he said, in as neutral a tone as he could manage, "my integrator did not tell me you were here."

"That is because it does not know it."

"To whom are you speaking?" said the integrator.

"Never mind," Imbry said. "Put yourself on standby."

"Done," said the device.

Imbry would have liked to ask Wellam Krim how he had managed to enter his operations center and wait there without its defenses being activated. But there was no point; the Krims' trade secrets were closely guarded. Besides, they had more important matters to discuss.

"How is Barlo?" the fat man said.

"Dead." A pair of lines appeared at the corners of the patriarch's mouth.

"And his spouse and child?"

The lines deepened. "Also dead."

"And how do you view my part in these deaths?"

From beneath two thickets of white, bushy brows, dark eyes burrowed into Imbry's. "At present, with a certain degree of ambiguity."

"May I explain?"

"That is one of the reasons I am here," said Krim. "Begin."

Imbry related an abbreviated version of what had happened to him since he had received an invitation to buy a set of knuckle-knackers from the old man's grandson on the Belmain seawall. Wellam Krim listened without interruption until the tale was told, then said, "The man who caused Barlo to drown in Mornedy Sound, he is dead?"

"Yes. I saw his body."

"But he was made to do it by someone else?"

"Someone," said Imbry, "I have not yet identified."

"But you have identified candidates."

"Three. In ascending order of likelihood: Popul Deep, Tamarac Firzanian, and Ayalenya Chadderdan."

The Krim of the Krims said, "Barlo had middled for all of them. Deep, I discount absolutely. Firzanian?"—his face was still for a moment, eyes narrowed—"he might act brashly against you, but not against one of us."

"That leaves Chadderdan," Imbry said.

"She is new, though her references were sterling."

"Did you investigate her thoroughly?"

Sadness suffused the old man's face. "Barlo did. She was his client."

"Integrator," Imbry said.

"Here," said the voice seemingly beside his ear.

"Where is Ayalenya Chadderdan?"

The reply was instant. "She departed Old Earth on the Amboy Fleet's *Prestige* five days ago."

"Where bound?"

"Holycow. And she had an open ticket."

The old man said, "Holycow is a transit point to more than a dozen foundational domains and three times that many secondaries."

"And with an open ticket," Imbry said, "she could be going to any of them, or even beyond."

Wellam Krim stood up. Stooped with age, he nonetheless radiated power. "We will find her," he said.

"Please let me be there when you do," said Imbry.

"You need have no doubt of that," said the old man. "When I said 'we,' I did so inclusively."

"I see," said the fat man.

"I hope you do." He fixed Imbry with a look that Imbry knew he had to meet. "We have done business, you and I. This is more than business. And you are part of it."

"Yes," said Imbry. "I am."

"I will book tickets on the next liner to Holycow. From there we will charter a ship."

"I know," Imbry said, "a good one."

The patriarch nodded. "Be ready to leave. I will send a volante to collect you. At which club will you be staying?"

"Quirks, I think," said Imbry.

Krim turned to depart, looked back at Imbry from the doorway. "Don't make us have to look for you."

Imbry raised one hand, made the halfworld gesture that signaled unalterable commitment. The old man pursed his lips and nodded again. Then he was gone.

"Integrator," Imbry said, "book me a room at Quirks."

"Done. I believe the rear door just opened and closed, though the who's-there said it did not happen."

"It does not matter," Imbry said. He placed his hands in his pockets. In one of them his fingers encountered the recording bead that contained the analysis of clitch that the Archives on Odlum had performed and transmitted to the *Pallistre*. "Integrator," he said, "deploy the research and communications matrix."

The scarred piece of furniture unfolded itself and said, "Ready."

Imbry inserted the bead into a receptacle and had the device display the analysis. An unlikely molecular structure, fantastically complex, appeared on a screen in the air. He studied it and said, "Where have I seen that before?"

"Here," said his integrator. It displayed a simplified version of the diagram. The attribution line underneath the schematic referenced "*Nineteenth-Aeon Ceramics: A Summing Up* by Shinath, Baron Mindern." It was his rendering of the long-sought-after secret ingredient that made possible the blazing glazes that colored Nineteenth-Aeon pots and vases.

Imbry found the small valise he had brought with him from Tintamarre. In its bottom, wrapped in some soiled small clothes, was the lump of clitch.

"Integrator," he said, "arrange for the purchase of a potter's wheel, a tub of finest white clay, and a first-class kiln."

"Done."

"And have my snouts start a whisper that Imbry is on the trail of a perfect Nineteenth-Aeon pot, previously unknown."

"Notifications have been sent."

He decided he would take the clitch to Quirks and have it placed in the club's secure facility. Nothing short of a direct command from the Archon could broach that safe.

"Were you expecting," said the integrator, "a ticket to be booked for you on the Graz Line's *Prominence*?" said the integrator.

"Yes. When does it leave?"

"Late tomorrow afternoon."

"Then advise the kitchen at Quirks that I will want their finest offering tonight and a good, soft bed to digest it in."

He rubbed his hands to clean the smear of clitch from his fingers. The future beckoned radiantly, he thought, though not so brightly for Ayalenya Chadderdan.

THE END

THE END

ABOUT THE AUTHOR

Matthew Hughes writes science-fantasy in a Jack Vance mode. His latest novels are *Hespira: A Tale of Henghis Hapthorn* (Night Shade), *Template* (Paizo), and *The Damned Busters* (Angry Robot). His short fiction has appeared in *Asimov's*, *F&SF*, *Postscripts*, *Storyteller*, and *Interzone*.

He has won the Canadian equivalent of the Edgar, and been shortlisted for the Aurora, Nebula, and Derringer Awards. For 30 years, he was a freelance speechwriter for Canadian corporate executives and political leaders. At present, he augments a fiction writer's income by housesitting and has no fixed address.

Web page: http://www.archonate.com